SHADOWS OF FURY

THE SHADOW REALMS
BOOK 4

BRENDA K DAVIES

BRENDA K. DAVIES

CHAPTER ONE

COLE HELD Lexi in his arms as he studied the crone and his brother while they spoke. He couldn't hear what they were saying, but judging by the way their eyes continuously flicked to Lexi and him, *they* were the topic of conversation.

Of course, he couldn't expect anything less after what just transpired with Lexi and the harrow stone, Brokk's face had drained of color and Kaylia looked extremely uneasy, which meant that whatever they were discussing wasn't good.

He imagined they were talking about that Shadow Reaver bullshit the crones were muttering about while he was in their realm, but he didn't care. He'd done what was necessary to save Lexi's life, and even if it meant drawing *every* shadow in *all* the realms to him, he would do it again.

When Lexi shuddered, he squeezed her tighter as he tried not to recall what it was like to stare at her unmoving body while she lay on the floor. That stone had nearly killed her.

He glanced uneasily at the red stone, still lying on the ground only a few feet away. If he could have reached it without disrupting Lexi too much, he would have kicked the thing clear across the room.

Instead, he glowered at it before shifting his attention back to Brokk and the crone. His gaze locked with Kaylia's, and for the first time, true fear shone in her pewter gray eyes. She had a right to be afraid; she had to know he wouldn't let her put Lexi's life in danger.

Which meant she most likely wouldn't leave here alive.

"What should I do with you?" he asked.

Kaylia's shoulders went back as her elegant, blonde eyebrows rose. "What do you mean, *do* with me?"

Lexi stirred in his arms and lifted her head. She was still far too pale but alive and moving, and that was what mattered.

"You know what I mean," Cole said.

"You won't be *doing* anything with me. I'm free to do as I please."

When Lexi first woke, he'd released the shadows that came to him, but the ones inside him stirred at Kaylia's tone. Recalling how hostile they'd been, he tamped the shadows down again. He *would* keep them away from Lexi.

"No, you won't," he replied. "Not with what you know about her. I can't let you walk free with that knowledge."

"Cole," Lexi whispered.

He kissed her forehead before adjusting his hold on her. He made sure she was comfortable against the wall before releasing her and rising. Kaylia braced her feet apart as she faced off against him.

"It doesn't matter *what* you are," Kaylia said, "or what you can do. If you kill me, the crones will come for you. They'll hunt you down—"

"And what?" Cole demanded. "*What* will they do? I'll burn them *all* down to keep her safe, and anyone else who gets in my *fucking* way."

Kaylia gulped, but she stubbornly raised her chin. "Cole—"

Kaylia cut off whatever Lexi was about to say.

"You're not indestructible, and neither is she!"

Despite his resolve to keep the shadows suppressed, they shifted and stirred inside him. Their power swelled into his fingertips as they sought release. They ached to break free and destroy, but he fisted his hands against the impulse.

No matter what, he didn't want to make enemies of the crones. They would be far better allies than enemies. But he would unleash hell on them if it became necessary.

"Are you threatening her?" Cole's voice started taking on the hint of distortion it held while he was in the crone realm.

CHAPTER TWO

"WHOA! SLOW DOWN HERE," Brokk said as he stepped between them and held up his hands.

"Yes," Del said as he moved away from the fireplace and closer to Brokk.

Orin remained standing with his arm resting on the mantle. Though an amused smile curved his lips, his posture said he wasn't as relaxed as he was pretending to be.

Behind Cole, Lexi placed her hand against the wall and rose. "What is going on? What exactly happened with the stone, with *me*, and the curse? How am I still alive?"

When Kaylia looked at her, Cole growled as he stepped between them. It didn't dissuade Kaylia from speaking to her.

"The stone reacted to you in such a way because it is an *arach* possession, and it recognized *you* as its rightful owner. Unfortunately, the curse still had some effect on you, but the stone protected you from the full brunt of it, so you didn't die. Then *I* removed the curse from the stone so Sahira, this vamp—" Her lip curled in disgust as she jerked her head toward Brokk. "—and you wouldn't die."

Kaylia's gaze shifted back to Cole. "You're welcome."

"Thank you," Lexi breathed.

"Finally, someone with some manners. You're welcome," Kaylia replied with a tight-lipped smile that was far from warm.

"I'm Brokk, *not* vamp," Brokk said to her. "And maybe you should show some manners considering I'm standing between you and my brother who wants *you* dead."

Kaylia glared at him but didn't respond before turning her attention haughtily away. Cole was beginning to like her less and less. *No* one treated his little brother like that.

"You're not going to leave here knowing what you do about her," Cole told her.

"*I* saved her life."

"And you could destroy it by revealing what you've discovered."

"I aligned myself and the rest of the crones with you and your cause when I gave Sahira the harrow stone. There is no turning back for them or me."

"That was before you knew about Lexi," he reminded her.

Sahira and Varo appeared in the hallway. Sahira held a tray of cheese and apple slices while Varo carried one filled with glasses and two decanters. One decanter had a reddish liquid, while the other contained an amber one.

They couldn't see into the library where Kaylia and the others stood, but Cole's stance and Lexi's uneasy glance told them things weren't good. Sahira set her tray on one of the stairs, and Varo did the same before coming closer. They stayed to the side of Cole but positioned themselves so they could see into the library.

Lexi rested her hand on his arm and stepped out from behind him. "Thank you for everything you've done, including letting us use the stone," she said.

"Don't thank her; she's a danger to you," Cole said.

"No, I'm not," Kaylia replied as she focused on Lexi. "Not only did I save your life, but when I gave you and your friends the harrow stone, I put my own life, and the lives of those I love, at risk. I'm not going to turn you over to the Lord; he'll kill me once he learns of my role in this."

"She's clearly not the enemy," Lexi said.

Orin groaned and dropped his head into his hand. "Save me from the ones with hearts and scruples."

"Oh, shut up!" Lexi snapped. "She's helped us multiple times."

"Yes, please shut up," Del said. "You're not helping the problem."

"She cannot leave here with the knowledge of what you are," Cole said. "None of the other crones know of your heritage, and it has to stay that way."

"I wouldn't tell them," Kaylia replied. "Not until you're prepared for the war her existence will bring, or until you give me permission to do so. With her abilities—"

"What *are* my abilities?" Lexi interrupted.

"How do you not know?" Kaylia blurted.

"Lexi," Cole warned. "We can't trust her."

"But I do."

"For fuck's sake," Orin muttered.

"I trust her too," Varo murmured in his soothing way that took a small edge off Cole's distrust.

"Oh, goodie," Orin said. "Now we have *two* of you with scruples. We're never going to win this war."

"Yes, we will," Kaylia retorted.

Cole's eyebrows rose over the vehemence in her tone. She'd just gotten involved in this, but for the first time, he believed she might be on their side and wouldn't have to die.

"I trust her as much as I do you," Del said and shot a pointed look at Orin.

Cole suspected it would be a long time before his friend forgave Orin for imprisoning him. But they would work together, for Lexi's sake. That didn't mean either of them was going to like it… which was evident as they scowled at each other.

"Why don't you know about your abilities?" Kaylia asked again. "*How* have you managed to stay hidden for so long?"

"How did you end up with the harrow stone if it's an arach possession?" Brokk asked.

"What about my questions?" Kaylia asked.

"Later," Cole replied brusquely.

Kaylia sighed, and one of her eyes twitched as she spoke. "I knew some arach; that's how I ended up with the harrow stone. When the war between them was really starting to ramp up, my friend Fenmenor showed me how to use the harrow stone and gave it to me for safekeeping.

"I placed the curse on the stone because I wasn't as capable as an arach to guard it. I figured that when he returned for it, I would remove the curse, but I never saw him again."

Cole wasn't sure if it was an act or what, but he saw true emotion in the crone's eyes for the first time. That sheen in them might have been tears, but she blinked them away too fast for him to be certain.

"So, the arach trusted you," Lexi said.

"Fenmenor did, and I knew others too," Kaylia replied. "I can help you with your abilities."

"Do you know what her abilities *are*?" Cole demanded.

CHAPTER THREE

"WELL," Kaylia hedged. "No, not really. The arach were very private about that and kept a lot of what they could do hidden. But I can show you how to use the stone, we know they could withstand fire, and we also know they could throw fire. You must be able to do those things."

"Not yet," Lexi admitted.

"And why not? No one has answered that for me yet."

"Because we kept her powers suppressed from the time she was a baby," Sahira replied. "We believed it was the best way to keep her safe."

"Who did?"

"Me and my brother," Sahira said and nodded toward Del.

"They're my aunt and my dad," Lexi said. "They kept me alive and safe."

"She didn't know what she truly was until recently," Del said.

Kaylia studied Del like he was some kind of alien frog monster. "*You* took care of her."

"I told you, you have a lot to learn about vampires," Del replied.

"He's a great dad," Lexi said defensively. "I never would have guessed he wasn't my real father or that Sahira wasn't my aunt until they told me the truth. I've always been loved, and if you don't like them, then we *are* going to have a problem."

Cole smiled at the crone while her mouth opened and closed as she tried to form words and failed.

"We're not going to have a problem," Kaylia finally said. "I'm just surprised to learn such a thing about vampires."

"We're not monsters," Brokk retorted.

"Most of you are."

"That's enough," Lexi interjected. "I understand you may be able to help, but these are my friends and family. I won't let you treat them like shit. I'd prefer you didn't help with this if it means you're going to treat them badly."

Which meant Cole would have to kill her or lock her away somewhere.

Kaylia's shoulders went back again. "You need my help, and I can give it. Few are more in tune with nature and magical abilities than me. I am the oldest living witch, and I can sense and intuit things no others can."

"This is true," Sahira said. "Kaylia is an extremely powerful witch who has helped many master their abilities."

"Many *witches*," Cole said. "She knows what witches are capable of doing; she doesn't know what the arach can do."

"That is true, but I can help her figure it out," Kaylia insisted.

"And why would you do that?"

"She is"—Kaylia's eyes locked on Lexi's—"*you* are needed to defeat the Lord, and that is something I want. He has to die."

CHAPTER FOUR

"Why do you want him dead?" Lexi inquired as she studied the beautiful woman across from her.

Her aunt had called her Kaylia. The name tugged at Lexi's memory. She'd heard it in one of the many stories Sahira used to tell her about the different realms and the immortals who resided in them. She couldn't remember what Sahira said about this woman, but she had spoken of her.

"Because witches are about life and prosperity; the Lord represents nothing but death and destruction. If he has his way, he'll kill us all and destroy everyone and everything I love, and I won't allow that.

"I may have withdrawn from the witches' realm and most immortals, but I will not allow him to destroy us all when I can help stop him. And I believe *you* are the key to bringing him down." Her gaze flicked from Lexi to Cole. "You both are."

Lexi frowned. She sensed something darker about Cole; it was as if something had slipped into him....

Or maybe it broke free.

Slipping her hand into his, she squeezed as she tried to will the darkness away. When he met her gaze, his eyes crinkled, and the familiar twinkle lit them again. Though he would still kill Kaylia as quick as she could blink, he finally relaxed a little.

Then, Kaylia shifted her stance, and the twinkle left his eyes. Silver flashed through their Persian blue depths as the lycan half of him briefly broke through the composed dark fae half. Then, the silver vanished, and he collected himself once more.

A muscle twitched in his jaw when he returned his attention to Kaylia. His short, neatly trimmed, black beard covered the bottom half of his face, but it didn't hide that jumping muscle.

The dark fae part of him retained control, but not by much. It would only take one small thing to push him over the edge.

"I can help you learn your powers and how to control them," Kaylia said. "But I have to return to the crone realm before I can help; if I don't, they'll hunt you down." She stared pointedly at Cole.

He laughed, but the sound was far from amused. "Let them come for me."

"Cole," Lexi murmured.

"A war between the dark fae king and the crones and witches will not go unnoticed. I'm sure the Lord would be *very* interested in learning why it started. If he somehow hears that I gave you the harrow stone, then he'll figure out why you used it. He'll come for you and your brothers."

Lexi almost recoiled when Cole released a sound somewhere between a man and a wolf ready to pounce. His hand contorted in hers; the bones popped as the fingers bent into something different. Claws grazed her flesh before they retracted.

"Don't threaten me," Cole snarled.

"It's not a threat; it's the truth. They expect me to return. They know who I left with, and they saw what you could do. They know you are the Shadow Reaver, and they *will* come for you if they believe you've hurt me."

"Shadow Reaver?" Lexi asked as her father stepped forward, lifted his hands in a placating gesture, and spoke.

"No one is going to fight anyone," her dad said. "Kaylia could be a very valuable resource for us, and we are all on the same side of this. Or at least we all want to see the Lord taken down. Working together will benefit us all, and fighting each other will most likely ensure the Lord wins."

"And none of us want that," Brokk said.

"No, we don't."

A ripple ran across Cole's skin as his thick, corded muscles tensed. She couldn't tell if it was tension, power, or something more vibrating through him.

"This is a battle, Cole. It's going to be a long battle, and not only will it require a plan, but it will also require help," her father said. "And the first step in our plan has to be teaching Lexi how to use and conceal her abilities—"

"Conceal?" Kaylia interrupted.

"Oh yeah, she's going to be a great help when she's not even aware of what Kitten can do," Orin drawled.

Lexi gave him the finger. Kaylia may not exactly know Lexi's abilities, but he was well aware of how much she *hated* when he called her Kitten. He brushed some of the black hair out of his black eyes and smirked at her.

"You're not helping," Brokk told him.

Orin rolled his eyes, but his smile never faltered as he waved a hand at Kaylia. "And neither is she."

"We need a plan," her dad said. "Kaylia is the start of one."

"I don't plan with vampires," Kaylia retorted.

Lexi's eyes narrowed on the woman. Until recently, she believed she was half vampire like Sahira and Brokk, and her father was *full* vampire.

"Then you can't help us," Lexi said, her voice colder than she'd anticipated. "I told you, these are my friends and family. I don't know what your issue with vampires is, and I don't care, but you will treat everyone here with respect."

"That settles it then," Orin said. "When do we kill her?"

CHAPTER FIVE

KAYLIA IGNORED him as she kept her eyes locked on Lexi. "I have always found that you cannot trust a vampire."

"Maybe not all of them, but the ones here, you can," Lexi said. "In every immortal species, there is good and bad, but my dad, Brokk, and Sahira are some of the most trustworthy immortals I know. If you have a problem with them, then you can't help us."

When Kaylia took a deep breath, the muscles in her neck flexed. It seemed she was trying to figure out what to say and how to proceed.

"Without my help, you might not be able to stop the Lord," she finally said.

"That may be true, but you're going to have to trust those who mean the most to me," Lexi told her. "We're putting faith in you that you can help without betraying us. You need to put some faith in the fact that *no* one here would ever hurt me."

She didn't think Kaylia had to know about Orin keeping her father locked up and the truth of it hidden until recently. As much as he pissed her off, she still trusted him. He wouldn't do anything to betray Cole.

"Fine," Kaylia grated through her teeth. "I'll work with the vampires to help *you*."

It was what Lexi had hoped for, but she wasn't sure this was such a good idea. She had a feeling Kaylia could be a *big* help and extremely useful. If they didn't agree to work together, then Cole and Orin would most likely kill her. However, Lexi didn't know if she could get past her hatred of vampires enough for there not to be future issues.

Unfortunately, she didn't have much choice. She'd prefer if Kaylia didn't die, and she especially didn't want a war with the witches and crones. She obviously needed any help she could get to master her abilities.

"I'm not looking for charity from you," Lexi told her. "This is my *life* we're talking about, and right now, you're not helping to make it any better."

"I can assure you, that is not my intention," Kaylia said. She lifted her palm before her and whispered a few words.

As she spoke, Cole stepped protectively in front of Lexi, and black shadows slithered across the floor toward the crone.

"Don't," Cole cautioned.

Lexi gawked at the shadows as they slid down the walls toward Cole. A chill crept up her spine and over her skin. No one had answered her question about the Shadow Reaver, but it had to be Cole they were talking about. But what did it mean?

"Cole," she whispered.

The shadows stopped moving to hover near the two of them and Kaylia. The crone lifted her head and opened her hand to reveal a small blue flame that hovered in the air before her. With a wave of her finger, the fire moved up before going down again.

The flame shifted into a small bird that rose into the air before transforming into a dragon. A blast of orange fire erupted from the dragon's mouth before its mouth closed. Bringing her hands together, Kaylia smothered the flame.

"A glamour; nothing more," Orin stated.

"True," Kaylia said. "But many witches can't produce a glamour from nothing. I can."

"That's true," Sahira said.

"Whether you're a witch or not, I can teach you about control," Kaylia said to Lexi. "But first, you must tell me, what are you seeking to conceal?"

"When I'm in the sun or moonlight, something strange happens to me," Lexi said.

"Strange how?" Kaylia asked.

"We can discuss that more later," Cole said.

Kaylia looked about to protest, but she closed her mouth and gave a small nod.

The shadows retreated, but the memory of them still chilled Lexi's skin. She stared at Cole's broad back as his shoulders remained tensed and the muscles in his body quivered.

He was so much bigger than her as he towered a foot over her five-foot-seven height. His massive size and protective nature made his lycan half the most noticeable. But the shadows were a newer development, and she did *not* like them.

"What is the Shadow Reaver?" she demanded.

Kaylia glanced away from her as Brokk stepped out from between Kaylia and Cole. "It's a legend; one that, until recently, I was sure was nothing more than a story shared around the cauldron to scare kids."

Scare kids? Lexi did *not* like the sound of that.

CHAPTER SIX

"But now"—Kaylia focused on Cole again— "I know it's true."

"What is this legend?" Lexi asked in a tiny voice much smaller than normal.

"It is a legend about a dark one who can control the shadows and use them to destroy the world."

Lexi's stomach plummeted into her toes as words surged out of her mouth. "You can't possibly think that's *Cole*!"

"I do," Kaylia said.

Lexi started to shake her head in denial before stopping. Cole released her hand and rested it on her shoulder. He gave it a gentle squeeze that did nothing to ease the terror churning in her belly.

"Cole would never do that," she stated.

"He can control the shadows," Kaylia said.

"*All* dark fae can manipulate the shadows," Orin said.

"Not like him. He draws them to him, he calls them from all around, they respond to him, they *communicate* with him."

"Impossible," Varo said.

"No, it's not," Cole replied with a calm that was completely out of place with the anxiety clawing at Lexi's insides. "The shadows warned me when one of the crones was on the move in the crone realm."

"So, you think you are this Shadow Reaver?" her dad asked.

Cole shrugged. "Maybe, maybe not. Right now, it's not at the top of my list of things to worry about. The shadows help me, and I will use them to keep Lexi safe."

"Maybe…" Lexi swallowed before speaking again. "Maybe you should stop using them."

"I'll do whatever's necessary to protect you."

She frowned at him before turning to Kaylia. It wasn't the time for this when Kaylia could have the answers they sought.

"Do you know anything more about the Shadow Reaver?" Lexi asked.

"That is all I know," she said. "But there is also a prophecy about the Reaver."

"Prophecies are garbage," Cole retorted.

"Normally, I agree, but the first half of this one seems to have already come true," Brokk said.

"What is it?" Lexi asked, but she really didn't want to know.

"When the last light blooms, the Shadow Reaver shall rise," Kaylia said. "When the last light falls, the Shadow Reaver will destroy us all. I believe Lexi is that light."

"It would seem so," Cole replied with an indifference that mystified Lexi.

Why is he not more concerned about this?

"But since I intend to make sure nothing happens to Lexi, then we have nothing to worry about," Cole replied. "Do you know where this prophecy came from or who predicted it?"

"No," Kaylia admitted.

"It was probably something started as a way to scare children or someone else into behaving, like so many of them are."

"True," Brokk said.

"Have you always been able to control the shadows like this?" Kaylia asked.

"No," Cole replied. "The trials made me stronger."

But is that for the better? Lexi hated the doubt churning inside her, but she couldn't shake it.

"Now, we have more important things, such as *you,* to discuss," he said to Kaylia.

Lexi swallowed back the knot in her throat and decided if this Shadow Reaver revelation wasn't bothering Cole, then she wouldn't let it bother *her* either. That would be easier said than done, but she couldn't do anything about it now.

"I have to learn control," Lexi said to Cole. "And Kaylia can help me with that."

"So can I," he said.

"The arach magic isn't like fae magic," Kaylia said.

"And it's like the witches'?" Cole inquired.

"It's unlike any other immortals who ever existed; that's what made the arach unique. It's what makes us *all* unique, but I know I can help with this."

"I think we should give her a chance," Varo said. "She's the only one here who has ever known an arach, and one of them trusted her enough to put a powerful arach possession into her hands."

Lexi's tension eased as he spoke, and though he didn't smile, his nearly white-blue eyes shone with warmth. She'd never known him before the war, but she could tell he was far too thin. She wasn't sure he'd earned his skeletal frame during the war, but she suspected he did.

His face was gaunt, and his cheekbones stood out against his pale skin. Dark shadows circled his eyes, and a long nap would do him some good, but strength radiated from him as he gazed at Kaylia.

"I believe she's trustworthy," Varo continued.

"Why?" Cole demanded.

"I just do."

"I think we should trust Varo's judgment," Brokk said. When

Cole looked at him, Brokk elaborated. "He survived the war somehow."

Varo smiled at this. "It definitely wasn't because of my fighting skills."

Orin snorted.

"Trust his judgment, Cole," Brokk insisted.

Cole looked to Sahira, who stared at him before replying, "I think we can trust her."

"I *can* help," Kaylia insisted.

"And we need it," Lexi said.

She couldn't spend the rest of her life locked away from any source of natural light, and she had to learn more about her powers and how to use them. She wouldn't do any good in this world if she didn't know who she was and more about her abilities.

And this world was desperate for a whole lot of good.

CHAPTER SEVEN

COLE STARED at Lexi as she peered up at him from her vibrant, hunter green eyes with their beautiful flecks of emerald green. Hope shone in those eyes. Hope for the future and them, but mostly hope Kaylia could teach her more about who she was.

He couldn't lose her. They needed to learn what she could do, but he didn't know about trusting this woman, no matter what Varo and Lexi believed.

"I must go back to the crone realm so they can see I'm alive. I'll start training with her once I return," Kaylia said.

He didn't acknowledge her as he asked Lexi. "What do you want to do?"

He already knew the answer, but he wanted her to be sure this was right for *her*. She drew her bottom lip between her teeth as she looked from him to Kaylia and back again.

"I have to learn to control my powers, and I believe she can help us. I *have* to be able to go outside again," Lexi said. "I can't keep hiding."

"Why can't you go outside?" Kaylia asked.

Cole held a finger up to her as he studied Lexi. "This could be a risk."

"I don't think it is."

This was not the road he would have chosen. He didn't like the idea of killing any innocent, and Kaylia's death would be one of the many that haunted him, but he would slaughter her and go to war with the crones if it meant keeping Lexi safe.

However, he wasn't the one Kaylia *might* help, and he couldn't deny Lexi this if she believed it would make a difference. If the crone turned out to be a liar, he'd kill her later. Until then, between all of them, they could keep a close eye on her.

He turned back to Kaylia. "I'll take you back to the crone realm to make sure you don't tell them anything."

"After what they witnessed earlier from you, they won't want you there," she said.

"I don't care."

"What did they witness?" Lexi demanded.

"Are you going to tell her, or shall I?" Kaylia asked him in a defiant, taunting voice.

Cole smiled grimly back at her; maybe her death wouldn't bother him as much as he originally believed. "Why don't you tell her."

"They saw him call on the shadows," Kaylia said to her. "They saw them surround him, change him, become a part of him, and communicate with him."

Cole studied Lexi for some hint of revulsion on her face, but it remained expressionless as she spoke. "So, they saw his power."

Her hand found his again, and he slid his fingers between hers as pride bloomed in his chest. He sensed her uneasiness over this Shadow Reaver nonsense, but she wouldn't let it show to anyone else. Her faith in him would remain absolute to anyone who might question it, as would her love.

"If you come back with me, they won't believe I'm safe and working with you willingly," Kaylia said.

"You seem to think I give a fuck what they think," Cole retorted.

"Cole, don't," Lexi said.

"I'll take her back," Orin said.

"Oh yes, let's have gone through the harrow stone spell so you can go running around in public," Brokk said.

Orin scowled at him, but Brokk had a point.

"I'll go with her," Brokk offered.

Kaylia didn't look overly thrilled by this, but she didn't have any other options.

"Fine," Cole relented. "But if you're not back in ten minutes—"

"I have to gather some of my things," Kaylia interrupted. "That will take some time. I'll need at least half an hour."

"Fifteen minutes or I'm coming after you," Cole grated through his teeth.

"That won't be necessary," Kaylia replied with a smile.

"What is she supposed to tell the other crones about the person who touched the harrow stone? They were all there to hear what happened when we went to get her," Brokk said. "Are they supposed to be dead or alive?"

"Dead," Cole stated. "We can't have anyone else suspecting that an arach still lives."

"Consider it done," Kaylia said.

And with that, she opened a portal and walked into it. Brokk waved to them before following her through.

CHAPTER EIGHT

"WHAT ABOUT THAT?" Del asked and thrust a finger at the harrow stone.

Cole glanced back at where the red stone still lay on the ground. It no longer glowed, but he would never forget the way it shot toward Lexi before touching her and throwing her across the room... or the way it nearly killed her.

And then he recalled how it burnt Sahira and Kaylia when they tried to pick it up. The thing could stay there forever.

"Don't," he said and tugged on Lexi's hand when she bent to pick it up.

Her auburn hair fell across her face when she turned her head to look at him. "Kaylia said it's an arach possession. I should be okay to touch it now that the curse has been removed."

"*Should* be is far from definitely. That thing nearly killed you."

She brushed the hair back from her face as she rose again. "That's because it felt a connection to me; it was seeking my touch before. It didn't know it would almost kill me."

"It's a stone; it doesn't *know* anything," Orin said.

"It knows it belongs to *me*," Lexi retorted.

"She's right," Sahira said. "That stone is hers, and it recognizes her as its rightful owner."

"Then why is it so quiet now?" Varo asked.

"Probably because it used a *big* burst of magic when it flew across the room to get closer to her," Sahira said.

"And then another burst to almost kill her," Cole grumbled.

"That wasn't the stone's magic; that was Kaylia's," Lexi said. Before he could stop her, she bent and snatched the stone off the floor. Though the curse had been removed, he kept waiting for her to fly back again or cry out in pain, but she did neither.

Instead, as she cradled the stone in her hand, it started to glow again. The brilliant radiance bathed her face in a red glow before returning to normal again.

"So, does this mean I can duplicate things?" Lexi asked.

"I don't see why not," Sahira said. "It might require you to figure out how to use your powers first, but you should be able to work the stone."

Lexi smiled as she examined the stone. "I have to put it somewhere safe."

"I have somewhere," Sahira said. "Follow me, but everyone else *stays here*."

~

"Well, I guess your father could have come," Sahira said as Lexi followed her past the staircase. "It's not like he doesn't know about this."

Lexi didn't reply as they entered the kitchen; she and her father both knew about Sahira's safe. She stopped in the doorway as Sahira crossed the room.

Sunlight normally streamed through the kitchen windows to illuminate the room at this time of day, but all the curtains were closed against it. The unnatural darkness of the room was a bleak reminder *she* was the reason those curtains were closed.

She flicked on the light switch; nothing happened. The electricity was out again, but that was nothing new. Ever since the Lord's war, it often came and went. At one time, it was doing better, but it had become more unreliable recently.

"I'm sure it will be back soon," Sahira said.

"One of these days, it's not going to come back," Lexi replied.

"No, it won't."

Lexi dreaded that day. They'd adjusted to not always having power, but they also expected it to return a couple of times a day to heat the water and run their appliances.

As of now, it came and went often enough that the little bit of food they had in their fridge rarely spoiled. They would lose that luxury when the power was completely gone. They'd also lose the luxury of hot showers.

Sahira glanced nervously over her shoulder. "Did anyone follow us?"

Lexi looked back to see Cole leaning against the wall where she'd left him, but his attention remained on the library.

"They're not paying attention," Lexi assured her aunt.

"Good."

Sahira walked over to the gray, stone back wall and ran her fingers across it until she found the rock she sought. She pushed on it.

A small panel swung open to reveal the safe beyond. Lexi was sure it was where Sahira kept the harrow stone before it decided to become her new best friend and almost killed her.

Lexi opened her fingers to study the red stone filling most of her palm. It wasn't glowing anymore, but she sensed power humming through it. She had no idea how to harness that power, but she *would* figure it out.

This was not what she'd wanted from her life. Before the war started, she was content to live at her manor, with her horses and aunt and dad. She'd loved her simple life, the joy the land and animals brought her, and felt secure in the love showered on her.

After the war, she'd learned to live with the hole her father's passing created inside her. They hadn't had much money, and things were falling apart around the manor, but she'd still loved her home, her aunt, and her life.

She'd never wanted it to change.

But change it had, long before she learned her father was still alive and was Orin's prisoner of war instead of dead. Cole's love had changed it for the better, and now that her dad and Sahira had revealed her true heritage, it was changing again.

This time, she didn't know if it was for the better or the worse. But she would have to find out because there weren't any other options. If she said she didn't want to do this, that she'd rather hide than learn her powers and face the Lord, Cole would take her from here and find somewhere safe for her to live the rest of her life… in hiding… as a coward.

She wrapped her hand around the stone again. No light shone from her palm, but warmth spread through her body as a small pulse reverberated from the stone.

It was happy to be in her possession. It was incredibly weird to think of a stone as happy, but it was.

All of this was so strange. She couldn't believe this was her life now, but it was, and she would do everything she could to reclaim the realm her ancestors lost in their mission to destroy each other.

When a loud knock on the front door reverberated down the hallway, she jumped and spun toward the door. She stared at it as the banging faded away. Cole pushed away from the wall as he met her gaze.

When the stone warmed in her hand, the overwhelming urge to protect it gripped her. There was *no* way a knock at her door was good news, not anymore.

Then she reminded herself it could be George, the man they'd hired to take care of the horses since her life flipped upside down. Still, she couldn't have the harrow stone out in the open when she had no idea who was out there.

When another reverberating bang echoed throughout the manor, she ran across the kitchen. Lexi skidded to a halt in front of the safe. If it were George, he wouldn't be so insistent unless something was wrong.

Lexi placed the stone in the back of the safe, behind Sahira's two books of shadows. Her mother had given her one of the books, and the other was Sahira's compilation of spells, herbs, and crystals, as well as other things she found useful or informative.

When she was a girl, Sahira never let her flip through the book her mother gave her, but she'd spent hours turning the thick pages of Sahira's. She'd been fascinated by the beautiful script and the pictures her aunt sketched throughout. The book was beautiful, old, and full of secrets.

Tucked inside with the books were rare stones and herbs. The herbs filled the air with their potent scent, but the safe was only half full. Hit by the sudden urge to reclaim the stone, Lexi almost snatched it back.

Instead, she closed the door and spun the dial before shutting the wall section next. When she turned back to the room, she discovered Sahira had returned to the kitchen doorway.

Sahira's familiar, a black cat named Shade, had his piercing gold eyes focused on her as he sat on the counter. She didn't need the wave of Shade's tail, or the next booming knock, to know something was wrong.

CHAPTER NINE

LEXI HURRIED to stand beside Sahira as the final, echoing boom of the knock faded away. Cole's focus was on the library, but she couldn't see what was happening in there... with the three immortals who were supposed to be *dead*.

When Lexi stepped into the hallway, Cole strode toward the front door. Lexi jogged to catch up with him. She had no idea who was out there, but a growing knot of anxiety was building in her stomach.

"Who is it?" she whispered to Cole when he stopped next to the door.

"Malakai," Cole growled.

The blood drained from Lexi's face. He could probably smell the bastard; lycans were renowned for their heightened senses, especially their ability to scent things.

This was *far* worse than she'd expected. She glanced into the library at her father, Orin, and Varo standing near the fireplace before looking at the clock.

She should have checked the time when Kaylia and Brokk left. At least five minutes had to have passed, right?

But they still had at least another ten minutes, and that was *if*

Kaylia returned on time. She didn't strike Lexi as the type of woman who took orders well, but then, neither did she.

However, it would be much better if Brokk was here, *now*.

The last time Cole and Malakai encountered each other was when Malakai attacked her in the barn. If he hadn't teleported out of there, Cole would have killed him.

She had no doubt he still intended to kill Malakai, but if Cole killed him now, the Lord would be pissed. The Lord favored Malakai.

He'd given the vampire a sun medallion to allow him to walk about in the day, and he'd made it clear he wouldn't tolerate Cole and Malakai fighting. If he killed Malakai, the Lord would make Cole pay, and they'd just gotten that monster off their backs by giving him the fake bodies of Orin and Varo.

"Lexi, come here," her dad said.

His face was full of strain, his jaw taut, and his eyes a vibrant shade of red. She hadn't told him about what happened between her and Malakai, there hadn't been time, but someone had… most likely, Sahira.

Varo's nearly white-blue eyes darted between the hall and the curtained front windows. Orin, for once, did not look amused as he stood with a hand on the hilt of his sword. They didn't need the three of them provoked into a fight.

"No," Lexi replied, and her dad's eyes widened.

She couldn't leave Cole to face Malakai alone. She was the only one who could keep him calm if this all went to shit, and she had a feeling that was exactly what the Lord was after.

He may favor Malakai, but he was looking to provoke Cole into doing something that would give him an excuse to make him suffer. And Malakai was the number one way to get Cole to lose his temper.

"Let me answer the door!" Lexi blurted.

"You can't go in the sun," her father reminded her.

Lexi almost slapped her forehead as she recalled *that* not-so-happy detail. If she opened the door… if she stepped *one* foot into the sun, she would ruin everything.

She may not be able to open the door, but she still ran to Cole, clasped his hand, and squeezed until he fixed his silver eyes on her. The lycan, whose mate was in jeopardy, was already trying to take over.

Lexi gulped. "Do *not* kill him. The Lord will make us pay if you do, and you just bought us time by bringing him Varo and Orin. We can't lose that reprieve now."

"It wasn't much of a reprieve if Malakai is here," Cole replied.

"He could be here of his own accord. This might have nothing to do with the Lord. He has stopped by before; you've been here when he has."

Maybe reminding him of this wasn't the best thing. However, she chose to believe Malakai's presence here, so soon after Cole's visit to Dragonia, was merely a coincidence.

Call her an optimistic idiot, but she preferred to hope for the best.

"And if the Lord did send him, it's because he's looking to bait you into a fight so he can punish you for it. You can*not* attack him."

Cole grunted in response, but at least it was a response. Then his hand tightened around hers, and his eyes shifted back to their beautiful, blue color.

"I won't attack him. I would never do anything to put you at risk. Stay out of the sun and out of Malakai's view."

Lexi reluctantly released him and looked to Sahira, who had crept up to join them. She was the only other immortal in the manor that others could see. As Sahira took up position behind Cole's back, she grasped Lexi's shoulder and nudged her toward the library.

"Go on now," her aunt encouraged. "I have his back."

There was a time when Lexi never would have expected those words to come from her aunt's mouth, and a time more recently when she wouldn't have been sure if she could trust Sahira, but she had absolute faith in her now.

"Thank you," Lexi whispered to her before retreating.

With a heavy heart, she stepped into the library and shoved her knuckles in her mouth as the front door opened.

CHAPTER TEN

COLE BRACED himself for once again seeing the man he despised. When he recalled what this bastard did to Lexi in the barn and the bruises on her face, everything in Cole screamed for Malakai's death.

As the memories ran through his mind, he tasted Malakai's blood as, in his wolf form, he'd bitten down on the vampire. He would taste that blood again, but unfortunately, today wouldn't be the day.

No matter how badly he wanted to beat Malakai into a bloody pile of mush, he *had* to keep himself under control. If he didn't, Lexi was right; the Lord would make all of them pay... and he would start with *Lexi*.

Cole would get her to safety and hide her somewhere the Lord would never find her before allowing that to happen. But once she was out of his grasp, the sick prick would go after the Gloaming.

Many of his people might have risen against him in the rebellion, but there were plenty more who hadn't and who counted on him to keep them safe. He might be able to get a lot of the dark fae out of the Gloaming before the Lord destroyed it, but many would perish, including women and children.

Those innocents would not pay because he lost control of his temper. He would not allow it.

With a hand far steadier than the rush of blood pulsing through him would have indicated, Cole turned the locks and opened the door. Sunlight streamed across him and into the hall, but Lexi remained safely out of it.

Standing in the doorway, Malakai had his forearm resting against the frame as he leaned a little forward. Because he was five inches shorter, he had to look up when Cole answered the door.

Seeing the vampire's dark brown hair, brown eyes, and lean frame again was like a punch to Cole's gut. In a flash, the lycan part of him tore free.

Joints and bones cracked and popped; the transformation started to take him over before he had a chance to process it might happen. His jaw extended, and his fangs lengthened.

Malakai's smug smile vanished; he leaned a little away as Cole started to suppress the lycan and regain control. Cracks and pops filled the air again as his joints and bones shifted back into place.

Malakai no longer smiled, but Cole did.

"King Colburn," Malakai greeted. "How delightful to see you again."

Malakai's singsong voice caused Cole's claws to elongate once more. When he rested his hand against the doorframe and gripped it, his claws pierced the wood.

He kept smiling as he looked past Malakai to the dozen or so members of the Lord's guard behind him. They stood so close together that they blocked his view of the yard and lake.

For all he knew, there could be more guards out there.

"Why are you here, Malakai?" Cole inquired. "Lexi has made it clear you're *not* welcome here."

"I'm sure Elexiandra would be more than happy to see me."

This soon-to-be-dead fucker lived in complete denial or was trying to piss off Cole. Either way, he was ensuring it wouldn't be an easy death.

"The Lord has sent me for two reasons," Malakai said.

"And those are?" Cole inquired.

"First, to inquire about the welfare of the lady of the manor," Malakai said. "He wants to make sure she's okay."

"She's fine," Cole said.

Malakai made a small *tsking* noise that caused Sahira to edge a little closer. "I see you're still trying to convince yourself that she didn't want it," Malakai asked. "I feel sorry for you. It must be difficult to be so wrapped around that whore's poisonous little finger."

Wood bit into Cole's palm as it splintered apart beneath his hand and pierced his flesh. No matter how hard he tried, he couldn't get his fangs to retract again. When his gaze dropped to Malakai's throat, saliva filled his mouth as he pictured tearing out his jugular.

"What is the second reason the Lord sent you here?" Sahira interjected.

She rested her hand on Cole's arm. Her touch didn't calm as effectively as Lexi's, but it served as a reminder that he had to maintain control.

One day, he thought as he held Malakai's eyes. *One day I'm going to destroy you, and I will bask in your screams.*

Malakai's smile grew as he took in Sahira's hand on Cole's arm. "Oh, how sweet. Do I sense a little side action here?"

"You're disgusting," Sahira replied. "And I want you *off* my property."

"It's time for you to go," Cole said.

"First," Malakai said as he held up a finger. "The Lord rules over all the realms and *all* the land, and he has sent me here. I'll leave after I accomplish his mission, and I can't reveal the second reason I'm here until I have proof the *first* is safe."

Cole knew the Lord had someone in the Gloaming reporting to him about what Cole was doing there, and now he suspected he had someone watching over them in the human realm too.

"Lexi's not coming anywhere near you," Cole told him.

"It's okay," Lexi said from behind him.

His shoulders hunched forward as the muscles in his back stretched and something popped. His shirt tore as his fingers dug further into the wood. He restrained himself from pulling the frame free of the wall.

His lips skimmed back when he spotted her standing in the hall. He didn't want her anywhere near this bastard and wouldn't give him the satisfaction of seeing her again.

"I'm right here," Lexi said.

She took another step closer before stopping. She stood a few feet away from the sunlight to remain out of direct contact with it. If Malakai asked her to come closer, there would be a problem.

When Lexi's eyes met his, they shone with love and a plea for him to keep it together. The others remained in hiding, but they would charge out here to go after Malakai if things went bad. He had to keep it together to prevent that from happening.

"Now, you can go back and tell the Lord I'm exactly where I'm supposed to be," Lexi said.

"So you are," Malakai drawled. "How are you, dear Elexiandra?"

"I'm wonderful, Malakai," she replied.

Malakai didn't appreciate either her breezy tone or her words, as his smile vanished and his lips clamped together. Blocking his view of Lexi, Cole turned to fill the doorway again.

"Now that you've seen her, you can tell us what the second thing is the Lord wants?" Cole asked.

Cole knew something bad was coming when Malakai's smile returned.

CHAPTER ELEVEN

BESIDE HIM, Sahira stiffened, and her hand clenched on his arm. Cole's body tensed as he prepared for what was about to come.

"Cole," Lexi whispered.

"The Lord wanted me to tell you that since you like pixies so much, he felt you should have more of them," Malakai said.

A knot of dread formed in Cole's stomach. He knew Malakai was talking about *the* pixie. He never should have touched that pitiful, tortured creature in the Lord's room.

He should have walked away and left her there to suffer; he'd known he was taking a chance by putting her out of her misery, but he'd still done it. He'd been so sure he was alone in the room, so sure no one would know as she'd already been on the verge of death.

Cole originally planned to save her, but she was too far gone. Instead, her blood, like the blood of *so* many others, stained his hands. It would always haunt him, but he could live with that.

Or, at least he'd believed he could. But he'd fucked up, and the Lord knew it, and now Malakai was staring at him with the smug smile on his face. Cole glowered at him as wood crunched beneath his hand.

"Cole!" Lexi said more forcefully. "Cole, please."

Her "please" pierced through the growing haze of red clouding his vision. It reminded him he still had thousands of lives resting on his shoulders.

He'd screwed up with the pixie; he would *not* mess up again now.

Still smiling, Malakai stepped aside, and the guards around him followed suit until Cole had a clear view of the brilliant colors strewn across the green lawn. *Have the leaves fallen?*

But that made *no* sense. It was still summertime. Fall was fast approaching, but it would still be some time before the leaves changed color and fell.

Then what the hell…?

His question trailed off as he took in the beautiful mixture of colors. The colors were so entwined, he could barely discern the blues from the greens, reds, oranges, yellows, peaches, purples, and all the shades in between.

And then, he finally realized the colors did not come from leaves or a sudden bloom of wildflowers. The true horror of what lay before him sank in.

It was a slaughter.

"The Lord hopes you enjoy your gift," Malakai said as he turned to descend the stairs.

He stopped at the bottom and turned to face Cole again. The man mistakenly thought the distance might save his life, but he didn't realize the shadows beneath his feet were also the enemy.

"And he wanted you to know he's more than happy to provide you with more… if these aren't enough for you," Malakai said.

When Cole felt himself unraveling, he glanced over his shoulder at Lexi. She remained hovering in the shadows, her hands twisting before her as she stared at him. Her face was so pale that there were ghosts with more color.

Stay calm for her. Stay calm for her.

And he could do that, because there wasn't anything he

wouldn't do for her. Turning back to Malakai, Cole smiled. It was more a baring of his fangs that made Malakai blanch, but Cole didn't attack him.

"Tell The Lord his gift is greatly appreciated," Cole forced out through his teeth.

"Oh, I will."

Malakai's laughter followed him as he strode toward his horse. Gathering his reins, he swung himself onto the saddle and turned his horse toward his manor.

"Malakai!" Cole called before he could ride away. The arrogant prick turned in the saddle to look at him. "You know you're already dead, right?"

Malakai spun his horse back to face him.

"You're walking, talking, and breathing, but you're already dead," Cole told him. "Because it's only a matter of time before I kill you."

Malakai laughed again, but he didn't fool Cole; Malakai knew the truth. If he hadn't already pissed himself, Cole would bet he was about to.

Turning his horse again, Malakai nudged it in the side, and the animal took off. The Lord's guards fell in around him. Their horse's hooves trampled the bodies of the pixies littering the ground as they rode away.

Cole stared after them until they vanished. The Lord had told him to stay away from Malakai, but as soon as he got his chance, the vampire would die.

CHAPTER TWELVE

"WHAT IS IT?" Lexi whispered from behind him.

"Stay here," he said instead of answering her. "And keep away from the doorway and sun. They're gone, and I don't sense or smell anyone nearby, but someone could be watching us from the woods across the way."

"What's going on?" another voice interjected.

Cole glanced back to see that Kaylia and Brokk had returned. Kaylia held a satchel in her hand as she stood in the doorway of the library. Brokk passed Lexi as he walked toward him.

"What happened?" his brother asked.

"The Lord has given me a present," Cole replied. "And it would be best if you all stayed inside while I take care of it."

Brokk stopped behind Cole and stared out the door. He saw when his brother realized what lay scattered across the lawn as his eyes widened and his mouth parted.

"Why?" Brokk asked.

"What's out there?" Lexi demanded.

Kaylia strode out of the library doorway while Varo, Orin, and Del joined Lexi in the hall. Cole half closed the door as Kaylia approached. Tears shimmered in Sahira's eyes as she stared at Cole with a look of betrayal and confusion.

"Why did the Lord do this? *Why* did he call it a gift for *you*?" Sahira asked in a high-pitched, barely controlled voice.

"Because he's a sick fuck," Cole replied.

"But *why* did he do it for *you*?"

Cole was glad he'd told Lexi about what happened in the Lord's private solar, the pixies hung and tortured there, and the one he killed to stop her suffering. He'd known there would be consequences if the Lord ever discovered what he did, but he'd assumed he was alone.

He *had been* alone, but the Lord still knew what he'd done. *How*?

Cole didn't have an answer for that, but he certainly hadn't expected the sick *fuck* to do something like *this* as payback.

"Stay inside," Cole snarled at them.

He opened the door and ran down the front steps toward the field of pixies. He had no idea how to clean this up, but it had to be done.

Brokk's footsteps followed him down the stairs, but when softer footfalls came next, he glanced back as Sahira and Kaylia stopped at the bottom of the steps.

"Go back inside," Cole commanded.

Tears slid down Kaylia's cheeks as she bent to pick up one of the tiny, broken bodies. A small sob escaped while she stroked the pixie's silken wings. Then, she lifted her head and pinned Cole with a deadly stare.

"*Why* did he do this for you?" she demanded.

Though she looked ready to attack, Cole turned his back on her. He wasn't in the mood to argue with the crone. And if they started fighting, he might take his rage at the Lord out on her.

"Go inside," he told her. "The Lord's men were just here and could still be watching us. He'll find it suspicious if he learns you're here."

"*Why did he do this for you?*" she practically shrieked.

"Because I made the mistake of letting my conscience get the best of me. I won't let it happen again."

"That's not—"

Cole cut her off before she could continue. "I killed a pixie he was torturing in his solar. She was beyond saving, so I ended a dying creature's suffering. He's repaying my *stupid* act of kindness with one of cruelty. I should have seen it coming, but I wasn't expecting something this insane, and I believed I was *alone.*"

And he would live with the death of these innocent creatures on his conscience just like so many other things. He didn't want to look any closer, but he inspected the broken bodies surrounding him.

They looked like someone crushed them. He imagined their captors reaching into the nets, or whatever they used to gather this many pixies, and squeezing the tiny creatures to death.

He had no doubt Malakai enjoyed it.

"Now get *inside* before you destroy us all," he snarled.

"I'm sorry," she whispered, and the words stunned him almost as much as the Lord's gruesome gift.

He didn't have to look back as she ascended the steps. When the door closed, he shut his eyes and focused on the shifting currents of air around him.

Drawing on the air currents, he pushed the bodies together until they clustered in the center of the yard. Brokk and Sahira remained nearby while he worked.

CHAPTER THIRTEEN

IT WAS nightfall when they finished burying all the pixies in the woods on the other side of the lake. None of the Lord's guards were there, so at least he didn't have to worry about one of them reporting a strange woman at the manor.

The Lord would probably recognize Kaylia if he saw her, but he doubted any of his men would. Still, a report of a strange woman at the manor wouldn't go over well.

They kept the bodies away from the graves of Lexi's birth parents and took them deeper into the woods. She couldn't have this reminder when she visited them.

He wiped the sweat from his brow as he stared at the hundreds of new graves surrounding him. It would have been faster to bury them all in a mass grave, but every one of them deserved their own place to lie. He wished he'd known their names.

He shifted his attention to the manor. From what he could tell, the electricity hadn't come back as the glow of the lanterns flickered against the closed curtains. Moonlight shone down on the earth and reflected off the serene surface of the lake as crickets sang and the tree frogs chirped.

It was all so peaceful, but a churning storm simmered beneath his surface. The shadows were awake inside him, and they were *seething*. This impotent fury only made him madder as he had no one to take it out on.

One day, he would make all those who had a hand in this pay for it, but how many more innocents would die before the Lord and his followers were destroyed? And how much longer could he continue to play this cruel game?

Not much longer. He wasn't a pawn, and he was far too powerful to continue to stand by and allow the Lord to push him around and destroy innocents.

This had to stop, but first, Lexi had to learn about and come into her powers. He would play the game until she was better able to defend herself. Because once he stopped playing, the Lord was going to come after them with everything he had.

"It's done," Sahira said as she stuck the tip of her shovel in the ground.

Cole had told her many times to go back inside, so she didn't have to do this; each time, she refused. Often, with tears streaming down her face, she resolutely remained as they gathered and buried the bodies.

Now, dirt streaked her pretty face, her mahogany hair had slid free of its customary bun, and red rimmed her amber eyes, but no tears shone in them. Like his and Brokk's, dirt and sweat streaked her clothes.

"I need a shower," Sahira murmured.

So did he, but he wasn't ready to return to the manor. He'd caused this with his reckless action. He shouldn't have killed the pixie, but his conscience and the creature's cries had driven him to react instead of thinking it through.

Since meeting Lexi, the lycan part of him had made itself more known and often took over the more rational dark fae side. And he wanted to claim it was the lycan part of him that reacted so foolishly, but the sensible, dark fae part couldn't have left the defenseless creature to suffer either.

And now, he would have to look at Lexi again while knowing the blood of *these* brutalized pixies rested solely on his shoulders.

"You both should go back inside; I'm going to tour the perimeter and make sure no one is nearby," he told them.

"You never could have seen this coming, Cole," Brokk said.

"Couldn't I?" he asked.

"You said you were alone in the room."

He'd filled them in on the details of what happened while they were removing all the bodies. "I should have known he wouldn't leave me there without somehow having eyes on me."

"How would he do that?" Brokk demanded.

While disposing of the remains, Cole's mind continuously returned to the hideous portrait of the Lord glaring down at him from where it hung on the wall.

"The Lord is a warlock; he could have cast a spell over the portrait, or *any* of the numerous heads in that room, to watch over anyone who enters it," Cole said. "It could have been any number of things, and I should have suspected it. I was an idiot."

"You weren't an idiot, but you'll be one now if you think this is anyone's fault except *his*," Sahira said. "I would have done the same thing as you. I never would have left the room with that poor pixie still alive."

The burning amber of her eyes told him she believed her words were the truth, but while Sahira had a steel rod running through her spine, he couldn't see her killing one of these tiny creatures.

"You couldn't have killed her," Cole said.

"I would have done it," she insisted. "You can believe that or not, but it's the truth."

Lifting the shovel from the ground, she sank the spade into the earth. It remained standing in the air as she released it and turned to walk away.

"You can check the perimeter, and you probably should, but don't hide out here all night. Lexi deserves better," Sahira called over her shoulder.

Cole refrained from replying. Instead, he turned to his brother. "How did things go in the crone realm?"

"Fine. She only spoke with one other woman, and that was to say she didn't know how long she would be gone, but she would check in. Then, she gathered her things, and we returned."

"Do you trust her?"

"I don't like her."

"That's not what I asked."

"I know." Brokk ran a hand through his hair and tugged at the ends of it as he stared at the manor. "Yes, I think we can trust her. She's in this pretty deep now, and I think she hates the Lord more than she hates vampires."

"Which is a lot."

"Apparently," Brokk muttered.

"I'm going to check the perimeter now."

"I'll help you," Brokk said. "We'll each go in different directions so that it will get done faster."

"Fine," Cole said as he picked up his and Brokk's discarded shovels. He pulled Sahira's from the ground to return to the barn. "I'll meet you behind the manor."

CHAPTER FOURTEEN

LEXI ROSE from her chair in the library where she'd been sitting and talking with her dad. She'd nearly chewed her nails off over her concern for Cole, but it was good to get a chance to sit and talk with him.

It helped calm her even as she resisted her impulse to run outside after Cole. She didn't have to see what was out there; Kaylia had informed her with tears in her eyes.

After that, her dad spent the next few hours occupying her by asking questions about her life after he went missing. He filled her in on his life during that time, but since he was in a prison cell, his side of the conversation was a lot shorter.

She'd missed him so much and hadn't realized her heartache from his absence was such a constant, needling pain until it was gone. His smile and laugh made her smile; she loved the way his eyes twinkled with merriment.

Despite everything going on, having him back in her life and his love returned was such a gift. She cherished every second of it.

She'd been right; Sahira had told him about Malakai's attack in the barn. He asked her a lot of questions about her relationship with Cole, but when Kaylia and Varo joined them in the room, he handed her a book.

"It's been a while, but I'd like to hear you read to me," he said.

"I'd like a story too," Kaylia said.

She settled on the floor near the fireplace. She held a glass of wine, and her eyes were still bloodshot, but she looked better than earlier.

Lexi looked at the book her father had handed her, *The Wind in the Willows*. It was one of her favorites.

Lexi settled back in her chair as Sahira breezed into the room. Her hair was still wet from her shower, and she'd cinched her bathrobe at the waist. Orin had vanished into the tunnels hours ago; she had no idea where he'd gone, but she was glad she didn't have to deal with him tonight.

Varo went into the other room and returned with two chairs for him and Sahira. Opening the book, Lexi began to read as the clock in the other room ticked away the time.

She read for almost half an hour before the front door opened. Brokk entered first, and Lexi held her breath as she waited for him to close the door. She half expected him to return alone, but Cole stepped into the manor behind him.

Her breath rushed out. A part of her was convinced he wouldn't return. That he'd feel too ashamed or dirty or was beating himself up too much for something that wasn't his fault and stay away.

But this was one of the many things that weren't his fault, yet he blamed himself.

When his eyes met hers, the self-hatred and anguish in their beautiful blue depths tore her heart out and stomped all over it. She'd give anything to walk over, grab his elbow, and steer him back out the door so they could walk around the lake and talk, but she couldn't go outside anymore.

She was trapped inside, and he was trapped in his memories. Throwing her shoulders back, she stalked past Brokk, linked her arm through Cole's, and walked with him toward the stairwell. At least, in her room, they'd have privacy from the others.

They were almost to the stairs when Kaylia stepped out of the library. "Cole."

The two of them stiffened before turning to face her.

"What?" Cole demanded.

She wasn't the least bit put off by his brusque tone. "We're going to destroy the Lord. He won't get away with this."

"No, he won't."

"We need a plan."

"The plan is to sleep tonight, and we'll talk in the morning," Lexi said.

Couldn't the woman see he was exhausted?

"Do you know somewhere private, where no one else will see her, and where there is sunlight to expose her to?" Cole asked.

Kaylia tapped an elegant finger against the small cleft in her chin. "I know of an outer realm that will work. I often use it to meditate, and I've never seen anyone else there. It's not like most of the other outer realms; it's rather pretty."

"I'll go with you tomorrow morning to check it out," Cole said.

CHAPTER FIFTEEN

LEXI WOKE the next morning to discover Cole standing by her window. The sun's rays streaming over his naked frame illuminated chiseled muscles, broad shoulders, a tapered waist, and powerful thighs.

She now knew that the black ciphers running from Cole's fingertips, up his arms, and across his shoulders before going down his back were the tip of the iceberg.

The black markings covered him from head to toe when he wasn't keeping most of them hidden. With their sharp edges, the black, dark fae markings resembled flames and were as amazing and impressive as him.

When he turned to her and saw she was awake, he pulled the curtains over the window.

"You do realize you're standing there, completely naked, for anyone to see," she said.

"I don't care who sees me," he replied.

"Maybe *I* do."

For the first time in a while, a small smile curved the corner of his too kissable mouth. "I like it when you get jealous."

She frowned as she crossed her arms over her chest. "I'm not jealous. I'm just possessive of what's mine."

"What's the difference?"

"If I were jealous, that would mean I'm not sure of my standing in this relationship and us, but I'm not."

His hand fell away from the curtain as he turned to face her fully. She couldn't stop her gaze from drifting down his magnificent body. When they'd entered her room last night, he stripped out of his clothes and tossed them in the corner before going to shower.

When she looked now, his clothes were gone. She had no idea what he'd done with them, but he would never wear them again. After he got out of the shower, he'd crawled into bed with her and held her close while she fell asleep in his arms.

Looking at him now, the memory of the horror the Lord had dumped in her front yard faded as a small kernel of desire bloomed in her belly. He could chase away the rest of the memory; he could make it disappear and replace it with something better.

"What are you doing over by the window?" she asked.

Had he gotten out of bed while she slept to sleep somewhere else, and she hadn't noticed?

She'd believed his aversion to sleeping in the same bed with her was over, but she might have been wrong.

"Some of the Lord's guard rode by earlier. I got out of bed to make sure they kept riding," he said.

Her fingers clenched on the comforter as her gaze went to the window. "Did they?"

"Yes, but I suspect we'll be seeing them more often. We have to start your training so you can defend yourself better when the time comes."

His words doused her desire as her mind pinged back and forth like a soccer ball between two kids. What if she couldn't do this? What if she failed to figure out how to control her powers? What if her failure got Cole killed?

Her fingers dug deeper into the comforter as she took a deep breath to calm herself. Freaking out about things she couldn't control wouldn't do her any good. She could freak out if she failed.

But since she *refused* to fail, then she wouldn't ever have to freak out.

She threw back the comforter, jumped to her feet, and hurried to her bureau to gather her clothes. Before she got there, Cole stepped in her way.

Lexi came to an abrupt halt in time to avoid smacking into his chest. Tilting her head back, she looked up to meet the beautiful Persian blue of his eyes.

His nearness caused the hair on her arms to stand up as electricity crackled across her skin. His earlier words had doused her passion, but his closeness caused it to come alive again.

Since she stopped taking the birth control Sahira had given her with the suppressing potion, she'd started feeling and experiencing things with more intensity. One of those things was her attraction to him.

It had always been intense, but now as she licked her lips, she could taste him even though it had been hours since they last kissed. And as her nipples hardened, she recalled what it felt like to have his hands on them and nearly moaned.

An ache grew between her thighs as she became wet with need. Sex was the last thing on her mind when she got out of bed, but now, it was all she could think about.

When her eyes met his, she saw the same hunger in their silver depths.

~

COLE HADN'T EXPECTED to have Lexi staring up at him like she was now. He'd planned to return to the Gloaming, gather some clothes, check in with Niall, and make sure everything was fine before returning to visit this outer realm and make sure it was safe.

And now, the scent of her arousal, the flush in her cheeks, and the small breaths she took as her gaze roamed over him again made him forget his plans. Her striking, hunter green eyes with their flecks of emerald sparkled in the dim light of the room as she nibbled on her lower lip.

Lifting a strand of her long, auburn hair, he admired its deeper shades of red as it slid through his fingers. When she rested her fingers against his chest, he nearly groaned as she licked her plump lips, and her pulse quickened.

The shadows within him stirred in response. Despite their thirst for blood and power, even they wanted her, but he kept them locked away.

Releasing her hair, he rested his hand on the silken skin of her shoulder as he traced its delicate curve. He'd touched her so often that he knew her every curve and freckle. Yet, *every* time he touched her, it was like the first time all over again.

She excited him in a way no other could; she was his other half, his mate, and the woman he couldn't live without—the woman he planned to marry. And soon, he would ask her to do so.

Drawing her closer, he cupped her cheek before bending to kiss her. She tasted of strawberries and promises to come and, as her tongue touched his, power.

The sensation of her power crackling against his skin set his blood on fire and roused the appetite of his dark fae half. A delicious sound of desire rumbled up her throat and vibrated his lips.

She rocked her hips into him as her fingers curled around his biceps and dug into his flesh. Her hand caressed his flesh and slid down his stomach to clasp his cock.

As she stroked him, power swirled between them until the crisp scent of it filled the air. The aroma reminded him of the air during a thunderstorm as lightning split the sky and crackled on the air.

It wasn't quite the scent of impending rain between them but the odor of the *energy* a thunderstorm possessed. Holding her, he felt like he'd grasped the power of lightning in his hands.

Walking her backward, he pressed her against the wall before pulling his hips back. He kept her pinned against the wall but pulled his dick away from her. Not at all happy about it, she bit his lip in displeasure, but he had plans for her.

CHAPTER SIXTEEN

HE GRINNED as he slid his hands down to grip her waist before gliding them lower. She gasped as he teased her clit and slid his finger through her enticing wetness. Her breaths came faster, and the need in her eyes enflamed his own.

Dropping to his knees, he looked up at her beautiful, flushed face before kissing her belly. Her hands fell on his shoulders as his kisses moved lower. Her eyes darkened, and her head fell back against the wall as his mouth settled over her hot, wet core.

He tasted her and fucked her with his tongue and watched her breasts rise and fall with the rapid increase of her breaths as her hips arched into him. She was so gorgeous and *his.*

One hand rose over her head and flattened against the wall; the other dug into his shoulder as her hips swayed toward him. She bit her lip to muffle her sounds of ecstasy, but they still reverberated in his ears as he gripped her ass and drew her closer.

Her other hand fell to his shoulder, and her fingers bit into his flesh as her racing heart hammered in his ears. And then, with a muffled cry that caused his body to tense in anticipation, she came.

He savored the taste of her orgasm as her legs went limp. Catching her in his arms, he rose and carried her to the bed, where he laid her down. The taste of her lingering on his tongue brought the lycan part of him to the forefront.

But the fae part still wanted to play.

He walked over to her closet, opened the doors, and removed the belt from the white robe hanging inside. Lexi watched him from hooded eyes as she stretched alluringly.

Climbing onto the bed, he straddled her with his legs and held her eyes as he grasped her wrists. "Do you trust me?"

"Always," she answered without hesitation.

Taking the belt, he wrapped it around her wrists, gripped the end of it, and pulled her hands above her head. Her eyes widened a little, but she didn't protest as he tied the end of the belt around one of the bedposts.

And then, he started to play. He explored every inch of her with hands and tongue. He kissed, he nipped, and he sank his fangs into her to mark her as his mate. When he finished with her front, he grasped her hips and rolled her over.

She moaned when his mouth found her shoulder blades, and his fingers found her clit. He teased until she was panting and her hips were rising and falling, but he didn't give her the release she sought.

When he pulled his hand away, she muttered a curse and wiggled back toward him. Leveling himself over her, he used his thighs to push her legs apart as he clasped her bound wrists and leaned over until his mouth was against her ear.

"How badly do you want me to fuck you?" he inquired.

"So bad," she whispered.

"Tell me exactly what you want me to do to you."

Despite the blush creeping into her neck, she replied. "I want you to put your cock inside me and make me come. I *need* you to fuck me and make me come."

"As you wish," he murmured.

Cole's pulse raced with excitement as he grasped her hips and lifted them a little way off the bed. When she was on her elbows and knees before him, he guided his shaft into her.

The second he entered her, the instant their bodies joined, the power swelled on the air between them, and his fangs lengthened again. The dark fae part of him feasted on that power. The lycan part sought to claim its mate again.

Sinking his fangs into her shoulder, he growled as he drove deeper into her. With every thrust, the power increased until it crackled between them.

He lost himself to the exquisite sensation of her sheath clenching his erection, her body beneath his, and the rightness of holding her in his arms. She buried her face in the bed to muffle her cries when she came again.

The exquisite sensation of her orgasm wrenched his own from him, and his seed filled her. For a second, his hand closed around the lightning surging between them, and it filled him with power.

CHAPTER SEVENTEEN

LEXI RAN her fingers up and down the etched muscle of Cole's chest and stomach as she lay nestled against his side. His arm encircled her, and his hand clasped her bicep as he held her close. Tenderly, he kissed her forehead before lying back to stare at the ceiling.

"We should go," he said. "You should start your training."

"I know."

But she was reluctant to get up. In his arms, she was safe and secure. She could forget about everything working against them and trying to tear them apart.

"I think Kaylia can help us," she said.

"I hope so."

"At the very least, I think we can trust her."

"Hmm," he grunted in response.

She ran her fingers down his belly, tracing the ridges there as she contemplated everything they'd learned yesterday. There was one thing she'd been avoiding, but they had to discuss it.

"What do you think about this Shadow Reaver thing?" she asked.

Holding her breath, she couldn't bring herself to look at him as she waited for his response.

"Ever since the trials, I've had more of a connection to the shadows and can control them in ways I never could before," he said.

"So, do you think you *are* this Shadow Reaver?"

"If they have to put a name to it, they can call me that if they want. That doesn't mean it's true. But even if it *is* true, I'm still me, Lexi."

"I know," she whispered.

But she worried he wouldn't *always* be him. The shadows might twist and turn him into something else… something unrecognizable.

Her hand flattened against his chest, above where his heart beat so solidly. It was such a good heart, and it belonged to one of the best men she'd ever known.

He was honorable and kind but also harsh and brutal when necessary. He'd fought a war, but not because he wanted to fight it, and those he'd killed still haunted him. They always would.

He was strong and beautiful, and he loved her and his family with everything he had. She couldn't see the shadows ever corrupting him, but they had no idea what their futures held or where their roads would lead.

"Don't worry about me," he said as if he could read her mind. "I'm not going anywhere, and I'm not going to let anything take me over. I'm in control of me."

"What about the prophecy?"

"Prophecies are garbage. The few that have come true were simple things. I bet *no* one knows the history of this prophecy or where it came from, not just Kaylia. Prophecies have never been something to take seriously."

"And we're not going to start now."

Cole chuckled as he kissed her forehead again. "No, we're not."

But she couldn't shake the knot of anxiety lodged in her chest and throat. He was a good, honorable man, but she'd felt the darkness simmering inside him… and it was growing.

He was the strongest immortal she knew, but was he strong enough to withstand the power of the shadows? What if they corrupted him?

And it was so easy for power to corrupt. Would she lose him? Or what if something *did* happen to her, and it pushed him over the edge?

"If something ever happens to me, promise me you'll be okay," she said.

"Don't say that. Nothing is going to happen to you."

Resting her hand on his chest, she lifted her head to look at him. "With everything we're facing, one of us dying is a very real possibility."

Silver flashed across his eyes before he suppressed it. "I'm not going to let anything happen to you."

"Promise me, Cole."

His hand settled on the small of her back as he pulled her closer. "I will go on, but you're my mate, Lexi. A lycan never recovers from the loss of a mate."

This was one area where his dark fae side wouldn't save him. If he recognized her as his mate and had claimed her as such, then he would suffer the same fate as every other lycan who lost their mate—a lifetime of misery.

"I won't let you go through that," she said.

"Good."

"You still haven't promised me."

"I promise not to destroy everyone. Besides, while it's flattering they think I possess that kind of power, I assure you, I don't. The shadows make me stronger, but not enough to destroy everyone or all the realms."

Lexi nodded, but they both knew his powers were growing. Could he destroy the world now?

No.

But if he continued to progress and draw on the shadows, and if they continued to weave their way into him, it could be an entirely different scenario.

However, dwelling on the possibilities wasn't getting them anywhere, and all this anxiety was most likely for nothing.

As he said, prophecies were garbage, but she was still uneasy as she settled against him once more. Not only did she *not* want him to become a monster, but she'd prefer not to die.

She was going to have to work to learn more about her powers, and she was going to have to do it as fast as she could.

CHAPTER EIGHTEEN

LEXI STEPPED out of the portal Kaylia had created and into her first outer realm. With her hand, she shaded her eyes against the sun streaming down on her. As she did so, her hand began to glow in the red light cascading over her skin.

Through squinted eyes, she peered toward the sun. Unlike the sun in the human realm, this one was more reddish-orange as it illuminated the land and the blue sky surrounding it.

After the darkness of the portal, it took her eyes a few seconds to adjust to this bright realm, but once they did, she lowered her hand to take in the landscape. Before she could see much of this new realm, Kaylia breathed...

"Oh... my... Hecate."

Cole stepped closer to Lexi as she turned toward the crone who exited the portal behind them. Kaylia's gray eyes roamed over Lexi as her jaw hung open.

Lexi glanced self-consciously down as the scale-like marks that resembled a dragon broke out on her arms. They disappeared beneath the thin, dark green shirt she wore.

She couldn't see her eyes, but she imagined they'd already

turned gold. Her pupils had probably become slitted like she'd seen them when she was in Underhill.

At this point, she wouldn't be shocked if she sprouted a dragon tail too.

At least she didn't feel a burning sensation in her chest, so maybe she wouldn't start spewing fire like a dragon anytime soon. And she also didn't have wings. But she *really* would have enjoyed wings.

She could almost feel the wind beneath her as she soared high above the land like she had so many times in her dreams. Had those dreams been trying to tell her about her true ancestry? Or had a part of her been trying to escape the binds her dad and Sahira placed on her?

She'd never know the answer, but she suspected that's exactly what happened.

And now those bonds were down, and she was glowing like the north star on a cold winter night. She had no idea what any of this meant, but she didn't seem to be turning *into* a dragon. That was good; she much preferred herself the way she was.

But maybe becoming a dragon would be for the best. Then she could sweep into the palace and eat the Lord.

She cringed at the idea of eating anyone, but after what he'd done to the pixies, she couldn't wait to see him dead.

Kaylia's hand went to her mouth as she continued to gaze at Lexi. From the portal behind her, Orin, Brokk, Varo, and Sahira emerged into the realm. Unable to be in the sun without burning and turning to ash, her father grudgingly remained behind.

"Fascinating, isn't it?" Orin murmured.

Kaylia's hand lowered from her mouth. "I've never seen anything like it."

Lexi struggled to keep her disappointment hidden; she'd hoped Kaylia would know what this was. "You never saw this from the arach you knew?"

"No, and I've never heard of anyone else seeing anything like it, and this is something that would have gotten around. You certainly can't miss it."

Lexi ran her fingers over the silver markings on her arm. They looked like dragon scales, but it felt no different than normal when she touched her skin. Beneath the rays of the reddish sun, she looked like something entirely different, but she was still herself.

It was all so confusing.

"I've seen silver markings on an arach before," Kaylia said. "But *never* to this extent. There were only a few of them, and they quickly faded away. And I never saw or ever heard of an arach being covered in them or *glowing*."

"We've heard of the silver markings, too," Cole said.

Earlier, he'd returned to the Gloaming to get clothes and check in on things. While there, he'd donned a black fae tunic, formfitting brown pants, and sable boots. He'd also strapped on his father's sword; the hilt of it glinted in the sun streaming over him.

"Do you know what caused the markings to come out on the arach you saw?" Lexi asked.

"No," Kaylia whispered as she continued to gawk at Lexi. "This is amazing."

"That's because it's not *you*. I can't stop it once the sun or moonlight touches me. I have no control over this, and I can't go outside until I gain some. There has to be a way to conceal this. I can't be the only arach who did this, can I?"

"I... I..." Kaylia stared at her as she tried to form a response. "No, you can't be. Since both your parents were arach, this *has* to be something they could do too. Which means it is controllable. We just have to figure out how to do that."

When Cole returned to the Gloaming earlier, she took a shower, dressed, and went downstairs to wait for him to return. While there, she and her father told Kaylia about her heritage and how he saved her as a baby.

Kaylia couldn't hide her doubt over the fact that her dad, a *vampire*, and Sahira, a half-*vampire*, had willingly put themselves in danger for her. She may have been skeptical and didn't like having to rethink her stance on vampires, but she couldn't deny Lexi was alive, happy, and had grown up surrounded by love.

"What is the point of this?" Lexi asked as she waved a hand over her body. "Why am I glowing like this?"

"I have no idea," Kaylia murmured.

Orin snorted and rolled his eyes. "We're off to a great start with you."

Kaylia scowled at him while Brokk chuckled. The crone turned her angry look on Brokk before focusing on Lexi again.

"If I want to control something, like a glamour, I have to go inside myself and picture it happening. If I want"—she held her palm up before her— "a phoenix in my hand, then I picture a phoenix."

Kaylia stopped talking as she stared at her palm. A few seconds later, a small phoenix materialized there. The tiny, beautiful creature ruffled its feathers before bursting into flames and turning to ash in her hand.

When Kaylia blew the ash away, a multitude of colors swirled through it before it vanished.

"Parlor tricks," Brokk muttered.

It was impossible to ignore the increasing hostility between them. It surprised Lexi to see Brokk hostile toward anyone as he was usually more easygoing, but Kaylia's attitude about vampires had rubbed Brokk the wrong way.

Kaylia ignored him as, with three long strides, she closed the distance between her and Lexi. Clasping Lexi's wrist, she lifted her hand into the air and held it between them.

"You don't want to glow, so try to picture it going way," Kaylia instructed.

She made it sound so easy, and Lexi *longed* for it to be that easy. It would be wonderful if she stopped glowing and didn't have to worry about exposing herself and everyone else simply by stepping into natural light.

Closing her eyes, she pictured herself surrounded by the glow, and then she started to imagine the glow fading away and her skin returning to normal. It was so vivid in her mind she could almost *feel* it.

She could practically taste how badly she *craved* the image in her mind to become true. She yearned to walk free again in the human realm and the Gloaming and everywhere else, including this rocky outer realm with its red sun and craggy mountaintops piercing the sky.

In her mind, she was once again normal as she tipped her head back to bask in the sun beating down on her while she stood beneath its rays as a completely normal immortal once more.

When she opened her eyes, she swore her skin glowed brighter.

CHAPTER NINETEEN

BY THE END of the first day, Lexi was disappointed but hopeful. By the end of the third day, her frustration was growing, and the niggling fear she would always be like this was taking a firmer hold on her.

By the end of the first week, she was struggling not to cry in frustration. Not only was she no closer to stopping the glow, but she was also exhausted.

When she wasn't working with Kaylia to gain control of herself, Brokk, Cole, and her dad were training her to fight better. She was stronger and faster without the potion to suppress her strength, reflexes, and abilities.

Lexi had no idea what else was possible for her, as she and Kaylia were also failing to unlock that potential, but she could wield a sword far better than she ever could before. She still preferred a dagger and throwing stars, as she could maneuver the first better, and she didn't have to get close to her targets with her stars.

However, wielding a sword had its benefits. She was also learning how to battle someone in hand-to-hand combat, and it was kicking her ass.

Despite Sahira's healing potions and her own ability to heal faster without the suppression potion, she was still sore, bruised, and exhausted when she crawled into bed every night. She *swore* Brokk lived to sweep her legs out from under her so she would always fall on her very bruised and battered ass.

He laughed every time he did it, and Lexi was beginning to understand Kaylia's dislike of him. When he offered her his hand, she'd push it away and get up herself. She learned real fast to bounce up and away from him as the first time she rose, he swept her legs out again.

Cole had to leave after that move as the shadows stirred around him, his eyes burned silver, and he couldn't hide the outline of his fangs behind his lips. It was necessary for her to learn this and to realize she would always have to be on guard in a real battle, but he didn't like it.

Her dad worked with her on defense the most. At night, they moved the furniture in the library aside so he could drill her on keeping her hands up, watching her opponent's every move, and trying to learn their weaknesses.

She and Cole mostly worked on weapons training, though the three of them weren't against teaming up against her. She was so exhausted she could barely keep her eyes open at dinner.

Once, when she fell asleep at the table, she woke to discover mashed potatoes all over her face. Cole wanted her to take a day off; she refused.

She had to get through this, she had to learn, and she had to get better if they were going to defeat the Lord. The only problem was, she was getting better at fighting, weapons, and defense, but she wasn't making any progress when it came to her arach abilities... whatever those were.

And now, at the end of the second week, she was feeling more beaten down and hopeless than ever. She would not let this defeat her. She would figure it out, even if it took years.

Lexi tried not to think about the possibility it might take that long. If she did, with as exhausted as she was, she'd start crying and probably never stop.

She also couldn't think about the reality. And that was, they didn't have years before the Lord sought to destroy them.

While Kaylia worked with her one-on-one, Brokk, Orin, and Varo stopped coming to the outer realm. They'd shifted their focus to preparing Orin's troops for another war.

They'd also moved the refugees out of the tunnels beneath the manor. Lexi was sad to see them go, especially Jayden, as she'd grown close to the little boy, but with the revelation of what she was, she'd realized it was more unsafe than ever to have them beneath the manor.

Her father had made sure no one would discover the tunnels. However, if her heritage were revealed, the Lord and Malakai would tear her home apart or destroy it. If that happened, there was a chance the refugees could be uncovered and killed.

For now, the refugees all resided in the outer realm where Orin's prison was located, including the humans. It was dangerous to take humans into the Shadow Realms. When he first started gathering rebels, Orin had come to her to keep the mortals safe in her tunnels, but they didn't have a choice anymore.

The humans should be safe at the prison, but they wouldn't be allowed to leave it. She was sure they were all miserable there, as it didn't sound like the most hospitable place, but at least they weren't trapped beneath the earth anymore, and they would be safer.

And soon, those who could fight might have to do so again.

Although, with the way things were going for her, they might never have to fight. Or they would have to fight, but they wouldn't have an arach there to help them through because she was failing at tapping into her powers.

She hid it well, but Lexi could tell Kaylia was becoming annoyed that she couldn't figure out how to repress the glow or how to trigger Lexi's other arach abilities. If she even *had* any other powers.

Lexi was beginning to question if the arach exaggerated their abilities and didn't have any. It would explain why she was such an epic failure at this.

But no matter how much she was starting to hope that was true, it wasn't. The arach helped create the trials Cole went through, which meant they possessed powerful magic. They communicated with or controlled the dragons... somehow.

They were said to throw fire and withstand its blast, and Kaylia confirmed this was indeed a trait of theirs. She'd witnessed it.

So, her ancestors could create fire, but Lexi couldn't, or at least she had no idea how to do so. And she was too afraid to stick her hand in a flame to see if she could withstand its heat now that she'd stopped taking the potion.

She'd had enough of burns after Orin did it to her. She easily recalled the searing pain of her hand burning, smelled the crispy flesh, and heard the sizzle.

She was in *no* rush to do that again.

Now, as she sat in the reddish sunlight of the outer realm, she studied the rocky land. The sun shining off the black stones reflected hundreds of reds and oranges around her.

It was stunning, but she was beginning to hate this place that once offered such hope and now only represented frustration and bitterness.

Cole and Sahira stood by the portal. Today, Brokk and Varo had ventured back to join them while Orin went... well, she had no idea where Orin went, and she was too tired to care enough to ask him.

Cole scowled as he watched her and Kaylia. He considered Kaylia a threat, and if she wasn't going to be useful, he would neutralize that threat.

Lexi wasn't going to let that happen. Kaylia hadn't been able to help her, but she could help them in other ways. She was wise and powerful and had a lot of friends. They couldn't afford to lose having her on their side.

Besides, though Lexi was losing hope, she wasn't going to give up. There had to be *some* way to control and learn how to use her abilities.

Sitting cross-legged in front of her, Kaylia rested her hands on her knees as she studied Lexi with an intensity that almost made her squirm, but she managed to remain still. Beneath the rays of the sun, sweat beaded her forehead and slid down her nape. Her bun kept her hair from her neck, but she was still uncomfortably hot.

"We're going to try something new," Kaylia said.

CHAPTER TWENTY

"I'M UP FOR NEW," Lexi replied.

"We've been working on trying to get you to control the glow by imagining it doesn't exist, but I think we should work on trying to shield it from others."

Lexi clasped her hands in her lap and fiddled with her fingers. "What do you mean?"

From the corner of her eye, she saw Cole shift. He folded his arms over his chest as his eyes narrowed on Kaylia. She could tell he was trying to decide if this was something that could harm Lexi.

"We're trying to control your arach abilities like they're those of a witch or a dark fae." Kaylia flicked a glance at Cole. "Many are aware the dark fae hide some of their ciphers to keep the true depth of their power a secret from *everyone* else."

Cole most certainly did. It was something Lexi had always suspected, but she never could have guessed the amount of ciphers covering his body until he revealed them to her. She doubted anyone, even a dark fae, would ever suspect his ciphers covered him from head to toe.

"How do you keep your ciphers hidden?" Kaylia asked.

"I'm not giving away the secrets of my species," Cole replied.

"This isn't about revealing secrets or learning new ones; this is about helping *her*. How do you hide them?"

Cole stared stonily back at her while Brokk and Varo shifted uncomfortably beside him. When Cole's steely eyes met Lexi's, they softened, and a smile curved the corners of his mouth.

"I simply imagine they're not there," he admitted. "Just like you do with a glamour."

Brokk's face scrunched up at this revelation, and Varo gave a small nod.

"But that's not working for her." Kaylia focused on Lexi again. "You're not a dark fae, and you're not a witch, so we're going to have to try something different, and hopefully, it will work.

"I've seen the silver markings of an arach; you've heard about their marks, but not anything like this, which means they keep this hidden, not through imagining them gone, but some other way. I believe that way might be some kind of shield, and sometimes, they experienced cracks in their protection.

"Those cracks allowed others to glimpse what lay beneath the shield... the marks. I think we're seeing all they hid beneath their shield with you. So, we'll create one that will either keep natural light out or stop others from seeing this.

"You have to try blocking out the sun, but we're going to do it in small increments. Lift your hand."

Lexi lifted her hand into the air. The golden glow emanating from her skin and the silver markings were beautiful, but she would give anything to sit outside again without turning into a glowstick.

"Now, I want you to imagine... no, not imagine. I want you to *create* a block or shield or whatever feels most natural to you to stop the light from touching your skin. If that doesn't feel right, try creating one to block others from seeing this."

Kaylia waved a hand at the golden glow emanating from her before tracing one of the scale-like, silver etchings.

"Create a shield around you that will keep your fingers

protected, and as it expands, your fingers will be normal again. But you have to work to make it a reality."

Lexi shot her an irritated look. "Do you think I'm not trying? Do you think I *enjoy* being locked in my house while worrying that everyone I love could die if anyone sees me? Do you think this is *fun* for me? I'm exhausted, frustrated, sore, and done with all of it, but I'm still here."

"I know you're trying," Kaylia replied in a placating tone that set Lexi's teeth on edge. "But it's time to try something new."

For a moment, Lexi was certain Cole would never get the chance to kill Kaylia as her fangs throbbed, and she almost punched the crone in her beautiful face. Then, she took a deep, steadying breath and reminded herself that Kaylia was only trying to help... even if she was *infuriating* at times.

She still wasn't sure if Kaylia actually liked her or was just here because she intended to bring down the Lord, but there were times when she liked this woman. Right now was not one of them.

"Please, try," Kaylia urged. "And start with something small, like your fingertips."

Lexi pulled her shoulders back and sat a little straighter. So what if everything else she'd tried had failed? This might be the thing that worked.

She tried not to let her past disappointments get the best of her. If she gave in to them, she would never succeed. Still, they wiggled at the back of her mind like worms rising from the earth on a rainy day.

Staring at her hand, she worked to create a shield to keep the sun from touching her, but it didn't feel right. She loved the sun and its warmth; she couldn't bear not feeling it against her skin as she basked in its warmth.

Her forehead furrowed as she tried to picture the shield the other way Kaylia described it as something to keep others from seeing her markings and the glow. She started with her fingernails.

The shield grew bigger and stronger in her mind until she could almost see it. It was like having a fine coat of wax around her fingers, one that kept the glow confined, but she could still feel the warmth of the sun against her skin there.

And then, for the briefest of seconds, the glow vanished and her fingertips were normal once more.

She emitted a strangled cry as she jerked her hand toward her. When she did, the shield crumpled and the glow returned.

"Did you see that?" She looked excitedly at Kaylia before whipping her head in Cole's direction. "*Did you see that?*"

"It was something," Kaylia said.

It was more than *something!* To her, it was *everything!*

Cole smiled as he came a little closer. "I saw," he assured her. "You're doing it."

"You have much further to go," Kaylia said.

The look Cole shot the crone caused Lexi's breath to suck in. When she turned back to Kaylia, her attention remained on Lexi, but the slight tensing of her jaw revealed her uneasiness of Cole.

Lexi hadn't seen anything out of control with Cole since Malakai arrived at her door, but she sensed the darkness and power simmering beneath his surface, waiting to break free.

She'd tried talking to him again about the Shadow Reaver, but he was rushing to get to the Gloaming. Since then, they'd barely had any time alone to discuss it.

After this, they would return to the manor, and he would go to the Gloaming and spend the rest of the evening there, getting things back under control while she worked with Brokk and her dad on more fighting lessons. She'd already spent the early morning working on them with Cole, but she had to get better.

One of the reasons she was so desperate to control her glowing ability was so she could return to the Gloaming with him. She disliked being separated from him and being unable to move around freely.

Over time, she might learn what else she could do. She'd come to accept that she might never know about all of her abilities, but she was determined to become strong enough to help bring down the Lord.

"Now, let's do it again, but we'll work on covering more of your hand this time," Kaylia said.

Turning to face the crone again, Lexi lifted her hand before her and concentrated on building another shield around her whole finger this time.

CHAPTER TWENTY-ONE

THAT EVENING, Cole left Lexi and Kaylia under the watch of Varo, Sahira, and Del as he returned to the Gloaming with Brokk. He had no idea where Orin had gone off to, but his brother was usually there when he left. However, Orin would probably turn up soon; he always did.

He still didn't trust the crone with Lexi; he never would, but she was *finally* making headway with his mate, and that was what mattered. As long as she didn't harm Lexi and remained on their side, he could ignore his dislike of her.

Brokk was a different story. His dislike of the woman who barely paid him, Del, or Sahira any attention was obvious. And it was growing stronger every day.

Now, as they strode down the hall, Brokk walked at his side with his shoulders back and determination etched onto his features. Neither of them was looking forward to this, but the council members had insisted on having a meeting.

Cole was not in the mood to play politics, but he couldn't deny them this. The Gloaming was still recovering from the destruction the rebellion created.

Too many dark fae didn't have homes. They remained

ensconced in the houses that once belonged to the king's soldiers who didn't survive the Lord's war.

For now, those homeless dark fae were content with their new residences, but that wouldn't last. They weren't used to living on top of each other, with the remaining king's soldiers, and being inside the bailey where they had less room to roam freely. They were used to freedom, farming, and working the land.

They were building new houses on the charred land they'd already cleared. Cole hoped it would only be another month before most of those living in the bailey were in their new homes.

But he was sure some of the council wasn't happy with the way things were going. They'd also made it clear they believed he should be here more often, but training Lexi had to be a priority.

They could never know that, but she could be the key to taking down the Lord, and he had to make sure she stayed safe. He already felt like he spent too much time away from her, but there weren't enough hours in the day for everything he had to do.

It was a good thing he'd learned to survive on very little sleep while fighting in the war because he was only getting a few hours a night now.

They turned a corner as a ripple of annoyance ran through the palace. Before he endured the trials, Cole never felt anything from the palace, but he'd experienced the sensation of being connected to it more than a few times since then.

It wasn't daily, but he'd come to accept he had a strange bond with this mysterious place now. He'd always known it had a mind of its own, but he'd learned that it felt and experienced things too.

He suspected the palace's irritation was due to Becca's arrival for the meeting. His suspicions were confirmed when a door slammed down the hall and Becca squeaked. Cole smiled, and Brokk chuckled.

Before Lexi arrived here, the palace never did anything to Becca, but the building had protected Lexi from her before. Now, it was letting Becca know it didn't like her presence in its halls.

Just thinking of his ex, who wasn't really an ex but more a passing fling, irritated Cole. The shadows inside him stirred, and the ones in the hall shifted toward him.

Cole suppressed the shadows inside him, but the ones in the hall continued to twist as he and Brokk turned another corner. Brokk glanced at him but didn't speak. Cole was aware his brother, Lexi, and the others were concerned about him. It wasn't necessary.

He could and *would* control this.

He would not become the Shadow Reaver the crones had whispered about, and he most definitely would *not* allow anything to happen to Lexi. Prophecies rarely ever came true, most immortals knew this, but enough had come true over the years that some foolish immortals put faith in them.

As they walked, Cole replayed the prophecy in his mind... *When the last light blooms, the Shadow Reaver shall rise. When the last light falls, the Shadow Reaver will destroy us all.*

If the ridiculous prophecy was true, then Lexi most certainly was the part when the last light blooms. She was the last arach, and she was definitely light. There was no denying that.

And he'd certainly become more like the shadows as they moved through and around him, but Lexi would never fall, and he wasn't going to destroy them all.

However, he couldn't deny that the shadows inside and around him were growing stronger. Their power, and the promise of the destruction they could wreak, whispered to him daily.

He'd dreamed of the death they could unleash before. It haunted him, but he refused to believe it could ever become a reality. The shadows were malevolent and violent, and he felt their malignant presence inside him every day.

He suspected he would have to battle their presence for the rest of his life, but he would *not* give in to the darkness growing inside him. Even if something happened to Lexi, he would never destroy innocent people like that dream indicated.

He'd killed countless immortals over the years, but he was not a ruthless, vicious killer. He did what was necessary to survive and protect those he loved; he did not destroy innocents or enjoy watching others fall.

That was the Lord. That was *not* him.

His nightmare had been wrong, the prophecy was false, and he would make sure neither of them ever came to fruition.

Lexi had pushed the nightmare away by curling up against his side while it was happening. Every night he slept with her, she continued to keep it, and his dreams about the war, at bay. She was the light that chased his nightmares and the shadows away.

When they arrived at the main hall, where the council usually gathered, Cole stopped in the doorway to take in what remained of the dark fae who held power in this realm. Becca was rubbing her nose as she settled into the chair beside Elvin. Alston and Finn sat on the other side of the table.

After he killed Aelfdane and Durin, Cole appointed Brokk to the Council. His chair at the head of the table remained empty, as did the one directly to the right of it. His brother now sat in that other empty chair.

The other members weren't thrilled with his decision, but he didn't care. After the trials and the rebellion, he was not in the mood to kowtow and especially not to these pampered pricks who'd never fought a battle in their lives.

And especially not to Alston, who pushed his son into the trials when he had to know his boy stood no chance of surviving. But Alston had wanted the throne, just not bad enough to risk his own ass.

Alston never would have survived the trials either, but he'd had a better chance than his son. Cole hadn't forgotten that detail about this man. Not only did it make him not trust the coward, but he still intended to make him pay for it.

The dark fae at this table were born into wealth and power in this realm. When their ancestors passed, they inherited their money, lands, and place at this table. The only one who had proven he deserved a place here was Elvin, but even he'd never been in a battle.

Elvin cared deeply about the realm, which was more than he could say for the other three. They relished their power and wealth but didn't give a shit about the dark fae who resided in the Gloaming… unless those fae could somehow increase *their* power.

Cole strode across the floor, pulled out his chair, and sat while the others remained standing. Brokk settled in beside him. Cole studied the council as he leaned back and clasped his hands on his stomach.

He kept his impatience to have this over hidden from them. Alston, Finn, and Becca would attempt to drag it out for a week if they suspected how badly he wanted out of this room and away from them.

Every night, he went to the Gloaming because, as king, he had a responsibility to this realm, but he was anxious to return to Lexi. She was safe with the others. They would keep her safe, but he still hated being separated from her, especially when Malakai was out there and when the Lord would happily see her dead.

She'd made progress today. Many would see it as small progress, but after the way she'd struggled for the past two weeks, he viewed it as a huge leap forward. And given her determination to learn and do this, she would have it mastered soon.

"Where have you been?" Becca demanded.

Cole's attention shifted to the beautiful dark fae whose black hair hung to her chin. Her almond-shaped, black eyes narrowed on Cole as a smile played across her lips. She was gorgeous, she knew it, and he felt as much for her as a mushroom.

"It's in no way *any* of your business what I do or where I go," Cole replied.

"The Gloaming is in ruins, and you are out gallivanting around with—"

Cole's nonchalant attitude vanished as he slammed his hand on the table before she could say something derogatory about Lexi. Its sound reverberated throughout the grand hall and bounced off the walls until it faded away. Until then, no one spoke, and he was sure Becca didn't breathe.

Along the walls, the shadows created by the flickering torches in their sconces twisted and turned toward them. Some slithered toward Becca, who stared defiantly back at him, but she couldn't hide the apprehension in her eyes.

Beside him, Brokk stiffened as the shadows crept forward. None of the others had noticed their insidious movements yet, but his brother had.

CHAPTER TWENTY-TWO

"I AM YOUR KING," Cole said. "Do *not* speak to me like that again, or you will regret it."

Becca blanched as he contemplated tossing her into the dungeon. She would do well with the rebels they imprisoned during the rebellion and the ones caught afterward.

The bounties he'd placed on the rebels who fled the realm had proven successful in rounding them up. There were many eager to collect the reward money.

Because of that bounty, the head of his guard, Niall, and some other guards managed to capture the remaining rebels. Cole was letting them all sweat it out in the dungeons before announcing their death sentences. He could not allow any traitor to walk free.

She may not have been part of the rebellion, but he had no problem adding Becca to the guest list for a week or two. Maybe then, she'd learn how to hold her tongue around him and Lexi.

"Now," he said as he kept his eyes on Becca. "Brokk and I are here because the council had business to discuss. So, what is it?"

Becca stared at him while the shadows crept closer. They encompassed the bottom of her chair but went no further.

Cole smiled at the idea he could destroy her without moving

from his chair. The power of those shadows and the knowledge of that thrummed through his veins as he stared at Becca.

Elvin cleared his throat before speaking. "The dragon has not returned to Underhill. Perhaps we should call back the troops you left there so they can help with rebuilding the homes here."

Cole finally tore his attention away from Becca to Elvin. He pondered the man's words as he studied his black hair, eyes, and dark skin. Elvin was a handsome man, but Cole had never seen him at any of the establishments so many of the dark fae frequently visited for pleasure.

Elvin had tied his life to the Gloaming centuries ago, but he had to have sexual partners. After all, he was a dark fae, and they required sex and food to survive. Rumors whispered that he had mistresses, but Elvin never brought them out in public.

"We'll wait a few more days to be safe," Cole replied. "We don't need a dragon destroying Underhill after our lands have burned."

"Very well then." Elvin licked his finger before turning the first page of the stack of papers sitting before him. "We require more wood for the building."

Cole listened as Elvin ran through the list of problems that had arisen since last night. Finn and Alston remained silent throughout it all while Becca crossed her legs and swung her foot in irritation.

Her gaze remained focused on the back wall as her irritation increased. She was bored, but then again, so was he. Many of the problems were the same as yesterday, and most of them would remain problems until they finished erecting the new homes.

He tried to focus on Elvin, but his mind kept traveling back to Lexi and what happened earlier. By the time Kaylia called a halt to their training session, Lexi had managed to shut off the glow to her entire hand.

Sweat coated her body and cleaved her clothes to her flesh. Exhaustion emanated from her, but she beamed with joy when she turned to him. Her exuberance brought an answering smile to his lips as he embraced her and lifted her off the ground.

It was good to see her so excited and happy about something again. She'd done nothing but beat herself up for the past two weeks while also pushing herself relentlessly onward.

She had a ways to go, but she was making progress, and he'd bet she was sitting in her room, working to keep her shield up against the moonlight. He'd told her to rest, but he'd been telling her that for weeks to no avail.

The shadows under her eyes made it clear she wasn't listening, even if she usually was asleep by the time he returned from the Gloaming. They were both going to take a day off soon, and he would make sure she relaxed and enjoyed herself.

When Elvin started to restack his papers, Cole realized he'd finished speaking.

"I'll send men out to cut down more trees at the edge of the forest," Cole said.

No one would enter the woods to fell the trees but staying at the edge of the forest should keep them safe from what lay within. But they didn't have a choice; there wouldn't be any more new homes without more wood.

"The sooner the homes are built, the sooner most of these problems will vanish," Cole continued.

"I agree," Elvin said, and Becca released a small snort they all chose to ignore.

"For now, it's time for me to return to the field and the building," Cole said.

Though they weren't doing much rebuilding at night, they did have a small group who continued to work so they could get done faster. He and Brokk often joined this group for a few hours before returning to the manor.

Tonight, the idea of swinging a hammer exhausted him, but he had to return to the field and the people working there. There had already been one rebellion since he took the throne; he didn't need another group becoming unhappy with their lives and trying to take over.

Seeing him out there, helping them get their lives back on track, was one of the best ways to earn their loyalty. They also deserved all the help they could get.

They were simple folk who got caught in the middle of a power struggle; their lives were destroyed because of it. The least he could do was hammer some nails for them.

When he rose from his chair, the others rose too.

"Of course, Milord," Finn murmured as he stifled a yawn.

While Elvin had helped with the rebuilding, the other three wouldn't dare get a speck of dirt on them or, worse, a callous. Cole didn't bother to reply to Finn before he turned and walked toward the open doors leading into the main hall.

After a few seconds, Brokk fell into step beside him. "Assholes," Brokk muttered.

"That they are," Cole agreed. "Except for Elvin."

"They all annoy me."

Before they made it to the main palace doors, one of them swung open to reveal the night beyond. No one had opened the door; this was the palace's doing.

As they stepped outside, the scent of smoke and death lingering in the air greeted them. But beneath those acrid aromas, he also detected the verdant smell of his home.

The Gloaming had always been a lush land, full of many plants and crops the dark fae tended and harvested. Charred earth had replaced that verdant land, but green grass was already popping up through the blackened ground.

A small fire burned outside some of the homes inside the bailey. Gathered around it, a group of dark Fae talked and laughed as they drank mead and roasted something over the fire. This was not their home or the land where they liked to reside, but they made the best of their new circumstance.

When the stable boy saw him, he rushed into the barn. A few

minutes later, he led Cole's black stallion, Torigon, outside. In his other hand, he held the reins of Brokk's large, bay stallion, Aspri.

Cole patted Torigon's neck before taking the reins and mounting the horse. When they spotted him, the farmers around the fire called out and waved.

Cole returned the greeting before directing Torigon toward the open side door in the palace's lethal fence. They rode out into the fields.

It was going to be another long night, but he would do what was necessary to keep his people happy and safe.

CHAPTER TWENTY-THREE

OVER THE NEXT WEEK, Lexi worked to spread her shield over her whole body. When she wasn't in the outer realm with Kaylia or training with her dad, Brokk, and Cole, she would sit in her room near the window.

She remained on the floor where no one could see her if they happened to pass by and look up at her window. Or if the Lord sent some of his men to watch over her... which was a possibility.

She'd often find a spot with enough moonlight to practice some more with her shield. It never lasted long as the moon's ever-changing arc through the sky meant she only had a limited amount of time before its light was gone, but it was still *something* more.

She was getting so much better at it too.

Today, she sat beneath the sun as Cole inspected the note Kaylia had written to the crones, telling them she was safe but would be gone longer than she'd anticipated. That was the extent of the message, but he kept checking it for some kind of hidden message.

She didn't know why he was so worried about it. Kaylia was trying to help, but Cole and Orin remained distrustful of her.

Finally, Cole called a crow and slipped the message into its beak. The crow flew through the air and vanished into the portal it opened.

Lexi closed her eyes as she returned to concentrating on her shield. She had only her left foot left to pull inside it, and once she did…

The shield slid into place over her toes with a click only she could hear and one that was entirely in her mind. But to her, it was like the final piece of a puzzle sliding into place.

It was complete. It was a whole. And when she cracked open her eyes, she saw the glow was gone. Completely. Fucking. Gone.

Tears sprang into her eyes. She became so overwhelmed with emotion and relief that she had no control over them. They flowed down her cheeks and dripped off her chin as sobs shook her shoulders.

She'd never seen anything so wonderful. No, that wasn't true.

The glow was beautiful, and it felt *right*, but so did walking outside without having to dread being destroyed by the Lord… and anyone else who saw her.

Kaylia knelt beside her and rested her hand on her shoulder. "It's okay. You did it. It will get easier for you now."

"*We*… did… it," Lexi breathed between the embarrassing sobs she couldn't get under control. She was far more exhausted than she'd realized.

A soft footfall behind her alerted her Cole was coming. "Leave us," he commanded gruffly.

Kaylia didn't make a sound as she rose from Lexi's side and walked toward the open portal leading into the manor. When Cole sat across from her, the tears in her eyes caused him to blur before her.

She tried to wipe them away, but the annoying things were falling too fast for her to control. Leaning forward, Cole rested his fingers on her knees. A small shiver of rightness shot through her.

They'd barely had any time together recently, and they spent most of it training. That could change now that she could keep herself shielded. She would have to remember to always keep it in place.

He smiled as he used his thumbs to wipe away more of her tears.

"I did it," she whispered. "I *finally* did it."

"I never had any doubt."

A small, choked laugh escaped as her tears finally dried. "That makes one of us."

"You're the most stubborn immortal I know; there was no way you weren't going to figure this out."

"What if I can't keep it in place for long?"

"The other arach were often out in public for extended periods. They must have kept a shield in place all that time. You will too."

"What if I can't?"

"How can you still doubt yourself? Look at all you've accomplished."

The urge to crawl into bed and not move again for a week hit her. "I'm so tired."

"I know." Taking her hand, he kissed her knuckles. "You're going to take a break now and rest."

"I can't take a break. The Lord is going to come back for us; we both know it."

"Yes, but if you're too tired to function, then you won't do anyone any good." Unfurling his legs, he rose in a movement so fluid and graceful it awed her. "Come on."

When she slipped her hand into his, he pulled her to her feet. On legs that felt more than a little wooden, she followed him into the portal and emerged in the library.

At first, no one was around, but as they made their way into the hallway, Sahira poked her head out of the kitchen. Over her shoulder, Kaylia was stirring something on the stove as Varo chopped an onion. Her dad had gone with Orin and Brokk to the prison realm. They must not have returned yet.

"Congratulations," Sahira said before vanishing into the kitchen again.

Cole slid his arm around her waist and led her upstairs to her bedroom. He sat her on the bed before going into her bathroom. Seconds later, the faucets turned on and water poured into the tub. When he returned a few minutes later, a plume of steam followed him out the door.

With tender care, he undressed her before leading her into the bathroom and helping her into the tub. The warm, steamy water scented with lavender, eucalyptus, and chamomile from one of Sahira's mixes felt like heaven as it engulfed her.

Though she'd forgiven her aunt and dad for keeping her true identity a secret from her, being around one of Sahira's mixtures still made her a little nervous. But right now, she didn't care if this bath made her sprout horns; it felt too amazing to leave.

Cole sat on the edge of the tub and picked up her loofah. With tender care, he worked his way over her body as he bathed her while massaging the knots from her tense muscles. By the time he finished, she felt limp and boneless.

When the water started to cool, he helped her rise before enveloping her in a large, fluffy towel. Lexi plodded into the bedroom and crawled into bed. As soon as her head hit the pillow, she fell asleep.

CHAPTER TWENTY-FOUR

ONCE LEXI WAS ASLEEP, Cole went downstairs to see if Brokk had returned. Tonight, he would stay with her while his brother returned to the Gloaming.

When he entered the kitchen, he discovered they had returned from the prison. They sat around the island in the kitchen, eating the roasted chicken set out before them.

"How is she?" Del inquired.

"Exhausted and sleeping, finally," Cole said. He shifted his attention to Brokk. "I'm going to stay here tonight; you'll have to return to the Gloaming without me."

"Of course," Brokk murmured.

"I think we still need to get our hands on a dragon," Orin said.

"You can't be serious," Kaylia stated.

"Oh, he's dead serious," Brokk replied.

"And he's dumb enough to end up dead if he tries to capture a dragon," Del said.

"Yet I managed to capture you, so I guess that makes *you* dumber than me," Orin taunted.

Del's chair scraped across the floor as he rose.

"Enough," Cole said as he stepped up to the island and lifted a chicken wing from the plate. "One of these days, you two can beat the shit out of each other, and I won't stop it, but today is not that day. We have too much happening for you two to be out of commission for any amount of time."

They continued to glower at each other before Orin shifted his attention to Kaylia. "Yes, I am serious. She's succeeded in controlling her glow. Now, it's time to see what else she can do, and the greatest asset the arach had was their ability to work with the dragons."

"As far as we know," Sahira said.

"What do you mean?" Cole asked.

"I mean, we have no idea what Lexi's capable of doing. Kaylia is helping her, but we may never be able to unlock all her potential. There's a reason for that glow; we don't know what it is, but it's important, or it wouldn't exist. She might be able to work with the dragons, or she might not."

"And that's what we have to find out," Orin said. "If we can take them away from the Lord, then that is a huge game changer. *Huge.* That man wouldn't have anything without them."

"And if she can't, then we're just putting her in danger," Del said.

"I wish we knew the reason for the glow," Sahira murmured as she picked at her green beans.

"Maybe she can harvest the power of the light and turn it into something?" Varo suggested.

Cole rubbed at his beard as he pondered this. "Maybe, but I've touched her while she's been glowing, and it didn't affect me in any way. If she were harvesting the power of the light to use as a weapon, then she would have accidentally turned it loose on one of us by now."

"I agree," Kaylia said.

"It has to be used for something other than lighting up the night," Orin insisted.

"No one is arguing that," Del said as he sipped a goblet of

blood. He was the only one at the table not eating. "But it's not something volatile... or at least not so far."

"We need a dragon," Orin insisted.

"And how do you plan to catch one?" Brokk snapped.

"Well, that's easy enough." When they all stared blankly at him, he smiled. "With bait."

"What kind of bait?" Cole asked skeptically.

Orin's smile was not reassuring. "Why, something a dragon would eat, of course."

"Of course," Cole muttered and bit into his chicken.

"It would eat you," Sahira said.

"I'm warming up to this dragon idea," Del said as he set his goblet down. "Do we take Orin to an outer realm or stake him outside and see if one hears his screams and comes to eat him?"

"Don't be silly," Orin replied. "I'm far too handsome to be dragon bait."

"I don't think they care what you look like," Varo said.

"We'll find more appealing bait than me. Something bigger. Maybe a giant."

"Good luck with that," Brokk muttered.

At the same time, Kaylia snorted, "You're insane."

"Maybe a little," Orin admitted.

"A giant would stomp you into the ground," Kaylia said.

"I'm too fast for that."

"Your humility will get you killed," Varo said.

Del lifted his goblet in the air. "We can hope."

"Don't expose yourself," Cole said to Orin. "We worked too hard to keep your existence a secret to have you blow it."

"I would never," Orin replied.

Deciding to ignore his brother, Cole shifted his attention to the others. "I'm going to take Lexi away tomorrow. It's time for her to take a break. We can work on trying to unlock her other abilities after that."

"I think that's a great idea," Del said.

Cole still hoped Del considered it a great idea after talking to him. "Can I speak to you privately?"

"Of course."

Del set his drink down and followed Cole from the room. Cole almost went for the library but changed his mind and entered the sitting room on the other side of the hall. He had to see Del's face while they talked.

He waited for Del to settle onto one of the antique, blue chairs before sitting on the couch across from him. It took all Cole had not to tug at the collar of his shirt. He hadn't expected to be this nervous about any of this.

"Is everything okay?" Del asked.

"I plan to ask Lexi to marry me tomorrow."

Del's eyebrows shot up as his mouth parted. Cole hadn't expected to be so blunt about it, but he didn't like feeling unsettled.

"And it will mean a lot to her if you approve the union." It would mean a lot to Cole too; he considered Del a friend, but he refrained from saying so. "I hope you will accept this and be happy for us."

Del grinned and laughed his deep, hearty laugh before jumping to his feet. "Of course I'm happy for you. I can't imagine a better son-in-law."

When Cole rose too, Del embraced him in a crushing bear hug that nearly cracked a rib. The vampire was smaller than him, but he was powerful, a warrior, and excited.

Until now, Cole hadn't considered that Del, a man he liked and respected, would become his father-in-law. He smiled over the knowledge as Del clapped him on the back.

Breaking free of his paralysis, Cole gave his friend a brief hug back. "Don't tell the others."

"Your secret is safe with me."

CHAPTER TWENTY-FIVE

BEFORE LEXI WOKE the next morning, Cole returned to the Gloaming to collect the rings his father had given him when he learned Cole had found his mate. Lifting them from the box where he'd stored them, he examined the silver bands made of fae metal.

His father's was thicker than his mother's more delicate band. For years, the rings hung on a chain around his father's neck, but he'd given them to Cole shortly before his death.

Cole's fingers closed around the rings as his father's laughter briefly drifted through his mind. He didn't often allow himself time to grieve the man he loved so much, but anguish stabbed his heart as he recalled the love the man radiated.

Before he was seven, there was a time when both his parents wore these rings. He had few memories of the time before his mom's murder, but he vividly remembered walking behind his parents one day as they held hands while crossing a field.

The sunlight glinting off their rings emphasized their bond and love for each other. He'd smiled as he basked in their love. He'd been so confident nothing could ever destroy their love for each other and him. So sure nothing would ever disrupt his secure world.

His mother's dark brown hair flowed around her face as she turned back to him. Her blue eyes, so similar in hue to his, shone with love as she released his father's hand to reach for him.

"Hurry up, slowpoke," she called to him.

He'd run to catch up with them and slid his hands into both of theirs. He recalled the warmth of their flesh and the brightness of their smiles as they beamed at him.

His mother died less than a month later, and all the security he felt on that day vanished. He still had his father's love, but there was always a hole in both their hearts after she died.

And now, he would build a family with Lexi and start it by placing this ring on her finger. He didn't see them as bad luck. Instead, he saw them as a start to a life built on love.

He slipped the rings into his pocket and went out to the hall. There, he retrieved a blanket from the nearby linen closet and tucked it under his arm before descending the stairs.

He went to the kitchen first; the cooks were starting to arrive for the day. When they saw him, they stopped in their tracks, and one woman became so pale he thought she might pass out.

"My Lord!" another woman blurted. "What are you doing here?"

He didn't blame them for being surprised to see him; he couldn't recall the last time he entered the kitchens. It was probably as a boy looking for treats.

"I'd like a basket prepared with fruits, cheeses, and some bread," he told them. "I'll be back in a few minutes to get it."

He didn't wait to see if they would obey his command. Heading for the back exit, he left the kitchen and entered a small hallway. Stopping outside one of the many doors lining the hall, he opened it to reveal a spiraling set of stairs. They rattled beneath his feet as he descended into the room below.

Quickly perusing the shelves, he found what he was looking for before returning upstairs to the kitchens. The head chef, Chandra, had arrived since he left. The woman had ruled the kitchens since he was a boy, but today she wouldn't chase him out of here for stealing a pastry while also surreptitiously slipping him one to eat.

"It is good to see you, milord," she murmured.

"You as well, Chandra."

She smiled as she handed him the basket. "Enjoy."

"I will. Thank you."

Her smile slid away as she turned, clapped her hands, and started barking orders that made him wish she'd commanded troops during the war. He was glad to see the years hadn't changed her.

Shifting his hold on the basket, he smiled as he left the kitchen to return to Lexi.

∾

HE WAS LYING BACK in bed beside Lexi, with the rings burning a hole in his pocket, when she woke a few hours later. Her sleepy, beautiful smile warmed his heart, and he leaned over to twirl a strand of her hair around his finger.

She leaned into his touch before her eyes shifted to the window. When she saw the sun's rays streaming through it, she bolted upright so fast that he tugged on her hair before unraveling it. She didn't notice as she started to swing her legs out of bed.

"I overslept! Kaylia must be waiting for me."

Cole grasped her arm before she could leap out of bed. "You have the day off."

Her head spun toward him, and her brow furrowed. "I can't do that."

"Yes, you can, and you *are*. We're both taking the day off to relax."

"Cole—"

"You've been working nonstop for weeks. Burning out and exhausting yourself isn't going to do anyone any good. You need a break, and you're going to get it. One day away won't hinder your progress. It will probably help you."

She remained rigid against his hand before relaxing and giving him a sultry smile. "And what are we going to do with our day off?"

His body reacted as if she had her mouth around his cock, but he had bigger plans than sex. Though, he would make sure to work it in at some point today. Ignoring the ache in his dick, he poked the tip of her nose.

"You're going to have to get ready to find out," he told her.

Laughing, she leaned over to kiss his cheek. He released her as she leapt out of bed. He admired the sway of her hips as she gathered her clothes and disappeared into the bathroom.

While she showered, he opened a portal and waited for her to return.

CHAPTER TWENTY-SIX

LEXI EXITED the portal behind Cole and stepped into a realm so green it was like entering the Emerald City. Rolling hills vanished over the horizon before rising from the earth as snow-topped mountains in the distance. White, fluffy clouds obscured some of the high peaks, but there weren't many clouds in the sky.

Cole led her over the top of one of the hills covered in lush, green grass. As they climbed to its summit, a waterfall came into view. Her mouth parted with a small breath as Cole led her toward the river flowing into the waterfall.

Stopping at the edge of the water, Lexi leaned over to peer down a hundred feet to where the water streamed into a pool so clear she could see the purple stones lining its bottom. A smaller stream traveled away from the pool. There it disappeared into the rocks of the cliff face a hundred feet away from the waterfall.

More green grass covered the earth below. Red, yellow, and blue flowers bloomed in abundance. The aroma of those flowers filled the air with a sweet scent, but it wasn't overwhelming.

The sun shining down on them reflected across the surface of the crystalline pool and river. She glanced nervously at the brilliant orb before making sure she hadn't started to glow.

Cole had instructed her to put up her shield before they left the safety of her room, but she worried she'd lose control and it would fall apart. Glancing nervously around, she searched for anyone else, but the land around them was empty.

"Where are we?" she asked.

"The Gloaming," he said. "I discovered this place when I was barely out of my teens. We're far from the palace, farms, or any other homes. If anyone else knows about this place, I've never seen them here."

"It's beautiful."

"Come."

When he held his arm out to her, she slipped hers through it and followed him around to the other side of the hole carved into the earth. Once there, she saw a rocky pathway that wasn't visible from the other side.

Spray from the waterfall made the rocks slippery, but his feet were sure against the surface, and he helped to steady her when she slipped. Her hair and clothes clung to her face and skin as they grew damp with water, but her heart raced with excitement as they got closer to the bottom.

They arrived at the pond, and Cole led her around to the other side. There the water narrowed into a smaller stream; he released her arm and jumped across it. Turning back, he held his hand out to her, and she took it to follow him across.

When they reached the center of the lawn, with all its beautiful flowers, Cole set the basket he'd been carrying down. While he removed a blanket from inside and spread it across the thick grass, Lexi watched a beautiful, yellow butterfly flit from one flower to another before soaring high and departing over the edge of the small canyon.

She crept closer to the water and stopped at its edge. Holding her hands out before her, she twisted them over as she basked in the warmth flowing over her perfectly normal-looking skin. She was *outside* again, and she looked *normal*.

Lexi laughed as she held her hands out at her sides, tipped her head back, and spun in a circle as the sun beat down on her. It was all so fantastic.

She was impatient to unlock more of her abilities but excited to be here, with him, on this beautiful day. When she stopped spinning, she turned to find Cole with a bottle of something in his hand.

He didn't move as he stared at her with such awe and love it stole her breath. Then, he broke eye contact as he set the bottle down.

He'd already laid the food out on the blanket, set out candle-holders, and lit the two white candles in them. When one of the flames went out, he waved his hand at it, and the fire leapt from one wick to the other, so they both blazed again.

He pulled out two glasses next and set them on the blanket before uncorking the bottle of champagne and filling them. Her heart melted while she watched him.

He'd brought her here to relax, but he'd put so much effort into making it a lovely, romantic day. That knowledge only served to reinforce how much he loved her.

Not that she'd ever doubted it, but they'd never had the chance to share time like this, and he'd gone out of his way to make it a wonderful day. Seeking to wash her hands before joining him, she knelt beside the pool.

She dipped her hands in to discover the water was warm, something she hadn't been expecting from a river-fed pool. Once they finished eating, she would strip and jump in. She couldn't wait.

She was about to rise when Cole knelt at her side.

"Would you like to go for a swim?" he asked.

Lexi glanced back at the beautifully laid blanket. "You just got everything set up."

"It will still be there afterward."

"The candles might not be."

He smiled as he leaned closer. "This day is about you and what *you* want. If they are gone, there will be plenty more candles in our future. Do you want to swim?"

Lexi bit her lip as she glanced between the candles and the pool. She missed swimming in the lake outside the manor all the time. That was before the war, before things became difficult, and before they told her that her father was dead. It had been so long since she had the time to swim, but today was just them, and they had all day to do whatever they wanted.

She looked at the blanket. He was right; it would still be there. This was what she wanted now.

Rising, she tugged off her shirt and unhooked her bra as she kicked off her boots. His eyes flashed silver when she wiggled out of her pants and underwear. Heat flared through her body as his eyes leisurely perused her.

She'd definitely made the right choice as every part of her reacted to his obvious arousal. With a grin and a small crook of her finger, she beckoned to him before diving into the pool.

She inwardly sighed with joy, and as the warm water engulfed her, the stress of the past few weeks eased. Kicking, she propelled herself to the bottom.

Her fingers brushed against the purple stones, and she opened her eyes to examine the different hues within the rocks. It was all so beautiful, so magical, and amazing.

When her lungs started to burn, she twisted around in the water, planted her feet against the stones, and pushed herself up. Water streamed past her as she kicked her way to the surface and broke free.

She gasped in air and laughed. Turning in the water, she searched for Cole and found him standing where she left him.

His fingers rested on the ground as he knelt to watch her. His eyes glinted silver in the sun, and the thick length of his erection evidenced his desire, but he didn't jump in after her.

With a few kicks, she propelled herself to the opposite side.

Everything in her yearned to go to him, but she was in a teasing mood today.

Arriving at the other side, she rested her arms on the rocks and turned to face him. "Aren't you coming in?"

"I'm enjoying watching you."

The low rumble of his words caused her nipples to harden. Turning, she rested both her elbows on the shore behind her and lifted herself, so her breasts were visible. When his gaze dropped to them, his growl was one of a lycan for its mate, but he still didn't come for her.

Lexi released the shore and, on her back, swam out a little way so he could get a good view of all of her. When a blush started creeping into her cheeks, she dove down again.

One of these days, she wouldn't blush so often, but she refused to let him see it now. She was no mermaid, but she felt like one as she twisted and turned beneath the water.

It had been years since she had a day of no responsibilities. She'd forgotten how fun it was to swim and play and simply be. She delighted in the freedom Cole had given her today and her power over him as he watched her every move.

CHAPTER TWENTY-SEVEN

LEXI DIDN'T KNOW how long she played, dipped, swam, and teased him by breaking the surface and running her hands across her breasts and down to her belly before diving under again. Sometimes, she floated on her back and leisurely caressed herself while he watched.

She brought herself to orgasm once, crying out at the release her finger gave her, but it wasn't enough. She wanted more; she wanted *him*.

But the stubborn man remained on the shore. He didn't bother to stroke his cock as he watched her with intense concentration.

Finally, when she was about to crawl from the water, push him onto the ground, and have her way with him, his arms enveloped her. When he pulled her up against his solid chest, a rush ran through her.

His skin against hers, and the strength of his arms, was as right as this beautiful day.

She leaned into him as he pulled her back against his chest and kicked toward the shore. Resting her head on his shoulder, she turned her cheek into it and inhaled his familiar, allspice scent.

At the edge of the pool, she rested her hands against the rock, and his hands came down beside hers. His erection pressed against her back as he turned his mouth into her ear.

"You are so *fucking* beautiful," he breathed in her ear.

She turned her head to meet his silver eyes. The way he studied her set off a small alarm in her head. Were they really here for a break, or had something happened? Was he going to have to leave for a while or go back to war again?

"Is everything okay?" she whispered.

He kissed her cheek and then her temple. "Everything is perfect."

"You're not going back to war, are you? Has there been another rebellion?"

"Not today, but I'm sure another war is coming."

"I'm sure there is, too," she murmured.

When sadness started to creep in, she shoved it away. Today was *not* the time or place for that; today was for *them*.

She took her hands off the rock and twisted to face him. Wrapping her legs around his waist, she draped her arms over his shoulders and smiled as she met his silver eyes.

"So, what do you feel like doing now?" she asked as she rubbed against his shaft.

His gaze fell to her lips before he kissed her. A current of electricity ran through her as he teased her lips with his tongue before slipping inside to taste her.

Her toes curled in response to his kiss. She pressed against him as his kiss chased away the sadness. It was impossible to think of anything else while he kissed her senseless.

The water lapping against her skin and his hands caressing her stoked her lust higher, but he still didn't put out the flames of passion he created. She felt special, protected, loved, and sheltered in his arms.

She also felt stronger.

His faith in her never wavered. Even when Lexi was certain she'd never master the abilities she knew about, he remained positive she would. He never doubted her, and his absolute faith in her only made her love him more.

He didn't want her involved in the battle against the Lord; he would far prefer she remained out of it and safe, but he believed she could handle it and never tried to stop her. Instead, he worked to make her stronger and better at protecting herself against the monsters out there.

Every time she thought she couldn't love him more, he did something to prove her wrong.

His hand slid up to cup the back of her head. His fingers threaded through her hair as he pulled her head gently back, and his mouth fell to her neck before touching upon her collarbone. Another unexpected hunger tore through Lexi, and she shuddered as her fangs lengthened.

Before learning she was an arach, she would have written it off as a vampire's thirst, but now it was the thirst of a different creature. One more powerful than the half human, half vampire she'd always believed herself to be.

Seeming to sense her hunger, Cole lifted his head, and his silver eyes met hers. For a second, black crept through the whites of his eyes. Behind him, the shadows on the ground stirred.

Her hunger had awoken something darker in him, something just as ravenous. Cole's jaw clenched as he battled to keep the blackness away.

She was once again staring into the gaze she'd always known before the trials changed him. Neither of them knew exactly what the full extent of those changes would be, but she had no doubt they would get through them together.

He brought her mouth down to his neck. Blood pulsed against her lips as the beat of his heart thundered in her ears.

"Feed, Lexi," he commanded.

When she sank her fangs into his neck, his hand gripped the back of her head. His powerful blood filled her mouth and infused her body with strength. Whimpering, she squirmed closer as his blood eased one hunger but heightened another.

Knowing what she needed, he grasped her hips and guided her down his dick. She moaned as her fingers dug into his back. The feel of him inside her and his blood filling her made her half mad with yearning.

One of his hands gripped her ass while the other remained braced against the side of the shore as she rode him with a desperate, fevered abandon. She needed it harder and faster as she thrust her hips against him and dug her fingers into his back.

As their sexual energy filled the air, she felt the tug of him feeding on her. She experienced the strength and vitality she gave him through his blood, which excited her more.

The rising tension building inside her broke on a crescendo that had her releasing her bite as her head tipped back and her body exploded with pleasure. A tingling wave ran across all her nerve endings.

Every one of those nerve endings became super-sensitized to the water around her, Cole's body, the currents of air, and the rush of his seed filling her. She felt each pulse of his cock inside her as exhaustion washed over her.

When he pulled her from the water, she collapsed onto the grass, curled up against his side, and fell asleep.

CHAPTER TWENTY-EIGHT

LEXI WASN'T sure what time it was when she woke, but the sun wasn't shining as brightly, and clouds had crept across the sky. Cole's arms still enveloped her, and something warm was draped over her.

She looked down to discover a white robe covering her. *Of course, he would have thought of that too.*

When she rolled over to face him, she discovered him awake and staring down at her. He ran his hand over her shoulder and down to her hip, where it settled.

"I shouldn't have fallen asleep," she said around a yawn.

"You needed it."

"But this is our only day together."

"We'll have *many* more days together."

"I know, but not many where it's just *us,* and we don't have to worry about... about... *everything.*"

"One day, that will change, and we'll have plenty of time to enjoy each other without so many worries."

"I can't wait."

He caressed her cheek with his thumb and traced the contours of her lips. "Are you hungry?"

Despite the fact he'd eased two of her hungers earlier, her stomach rumbled in response.

He laughed as he released her and rolled away. "I'll take that as a yes."

He lifted the robe from her and tucked it under his arm before offering his hand to help her rise. The air brushing against her skin wasn't unpleasant, but she was glad when he draped the robe around her shoulders.

She slid her arms into the baggy sleeves and tied it around her waist. Lexi walked with him over to the blanket and settled herself on it. The candles had burnt out, or he'd put them out, but enough of the candles remained for him to relight them.

The champagne had been recorked, and as she sat, Cole uncorked it, poured her a glass, and handed it to her. She took it and smiled as she sipped the bubbly liquid. It fizzed on her lips and tongue in a delightful way.

Her father had let her have a few sips of his champagne when she was younger. It had always been on special occasions like New Years and birthdays. After she learned of her father's death, she got drunk with Sahira one night, but that was on wine and whiskey.

It had been so long since she tasted champagne, she'd forgotten how much she enjoyed it.

～

COLE SMILED as Lexi laughed and took another sip. A beautiful flush stained her cheeks as her eyes twinkled and her nose scrunched up in the most delightful of ways.

He'd never seen her look more beautiful as her still damp hair tumbled around her shoulders and fell down her back in waves. Handing her a plate of cheese, bread, and fruit, he chuckled when her stomach rumbled, and she nearly ripped the plate from his hand.

When she leaned against his side, he settled his arm around her waist as he made his plate. They ate in silence while watching the waterfall.

He'd never been this content or happy before. He didn't want it to end as he put his plate aside, but he'd come here for a reason.

After she finished, he took her plate, set it on the ground, and drew her into his arms. He held her for a while before shifting his hold so he could see her. Clasping her chin, he kissed her tenderly before releasing her and leaning back.

He slid his hand into one of the pockets on the side of the basket. His fingers brushed against the two rings there, but he only sought his mother's ring. When he slid it out, he enclosed it in his hand as Lexi tipped her head back to bask in the warm sun.

While he watched her sleeping earlier, he was amazed and relieved to learn she didn't start glowing while she slept. She'd gained enough control of herself to maintain a steady shield even when not focused on it.

He didn't think she was ready for public yet, but he was confident she could return to normal life soon.

While her head remained tipped back, he lifted her hand off the ground, kissed her knuckles, and let his lips linger on her hand. When she lowered her head and smiled at him, he had no doubt she was the one for him as his heart skipped a beat.

Seeing that smile only fortified the certainty of his love for her. Kneeling beside her, he held her gaze as he lifted the ring for her to see.

"Will you marry me, Elexiandra?"

Her mouth dropped, and her eyebrows rose. Her gaze went from him to the ring and back again. Tears brimmed in her eyes, and her face lit with such radiant joy that his heart soared in response.

She threw herself into his arms and cleaved to him as she cried, "Yes! Yes! Yes!"

Cole laughed as her exuberance tumbled them both back on the blanket, so he lay beneath her. Hugging her close, he savored how her body felt against his and the rightness of her in his arms.

Then he pulled back so he could gaze into her radiant face. "It's my mother's ring," he said as he slid it on her finger. "If you'd like something different—"

"No!" she blurted as she lifted her hand to examine the silver band on her finger. "It's beautiful and perfect." She wiggled her fingers. "So perfect it already fits!"

When she kissed him again, he pulled her closer as they once again lost themselves to each other.

CHAPTER TWENTY-NINE

WHEN THEY RETURNED to the manor, Lexi was eager to show everyone her ring. Varo and Brokk clapped Cole so hard on the back she suspected they cracked one of his ribs. Then, they each hugged her.

Her father wasn't at all surprised as he beamed from ear to ear while hugging her. Sahira and Kaylia stood with their mouths ajar as they stared from her to Cole and back again. Orin shook his head as he laughed.

"I knew you were a sucker," he said to Cole. "But I didn't realize how much of one you were."

"We're excited about it too," Cole told him, and Orin laughed louder.

"Better you than me, brother," he said as he slapped Cole on the back. "But congratulations. I'm happy for you."

"Well, I certainly wouldn't want to marry you," Lexi told him.

Orin slapped his hands over his heart. "Ouch!"

Then he lowered his hands and, to her astonishment, hugged her. Lexi stiffened against him; she could never forget he'd kept her father imprisoned while she was saving his life.

She couldn't forget that, if it wasn't for the fact Orin had suspected she was more than a human-vampire mix, her father would still be rotting behind bars. And she would still be mourning his death, even while he lived.

But, in the end, she gave Orin a small squeeze and pulled away. He loved Cole and was determined to make this world a better place by bringing down the Lord.

It was impossible to hate him when she remembered that, but it *was* possible to almost always to be pissed at him too.

"Welcome to the family, sis," Orin said.

"We're not married yet," she replied.

"You were family before he put a ring on your finger... at least to him. Now, you're family to all of us."

"Very true," Varo said.

"It's time to celebrate!" Brokk announced. "It's been a rather dull, stressful, and awful few weeks. This calls for drinks, laughter, and dancing."

Lexi opened her mouth to argue with him, she had to return to work tomorrow, but then she closed it again. She would never get engaged again, never have this day or night back, and she wasn't ready for it to end.

They'd all been working so tirelessly, and they may not all survive what was coming. What harm would celebrating do?

So, when Brokk and her father broke out the alcohol, while Varo and Orin moved all the furniture around the sitting room to make a dance space, she threw herself into the party. She couldn't recall the last time she laughed so hard, danced so much, or had such a fantastic time.

Her dad spun her around the room as they danced like they had when she was a little girl and would throw dance parties. Then he hugged her, told her how much he loved her and how happy he was for them.

"I love you too, Daddy," she whispered before he spun her away again.

As he did, he couldn't hide the sheen of tears in his eyes. But then he blinked them away, handed her over to Cole, and went to drink some whiskey.

Lexi relished every second of their celebration. She didn't know when any of them would get the chance to enjoy themselves like this again.

And it could all change tomorrow.

∽

THE NEXT DAY, though she was tired, Lexi resumed her training. She didn't do her early morning training with Cole, but she and Kaylia returned to the outer realm before noon.

For this trip, Kaylia brought fire with her. The fire had caught Orin's attention. He'd been heading out alone, to do whatever he did, but reversed direction and followed them through the portal.

Varo and Sahira also decided to join them, but the sun required her father to remain behind. He was not happy about it and scowled at Kaylia as she carried the torch past him.

"Don't hurt her," he'd growled.

"I have no intention of doing so," she replied before entering the portal.

Lexi stopped to kiss his cheek before following Kaylia through. A portal separated them, but Lexi swore she could still feel his irritation through it.

Brokk and Cole took up a position near the portal while Orin stood a few feet away. Sahira and Varo edged a little closer but remained ten feet away from her and Kaylia.

Kaylia jammed the torch's pole into the ground. Lexi eyed the flame as it jumped and sputtered. There wasn't much of a breeze on this sunny realm, and the fire righted itself to crackle on the still air.

"Now," Kaylia said. "We know for certain the arach had magical abilities, sort of like witches. That's why the harrow stone works for both of us, except the arach kept their abilities more secretive than the witches. We also know they have some kind of connection to the dragons, but we have no idea how to awaken that or how it works."

"That's because we have to get a dragon," Orin said. Then, he pinned his attention on Kaylia. "I know you agree that getting her near a dragon is the key to activating, or testing, whatever she can do with them."

"I don't agree to any such thing," Kaylia retorted. "Getting her near a dragon could get her killed, and she's *much* more useful to us alive than dead."

"Thanks," Lexi muttered.

"Well, it's true," Kaylia said. "I'd also prefer if you weren't eaten."

"Good to know."

Kaylia smiled at her, but it vanished when Orin started talking again.

"Still, you think it's the best way to find out how to unlock what she can do with the dragons. And let's face it, *that's* the ability we really need."

"We need them all," Kaylia stated. She turned her back on Orin, but her irritation with him was evident in the set of her jaw. "I watched an arach walk straight through a dragon's fire and out the other side. It was one of the most amazing things I've ever seen."

Lexi bit her lip and glanced at the torch as she realized where this was heading. Learning if she could withstand fire was necessary, but she would prefer not to endure it.

CHAPTER THIRTY

"We also know they can create fire with their hands and wield it like a dragon," Kaylia continued. "I've seen that happen."

Lexi turned her palms over to inspect them. She'd heard this about the arach too, but she couldn't imagine being able to create fire with her hands. It would be such a wonderful, strange thing.

"So, we're going to work on the fire. The ability to withstand fire should be easy enough; stick your hand into the flame and see what happens," Kaylia said as if it were the simplest thing ever.

"I tried that once," Orin said. "It didn't work out well for me, and she burned."

"It won't work out well for you if you try it again either," Cole warned.

"Not me, brother." Orin held his hands up. "I may be devilishly handsome, adventurous, and up for anything that involves a good time, but I'm not stupid."

"I beg to differ," Sahira muttered.

The smile Orin flashed her had probably melted the hearts of many women over the years.

"If you'd like, I can make you beg for many things," Orin purred. "And all of them will be enjoyable."

Sahira rolled her eyes. "The only thing I'd beg for from *you* is an exit."

Orin's laughter caused Kaylia to spin on him. She planted her hands on her hips as she glared at Orin and Sahira.

"If you two are done flirting, we have work to do here," she snapped. "If you're going to be disruptive, then leave. We certainly get a lot more done when you *aren't* here."

That shut them up, and Orin looked a little abashed while he dug the toe of his boot into the rocky ground. Sahira folded her arms over her chest as she stared at the flame.

Kaylia turned back to Lexi. "Now, let's see what happens when you play with fire."

Lexi stared at the fire dancing around the head of the torch. The orange and yellow color was as pretty as it was unnerving.

Orin sticking her hand into the stove's flame wasn't the first burn she ever had, and none of them were pleasant memories. Once, when she was a teen, she'd been unfortunate enough to knock a pot of boiling water from the stove.

She avoided most of the boiling water, but it got her toes and the very top of her feet. The blisters and pain were instantaneous.

Thankfully, she had Sahira's healing poultices and potion, but it had still sucked. It took three days before she could walk without a limp and another week before her skin fully regrew.

Now, she was going to willingly stick her hand into fire and bear the consequences of it. The logical part of her said this shouldn't be a problem because the potion suppressing her powers had worn off. But the emotional side of her screamed *NO!*

"You don't have to do this," Cole said.

But they both knew she did. She was an arach; she had the strange glowing ability and silver markings to prove it, so she *could* do this.

Taking a deep breath, she steeled her nerve, closed her eyes, and before she could think too much about it, she shoved her hand into the fire. She waited for the sizzle, the pop, and the agony sure to follow...

And nothing. There was no sizzle. No pop. No agony or cry as she jerked her hand away.

She cracked one eye open to make sure she hadn't missed and actually *had* put her hand into the fire. And there it was, sitting in the middle of the flame like it had every right to be there.

She gazed in astonishment as fire encircled her hand like it was giving a tender embrace. It warmed her flesh but didn't torch her skin or burn the hair from her arms.

The edge of her sleeve blackened but not enough to catch fire. She moved her arm a little further into the fire. The second she did, her blackened sleeve caught, and flames flickered to life.

Instinctively, she slapped the fire out. It didn't burn her other hand either as she succeeded in smothering it.

She lowered her arm and stepped away from the torch to examine her flesh carefully. There wasn't a single mark on her other than her scorched shirt.

"It worked," she breathed.

And then a rush of excitement ran through her. She was getting there. She was doing this! Slowly but surely, she was gaining new abilities and learning to control them.

Lifting her head, she grinned at Kaylia. "What's next?"

Kaylia smiled back at her. "Now we have to figure out how an arach throws fire. Learning to bring out your magical abilities will be more complicated, but I think we can unlock the fire."

"How?" Lexi asked.

"I'm thinking we either piss you off or put you in danger."

"What good will either of those things do?" Cole demanded.

"There's a reason they call it a fiery rage," Kaylia replied. "If making her mad doesn't work, then maybe putting her in danger will. Her survival instincts will kick in and might make the fire come out."

"See!" Orin declared. "I knew you wanted me to catch a dragon!"

CHAPTER THIRTY-ONE

OVER THE NEXT WEEK, Cole returned to the Gloaming every night while Lexi slept, or at least attempted to sleep. He wasn't fooled into believing she slept well; the circles under her eyes didn't lie.

However, she was doing better now that she could keep and hold the shield in place for long periods. She'd started venturing out of the manor again and returned to working with George and the horses for an hour every day.

Cole had met with George a couple of times to ensure he could trust the man around Lexi. Once he discovered he liked the middle-aged human, he made sure George was happy here and well paid.

The man took good care of the horses that meant so much to Lexi, she liked him, and Cole didn't want her to lose him. She was helping George again but didn't have the time she used to have for the horses.

Her training continued to take up most of her day. She still hadn't figured out how to unlock her fire ability, and that had become her main focus.

Orin had taunted her with reminders of how he kept her father locked away, and while she looked about ready to tear off his head, she hadn't set him on fire. Something, Cole suspected, that disappointed her a little.

Though Cole considered it a bad idea, he was beginning to wonder how they could safely put her in contact with a dragon. Everything in him argued against putting her in such a position, but they had to test her around the creatures at some point.

He was hoping for later when she had more control over *all* her abilities, but the Lord, and life, often had a way of throwing things into chaos.

A little over a week later, Lexi announced she wanted to return to the Gloaming with him. At first, he was against it.

The last thing they needed was for her to lose control while there, but she would be his queen, which meant the fae had to see her. And, at some point, they all had to trust in her ability to maintain control over her shield.

She trained with Brokk and her dad outside at night, and she often sat outdoors for her meals. She spent more time in the light than out of it now, and she hadn't slipped.

Even still, as she walked with him through the portal toward the Gloaming, the lycan part of him prowled beneath the surface. It begged to break free so it could take her away from this realm and put her somewhere safer.

No one would attack her in the Gloaming; he would ensure that. But if she had a slip while here, then whoever was reporting back to the Lord would surely tell them if they saw it.

He wasn't sure if the Lord would know what the glow and markings meant, but there was a good possibility he would. And even if he didn't, he'd still come for Lexi because he would be determined to learn more about her.

She shouldn't be here!

But she wouldn't remain locked away, and he couldn't keep her from the realm she would rule with him.

His mind knew these things were true, and she was strong

enough to get through this with her shield intact, but not only did the lycan prowl, but the shadows shifted and swayed around them.

"Easy." Lexi slid her hand into his. "I'm going to be okay. If I can sleep with the shield in place, then I can make it through this."

He could only manage a grunt in response as he strained to keep the lycan from taking control. Lexi squeezed his hand as she surveyed the portal.

"I wonder when Kaylia plans to teach me how to use portals," she said. "It was the one thing I resented not being able to do the most when I had no powers. I thought it was so awesome that every other immortal could travel from one place to another with such ease while I remained trapped in the human realm. I'm excited to learn how to create one."

"We should have thought of that sooner," he said. "It will be good for you to know in case you have to get away from somewhere fast. We've been so focused on unlocking your arach abilities that I forgot to teach you how to use an ability most immortals possess."

Lexi shrugged as they stepped from the portal. "I never said anything either."

"I'm pretty sure all immortals open portals in the same way. When it's time to return to the manor, I'll teach you how to do it."

She beamed as she rose on her toes to kiss his cheek. "That would be fantastic!"

He smiled too before recalling where they were... and what was about to happen. The Gloaming had a way of surprising immortals; it had certainly surprised him more than a few times over the centuries he resided here.

CHAPTER THIRTY-TWO

As he led her toward the door to the hall, a ripple of happiness rolled through the palace.

"The palace is happy you've returned," he told her.

Lexi blinked at him before glancing around his sitting room. "How do you know that?"

"It told me so," he replied with a smile.

Lexi looked as if she didn't believe him at first; then, she started to laugh. "If anything is going to do that, it's this palace."

Cole had to agree, but he knew many horrors came with the wonders. This place harbored a lot of secrets.

And it was more than content to keep them all.

He unlocked and opened the door before leading her into the hall and downstairs to the first level. Once there, the helots in the hall turned to face them. Shock registered on their faces, and one of them squealed before rushing toward them.

"Lexi!" Amaris exclaimed. "It's so good to see you again!"

Though she looked like she planned to run up to Lexi and throw her arms around her, she skidded to a halt a few feet away. Smiling, she clasped her hands before her and twisted them in the skirt of her dress.

Stepping toward her, Lexi held out her hands, and Amaris grasped them.

"It's good to see you too," Lexi said.

Amaris beamed at her, but then her smile faltered, and her gaze dropped to Lexi's hand. She released another small squeal, and when her eyes flew back up to Lexi's, they danced with merriment.

"Oh my! Is it…?" Her eyes darted to Cole before falling to the ring again.

"We're engaged," Cole confirmed.

Amaris squealed again and jumped up and down a little. "I have so many ideas for a wedding dress for you! And your hair!"

She reached for Lexi's hair before recalling herself and yanking her hand back. "Pardon me, milord and lady. I forgot myself. I'm sure you have plenty of ideas for your wedding dress and someone to make it."

"Don't apologize," Lexi said. "I'm so glad someone in this realm is excited for us."

"Many others will be too," Amaris assured her.

"I'd love to hear your ideas and would like nothing more than to have you make my dress," Lexi said.

"That's wonderful!" Amaris exclaimed. "I'm so happy for you both! Congratulations!"

Amaris backed away before turning and rushing to rejoin the other helots. They huddled together and kept glancing at them as Amaris shared her news. Everyone in the Gloaming would soon learn of their engagement.

"The dark fae don't know about us?" Lexi asked.

He was afraid to see hurt on her face when he looked at her, but she just appeared confused.

"Brokk is the only one I told. If I informed anyone else here, it would be all over the Gloaming by tomorrow, and it will be. As soon as it was public knowledge, they would expect to see you here again, and you weren't ready for that. Now, you are."

"I can be here whenever I'm needed."

He didn't tell her that he'd prefer if she spent more time *out* of the Gloaming; it would only upset her. But, for all its beauty and all the good within most of its residents, the Gloaming was also a dark place full of secrets and cruelty.

The dark fae thrived on the despair of others. They felt no regret over leaving mindless, sex-obsessed, shadow kissed immortals behind them. Neither did he.

This realm was not for Lexi, even if she was to be its queen.

Before they arrived at the front doors, they swung open, and a small gust of wind came through. The smell of smoke, burnt land, homes, and the dead greeted them.

To her credit, Lexi didn't cringe or recoil. She kept her chin high and her shoulders back as they stepped outside and stood at the top of the stairs.

When she'd asked to return with him, Lexi had insisted on being able to see the displaced dark fae and the land once more. She wanted to help them rebuild, and he couldn't deny her that.

The dark fae now residing within the bailey already admired her for riding out to him during the rebellions. If she helped them rebuild, too, they'd probably give her their hearts and loyalty.

And neither of those things was easy for anyone to win from a dark fae.

"The dragon head is gone," Lexi said.

"Yes," Cole replied. "I had it removed a few weeks ago."

"Why?"

"I'd made my point with it. All those in the Gloaming know I'm the one who slayed the dragon and stopped the rebellion. They'll think twice before trying to attack me again. I also didn't think you should have to keep seeing it."

Lexi sighed as she leaned against his side. "Thank you."

CHAPTER THIRTY-THREE

LEXI SPENT most of the day talking with the dark fae and helping to build one of the new homes rising from the land. She'd told Cole that if she could keep her shield up while sleeping, there wouldn't be any problem doing it here, but she was constantly aware of it.

A part of her mind always remained on the necessity to keep her shield intact. The reminder ran on an incessant, irritating loop in her head as she spoke with the different dark fae, carried wood, hammered nails, and laughed at the children darting through the construction site.

Their mothers chased after them, shooing them away as they giggled and dashed in different directions. One of the mothers threw a towel after them before they disappeared.

Lexi wiped the sweat from her forehead as the sun beat down at her, and closing her eyes, she worked her way through her shield again, making sure everything remained intact.

"Are you okay?" Cole asked.

Opening her eyes, she smiled at him and hefted another piece of wood from the dwindling pile. "I'm great."

"If you need a break—"

"Nope," she interrupted. "I'm enjoying this."

And she was. She loved working with her hands, being outside, and making a difference by helping these fae get back into their own homes. It had been a month since she felt this useful, and she enjoyed it.

By the end of the day, she had blisters on her hands, but she felt good as she stepped back to examine the wall she'd helped to erect. Wiping the sweat from her brow, she smiled at the building.

Some of the dark fae remained distant, but many thanked her for helping, and they all congratulated Cole on his engagement. Word traveled fast as even some of the council came to congratulate them.

Becca didn't join Elvin, Alston, and Finn when they rode up to see Cole. They all offered congratulations, but it was easy to tell they were *far* from thrilled about it. They didn't stay long.

She was sure Becca had also heard the news, but she did *not* expect Cole's ex-lover to congratulate them. Even if he believed Becca just wanted his power, Lexi was sure the woman was in love with him.

She was probably somewhere wishing Lexi dead and maybe trying to figure out a way to make it happen. However, Becca would be in for a surprise if she came after her.

Lexi may not have figured out a lot of her abilities, but she was faster, stronger, and a *whole* lot better at fighting now. Becca expected a weak half-human adversary, but Lexi would kick her ass.

When Lexi accepted the jug of water one of the fae handed her and drank it without hesitation, all those gathered close by stared at her. They had no idea what to make of their future queen acting like one of them.

Lexi recapped the water, grinned at the fae man who gave it to her, and flipped her hammer in her hand as she shifted her attention back to the wall. She liked that they didn't know what to make of her but seemed to like her.

If they hated or disliked her, she would be in for a lifetime of unhappiness in this land. It would make Cole's life miserable too, and that was the last thing she wanted.

So far, they were accepting, if not a little shocked to see her, for which she was grateful. No matter how much she enjoyed working the land, this was not normally the proper place for the well-bred nobility of the realms, and certainly not for a king or queen.

The dark fae would have to get used to this change. She refused to be locked in the palace, shoved into pretty dresses, and perched on a throne. And this wouldn't be the last time Cole helped the fae.

That was not the way she was going to spend the rest of her life. But then, if they succeeded in taking down the Lord, her rightful place would be on the Dragonian throne... which threw one more complication into her and Cole's relationship.

However, it would probably be the easiest one to figure out.

How difficult could it be to decide which throne you preferred to sit on that day?

"You like doing this work," Niall said as he came to stand beside her. Either he or Cole had been within ten feet of her all day.

"I do," she replied. "It's good work."

"It is," Niall agreed. "I just didn't think it was a queen's work."

"It is now."

His eyebrows rose as he chuckled. He would be more astounded when he learned about her true heritage, and she didn't doubt that everyone in all the realms would eventually know it.

That's what they were all working toward with her powers, after all. And once the secret was out, it would spread faster than news of her engagement.

She glanced around at all the people who had helped spread that news. She was sure they'd sent crows to the furthest areas of the Gloaming too, and she was happy they would all soon know Cole was *hers*.

Marriage was sacred to immortals; it lasted until one of them perished, and *no* one messed with that bond. Though, she was sure the Lord would try.

He'd probably enjoy doing so.

Lexi pushed thoughts of him aside. She refused to let that monster ruin her good mood. He would do so soon enough, she was sure.

Studying the scorched earth surrounding them, a small tremor ran through her as she recalled the blood, death, screams, and the monstrous craz that ravished the land during the rebellion. Unable to stop herself, she glanced nervously at the sky.

"The craz haven't come back since that day," Niall said; he must have seen the direction of her gaze. "It would be certain death for them now that we're not all fighting each other."

"How many more creatures like them live in the Gloaming?" she asked.

"Far too many for anyone to know the exact number."

That was the least reassuring answer ever.

"Do the other ones ever come out?" she asked.

"Not into populated areas like this one, or at least not until something draws them out, like a battle and blood. But in some of the more remote areas, they venture forth, and the few fae who live there have to deal with them. They don't come out of the forest either"—Niall waved his hand at the woods a half a mile away from them—"but if we enter it, we're fair game."

And she would bet many had lost that game.

While the rebellion was taking place, she'd opened the wrong doors to discover the forest and eyes on the other side. The palace tore the door away and slammed it shut, but she believed it gave her a glimpse of those eyes as a warning.

Whether that warning had been to stay away from the rebellion or the forest, she didn't know. But she couldn't stay away from the battle; Cole had needed her. However, she had *no* intention of ever entering those woods.

She glanced over at where Cole stood with a tall, thin man pointing at the top of the house they were currently building. Cole nodded at something the man said and replied, but Lexi couldn't hear them.

When she glanced up at the sun, a tiny voice in the back of her mind whispered, "Don't forget the shield."

The reminder gave her a jolt when she realized it had been a while since she last thought of the shield. It was holding up, but she'd intended to be vigilant about it, and she'd failed at it.

Shifting her attention to her shield, she reinforced its protective barrier. She didn't sense any weakening, which gave her comfort, but she wouldn't let her guard down again.

With her stomach rumbling, Lexi bent and picked up another board. She wouldn't leave this place until the others declared it a day. She had a home to return to; many here didn't.

CHAPTER THIRTY-FOUR

THE SUN WAS SETTING when the daytime laborers called it a day and trudged back toward the palace. Lexi sat in the saddle before Cole as he rode Torigon through the open side door.

As they passed through, she glanced up at the spike where the dragon head once resided. She was glad to see it gone, and not just because of what she was, but also because it had been hideous.

Cole pulled Torigon to a stop near the steps of the palace. A stable boy ran out and took the reins from him. He dismounted and removed his sword from where he'd hooked it over the saddle.

He settled the sword on his back before grasping Lexi by the waist and lifting her from the saddle. The boy led Torigon away as they climbed the steps. The palace doors opened to reveal Brokk on the other side, before they reached the top.

He'd opted out of coming to the Gloaming with them this morning. Instead, he'd made some excuse about visiting old friends, which Lexi took to mean women. He *was* part dark fae, after all.

And judging by the vitality radiating from him, and the healthy glow of his face, she'd been right.

"You decided to join us," Cole said as they arrived at Brokk's side.

"I came to help, but it seems I'm too late."

"You can always return to work tonight."

"I'm going to pretend I didn't hear that and come back tomorrow," Brokk said with a smile; Cole laughed, and Lexi shook her head.

"How did things go here?" Brokk asked.

"Great!" Lexi told him. "I helped build a house."

"I can tell."

Lexi glanced down at her filthy clothes and shrugged. She'd opted for fae wear since she was in their realm, and her yellow tunic was now mostly brown from dirt and sawdust. It hung limply off her and had sweat stains in some unflattering places, but she didn't care.

"It was fun," she told him.

"You're so weird."

Lexi gave him a playful push as Niall walked up the steps and entered the palace behind them. She hadn't trusted Niall when she first met him, but now she was extremely glad he was Cole's friend and protector.

The four of them were almost to the great hall entrance when a loud knock sounded on the palace doors. They all slowed before turning toward the doors as the echo of the knock faded away.

Lexi waited for the palace to open the doors and reveal whoever was on the other side. When they remained shut, an uneasy feeling ran down her spine.

If the palace trusted whoever it was, it would have granted them admission. The closed doors meant the palace did *not* want them here, which meant Lexi didn't either.

"Stay here," Cole said.

Lexi suspected he'd come to the same conclusion as her as he started down the hall. She almost tried to pull him back, but he was the king in this realm, and he couldn't ignore someone at the door simply because the palace didn't grant them entry.

Niall stepped closer to her while Brokk followed his brother down the hall. Brokk stopped a few feet away from the door, and his hand fell to the hilt of his sword. Lexi's heart thumped faster when Cole kept his sword sheathed.

But then, there were many immortals that the palace didn't openly welcome. If she wasn't with Cole, it might not open the doors for her either.

"I'll get it, sire!" a young helot called as he rushed out from one of the side rooms.

"That's okay," Cole assured him. "I'll answer it."

"But, milord—"

"Go back to whatever you were doing," Cole said brusquely.

The boy started to protest before closing his mouth and giving a crisp nod. He turned and scurried away.

Grasping one of the handles, Cole opened the door to reveal three men standing on the other side. Two of them gave a swift bow while the one in the middle remained standing.

Judging by their fairer hair coloring, they weren't dark fae. But they were most certainly the Lord's men as they wore his red and white colors.

CHAPTER THIRTY-FIVE

"KING COLBURN of the House of the Dark Fae?" the one in the middle inquired though he had to know who Cole was. Even if he'd never seen him before, Cole was known throughout the realms.

"Yes," Cole replied.

"This is for you."

The man held out a white envelope. The second Cole took it from him, the other two rose and clapped their heels together. None of them said anything else before the three of them turned and departed.

When Cole turned away from the door, it swung shut. He opened the envelope and removed the card inside as he walked toward them. He was still a few feet away when his face darkened, and the shadows on the walls twisted toward him.

His eyes were a vibrant silver when he lifted his head to look at them. Lexi's question died on her tongue.

Brokk didn't have the same problem as he inquired, "What does it say?"

A muscle jumped in Cole's cheek as his muscles swelled like

he was about to make the change into a wolf. Niall and Brokk edged away while Lexi strode toward him.

As she walked, she found her voice again. "What is it?"

Silver filled Cole's eyes when they met hers. "The Lord has requested our presence at a ball. Next week. To celebrate our engagement."

Some of the blood drained from Lexi's face as she looked from him to the invitation and back again. He'd suspected someone from the Gloaming was feeding the Lord information, but...

"Everyone here *just* found out," Lexi said.

"They did," Cole agreed.

"It's too fast!"

"No, it's not."

Lexi gulped; there was definitely a traitor in the Gloaming, but who? Cole believed it was Becca, and he was probably right, but there were so many here they couldn't trust. For all they knew, it was Becca and a dozen others too.

"Can I see it?" she asked.

When Lexi held out her hand for the invitation, Cole gave it to her. She stared at the neat handwriting for a minute before she started processing the words.

King Colburn,

I wish to congratulate you on your engagement. She is a fine young woman. To celebrate, you will both attend the ball I am throwing in your honor next Friday. Be there when the clock strikes 4 PM. I will take care of the guest list and all preparations.

Best wishes,

Lord Andreas of the Shadow Realms

Lexi gulped as she read it three more times. It seemed so innocent and like an honor for them, but she knew the Lord. This would *not* be an honor.

This was going to be bad. Very, *very* bad.

When she lifted her eyes to Cole's, she saw the stark reality of that knowledge staring back at her. They couldn't refuse to go; it would automatically make them enemies to the throne. He would label them as traitors and have them hunted for it.

But if they went...

If they went, the Lord would make them suffer. He might even try to kill one of them.

But they had no other choice. Far too many lives rested on their shoulders and especially Cole's. If they didn't attend this ball, the Gloaming would suffer.

"I'm going to need a dress," she said.

Cole's explosive curse made her wince.

CHAPTER THIRTY-SIX

COLE WAS in such a foul mood by the time they returned to his room, he forgot he'd told her that he would teach her how to open a portal. When he started to open one himself, Lexi grasped his arm.

"You were going to show me," she reminded him.

He started to say something but barely got out one word before closing his mouth and waving his hand at the portal. It vanished before it fully formed. Brokk crossed his arms over his chest and leaned against the door to watch them.

Her words were the first any of them had spoken since Cole told Niall to make sure the Lord's men left the Gloaming. He'd gone out the front door while Cole had stalked back to his rooms. She and Brokk had followed.

If the two of them were anything like her, a million different things had gone through their minds by the time they returned to Cole's rooms and the thought at the forefront of their minds was to *run, run, RUN!*

But they couldn't run. And the Lord knew it.

Not only would he destroy the Gloaming if they ran, but he

would also destroy her home and unleash his vengeance on other unsuspecting immortals and humans. He would make them all pay. But if she went, there was a chance he would kill them. There was also the horrifying possibility Dragonia would trigger something in her and make it impossible to control her abilities. Or it would activate something she had *no* idea how to handle.

Lexi's fingers twisted in her dirty shirt as she resisted the impulse to chomp her nails like they were a pepperoni pizza and she was starving.

"I have to know how to open a portal for when we go to Dragonia," she said. "Arach can open portals in and out of Dragonia. He'll *never* expect me to do it. It might be our only chance of escaping him."

"We're not going," Cole stated.

Lexi kept her alarm over this assertion hidden as the shadows behind him crept down the walls. "You can't refuse him."

"I am the king of the dark fae; I can do whatever the *fuck* I want."

They both knew that wasn't true, but she didn't think this was the time to point out they were *all* at the mercy of the Lord and his dragons.

"You're not returning to that realm," Cole said. "We have no idea how your abilities will react to it. You could step out of a portal and turn into a beacon for all to see."

"Then we'll go right back into the portal, or I'll open my own, and we'll get out of there. They won't be expecting that from us. Besides, I don't think that will happen. If the arach reacted to Dragonia, all immortals would have known about the glowing thing. Other immortals used to go in and out of Dragonia when the arach ruled there."

She *really* hoped she was right. No, she *had* to be right. If the arach couldn't control their glowing while in Dragonia, then everyone would have known about it. Word traveled fast among immortals. She just hoped she could maintain control of her shield while there.

"If we don't go, he's going to make the Gloaming and the human realm pay for it," she said.

"I'll go," he said. "While you remain behind."

Panic filled her at the idea he might try to leave her behind. If he went alone, he couldn't use a portal to escape if it became necessary. And it would prove essential if he disobeyed the Lord by leaving her behind.

There was *no* way she was going to let that happen.

"He'll punish you for that, Cole. You know we *both* have to go."

All around him, the shadows crept closer until they loomed over his back, making him appear even larger. Lexi kept her uneasiness over it hidden, but she *hated* them.

"Show me how to open a portal," she said.

A vein throbbed to life in Cole's temple as his gaze shifted from her to Brokk and back again. Finally, his shoulders relaxed a little, and he turned toward where he had started to open a portal before.

"It's difficult to do in the beginning; not because it's hard, but because it's something you're not used to doing. Once you're used to it, it becomes as easy as breathing," he said.

"To open a portal, you have to imagine the place where you're going. Draw it in vivid detail in your mind and, at least for all the immortals I know, a portal will materialize and lead you to the place you imagined. Some like to wave their hands to form it, others simply let their minds form it, and I do a combination of both."

"I like a good nod toward it once in a while," Brokk said. "I've also given a karate kick or two."

Despite the distress gnawing at her belly, Lexi chuckled. "I can do that."

She'd gotten a lot better at her kicks and punches over the past month. She was far from a battle-hardened warrior, but she could take an immortal down now. In fact, she might be able to take down two or three. She was a lot stronger and faster than she'd always believed.

"Close your eyes. Picture the library in the manor," Cole said. "Imagine your favorite thing about it and make it a clear, mental image. One so clear it's almost as if you could touch it."

Lexi closed her eyes and pictured all the books lining the shelves of her favorite room in the manor. She recalled their familiar, comforting scent as she visualized running her fingers over their spines while she searched for something to read.

She imagined the familiar warmth of the room when a fire was crackling in the hearth. It always felt like she was walking into a warm embrace when she entered the library, and Lexi smiled while picturing it.

When she felt like she was there, in the library, curled up in her chair with her favorite book, she gave a small wave of her hand.

"That's it," Cole murmured.

She opened her eyes to discover a small portal forming before her. It was nowhere near big enough to travel through, but it was there, and *she* had created it!

Lexi almost squealed, and she couldn't resist clapping her hands as she gave a small jump up and down. She'd just done the one thing she'd always resented not being able to do!

And, for once, it hadn't been difficult like *everything* else she'd struggled to learn since discovering her heritage. *Finally*, something was easy. *Finally,* she had progressed without feeling like it might break her first.

She hadn't realized how stressed and disheartened she'd been about it all until she nearly shouted with joy over *not* feeling like an incompetent idiot. Opening it had tired her a little, but she was so excited by this development that she barely felt it.

Cole rested his hand on her shoulder and gave it a small squeeze. "You're doing great."

He didn't know how badly she needed to hear those words. Rising onto her toes, she kissed his cheek and smiled at the familiar scruff of his beard against her lips.

"Keep picturing the library, and the portal will grow bigger," Cole said.

Lexi heard the turn of the pages while she read her book and felt its pages against her fingers. The portal swelled to a size that would allow them to walk through it.

"I did it," she breathed.

"You did it," Cole said as he hugged her. "It will only get easier for you."

She grinned at him before turning and running into the portal.

CHAPTER THIRTY-SEVEN

"You're not really going to go," Orin said as soon as Cole finished telling everyone about the Lord's invitation.

Once they returned to the manor, he'd asked everyone to join them in the kitchen. Thankfully, everyone had been present when they returned so he wouldn't have to tell this story more than once. He was not in the mood to repeat it.

"Do you think we have a choice?" Lexi inquired.

"Yes. Don't go."

"And then he'll hunt us down."

"Let him hunt you then! You're better off being on the run than dead."

"And if he's not bringing us there to kill us, are we supposed to spend the rest of our days hiding, like you?" Cole asked. "There's no one to bring him a duplicate of mine or Lexi's bodies."

"She's getting stronger. If we can get a dragon and learn more about her powers, we might be able to take him down soon. We can't do that if you're both dead," Orin retorted.

"He'll destroy the Gloaming."

Orin shrugged.

"You're such an asshole," Brokk muttered.

"We can't let that happen," Varo said.

"I'm going to do everything I can to keep it from happening," Cole assured him.

"Many of the dark fae could flee from there if he tried to destroy it," Orin said.

"But there are innocents who won't make it out in time and will die there," Varo replied.

"So what?" Orin retorted. "*Many* more will die if we fail in this. Those lives are a small sacrifice in the grand scheme of things."

"Orin," Varo whispered in a horrified tone.

Orin's gaze bored into Cole. "You know I'm right."

"You are," Cole agreed, and Lexi winced. "But that doesn't mean I'm going to run away. I won't allow him to destroy the Gloaming because of my cowardice."

Everything in him screamed to take Lexi and run as far and fast as possible. But she was right; she could get them out of Dragonia if necessary.

It would reveal what she was to everyone at the ball, but the Lord had backed them into this corner, and they would come out fighting if necessary.

Del's hands fisted on the countertop. "Why is he doing this?"

"To prove he can make us do whatever he wants," Cole said. "I don't think he's going to hurt Lexi; she's his leverage over me."

"And what if he decides to keep that leverage with him to use against you?" Kaylia asked.

Cole had asked himself this question more than a few times since reading the invitation. "I taught her how to open a portal. She's an arach, which means she can travel in and out of Dragonia through a portal of her own making. *No* one else in all the realms can do that. The Lord will never expect her to do it; we can get out of there if it becomes necessary."

"And what if an arach somehow removed the ability for all

other arachs to open portals in and out of that realm?" Brokk asked.

"That would take far too much magic to accomplish," Kaylia said. "The arachs were powerful beings, but not that powerful on their own."

"What if it was more than one of them who did it?"

Kaylia frowned as she pondered this. "No. I don't see any of them trying to do that. If it ever backfired, which spells that powerful have a way of doing, they could have ended up banning *everyone* from opening a portal in and out, including themselves. That's not a chance they would take.

"Besides, they would need a large group of arachs to pull off such a thing, and most likely the name or names of the arachs they planned to bar. There's no way they would have Lexi's name."

"You can't know that for sure," Del said. "You have no idea how their magic worked."

"True, but many spells are similar. It's the way witches or warlocks or the arach used them and got them to work that differs."

"So, she should be able to open a portal," Cole said.

"Yes," Kaylia said.

"This is a bad idea," Orin muttered.

"I *don't* like this," Del grumbled through his clenched teeth.

"Neither do I," Cole said. "He has an ulterior motive for this ball; I don't doubt it. But we can get away if it becomes necessary."

"And you'll be giving away our best secret and weapon against him if you do," Orin said. "Once he learns of her existence, he's going to hunt her with everything he has. He'll also know we're coming for him. If he never learns about her, we'll be far better off."

"I know," Cole growled. "Do you think I like this? Do you think I *want* to take her in there?"

It wasn't until Lexi rested a hand on his arm that he realized he was drawing the shadows toward him again. He released them as he placed his hand over the tops of hers. The warmth of her fingers and the feel of her skin soothed him, but anger festered inside him.

He hated being backed into this corner, and like any wolf who was, the lycan part of him strained to break free so it could destroy the one who had cornered him. But the Lord wasn't here. If Orin kept testing his patience, he might go for his brother instead.

CHAPTER THIRTY-EIGHT

"You should run," Orin said. "You're taking our one hope against him and leading her straight into Dragonia. What if she reacts differently in that realm? What if she can't control her ability or her shield fails?"

"Then we get out of there as fast as possible, and we go on the run," Cole replied.

"It doesn't matter what you say," Lexi said to Orin. "We've already discussed this. I *am* going. I'm a grown woman; I'll make my own decisions, and I'm not going to let one person die when there might be something I can do to stop it from happening."

Her hunter green eyes burned with determination as she stared at Orin. "You're the one who wants to catch a dragon; now, you won't have to catch one. I'll go to them."

Her words were like a bucket of cold water as Cole recoiled from them. "We're *not* going because of that."

"No, we're not," Lexi agreed. "But if we happen to have an opportunity with a dragon, then we're going to take it."

"And how do you plan to have an opportunity with a dragon?" Sahira asked incredulously.

"I have no idea," Lexi admitted. "But it could happen. Besides, it doesn't matter; we have to go. You all know that."

"I know no such thing," Del said.

Lexi leaned over the kitchen counter and rested her other hand on her father's arm. "He'll kill so many if we don't go. He doesn't tolerate disobedience."

"Your life is more important than theirs," Orin said.

"Is it?" Lexi asked.

"Yes," Orin and Cole said at the same time.

Lexi tipped her head back to meet his gaze. Her hand on his arm tightened.

"You're the last arach, Lexi. That means something," Cole told her. "Don't ever doubt it. And to me, your life means *everything*."

"And to someone else, their loved one's life means everything too," she whispered. "There are plenty of others who love their spouses, mates, and children more than anything. We are no more special than them."

"What you are *is* more special," Orin stated.

"I might not be able to do anything against the Lord," she said. "We can't figure out how to use my fire, and I have no idea how to control a dragon. Right now, I'm no better than most others against him. The only special thing I can do is open a portal in and out of Dragonia."

"It's only been a month, and there are no other arachs to help guide you on your journey," Del said. "With time, you'll learn more about what you can do. You're doing a fantastic job of learning your way."

"Am I? Or are you saying that because you're my dad?"

"You're too hard on yourself; you always have been."

"Even if that's true, we still have to go to this ball."

Del's knuckles turned white, and at the far end of the counter, Kaylia said, "That man will destroy you."

"Not unless I let him, and I won't let that happen. We'll go, and we'll get through it. If something goes wrong, we'll escape."

"This is such a bad idea," Sahira said.

"I think she has a point," Varo said. "If they refuse to go, they'll be on the run and locked away... like the rest of us. If she goes, she has an opportunity to touch base with her heritage. That might be what she needs to unlock some of her abilities."

"And if unlocking those abilities exposes her and gets her killed?" Orin asked.

"You all have faith she can stand against the Lord when the time comes, but you don't have faith she could escape Dragonia if it became necessary?"

"She's not ready yet," Del said.

"She doesn't agree, and I think that means she has more faith in her ability than even *she* realizes. I think we should trust that."

Lexi's mouth parted, and she stared at Varo for a full minute before smiling. "Maybe we should."

Orin threw up his hands in exasperation. "Oh great, let's risk everything on a bunch of maybes."

Cole didn't want to bring her anywhere near the Lord, but he found himself saying, "It's not a maybe. She *can* do this."

Because she could. She was stubborn, strong, and powerful. She needed more confidence in herself, but she would take this world by storm... once she figured out her abilities.

The radiant smile she bestowed on him told him he'd done the right thing when it came to her confidence. He just hoped he was doing the right thing when it came to her life.

CHAPTER THIRTY-NINE

LEXI SPENT the next week making sure her shield was as strong as it could be and trying to unleash her fire. She was successful with the shield but not the fire.

No matter how often Orin pissed her off or jumped out and tried to scare her, she didn't set him on fire like she wished she could. If he hid behind one more corner and jumped out to scare her, she was going to kick his nuts off.

Like send them flying into outer space *off*, that's how much he annoyed her.

It seemed that was the only time she saw him. He was mostly scarce throughout the day and night, but he managed to scare her at least once a day. He always failed to ignite her power, but he never failed to laugh when she screamed and jumped.

He'd gotten Brokk and her dad in on the action of hiding somewhere to scare her. It didn't matter if it worked or not; they all considered it hilarious to frighten her. She did not agree.

They were trying to figure out how to put her in danger to see if that would unlock her abilities somehow, but they couldn't come up with anything. Or at least not anything Cole and her dad would approve, so she didn't know if maybe that was the key to unlocking her fire. Lexi suspected that if danger was the key to unlocking it, going to Dragonia and facing the Lord might be the way to set it free.

During the day, she trained with Cole, her dad, and Brokk more. When they attacked two on one, she didn't best them, but she put up a hell of a fight and was doing better keeping them at bay.

Her dad still wasn't happy about her going to Dragonia but was determined to make sure she prepared for it. Though, Lexi didn't think she could ever prepare for what was about to come.

When she wasn't trying to unlock more of her abilities and training, she was in the Gloaming, standing before Amaris and her team as they fitted her for a dress she *loved*. The pale-yellow color was such a beautiful hue that Lexi couldn't help running her hand over the soft material.

She admired its subtle shade and the way the light danced across it. The dress hugged her waist before flaring into a full skirt that fell to the ground. Once she put her shoes on, the skirt would barely cover them.

It would be so wonderful to dance in it and to feel the material swaying against her legs as Cole spun her around. And then she realized that any dancing at this ball probably wasn't going to be fun.

Lexi gulped as she ran her hands over the silky material again. The bodice was formfitting. It hugged her waist in, while emphasizing and pushing up her breasts. It was sleeveless with gold chains across her shoulders that fell to her upper arms.

She felt beautiful in the dress and couldn't wait for Cole to see her in it, but she couldn't help fearing it might be the last thing she ever wore. And then she hated herself for being so morbid.

With a sigh, she shifted her attention back to Amaris and the others. As they worked, they talked about things happening around the palace and how fast the new homes were going up.

When she finished on the dress's hem, Amaris rose, stretched her back, and beamed at Lexi. "We're almost done."

"It looks amazing," Lexi said for the hundredth time since she'd tried it on today.

"I have something to show you."

Amaris walked over and lifted a sketch pad from one of Cole's sitting room chairs. She opened it and started flipping through the pages as she approached Lexi.

"I know you haven't set a date yet, but I couldn't help sketching out some ideas I had. If they're not what you want, let me know, and I can do whatever you envision, but I had to get the ideas out of my head," Amaris told her.

When she held the sketch pad up in front of Lexi, her eyes widened, and her mouth parted as she gazed at the beautiful wedding dress on the page. It was far more elaborate and bigger than she'd imagined, but it was gorgeous.

Amaris talked as she started flipping through the pages, showing dress after dress. "We can do so many different things with your hair, but I think it would look so lovely up and away from your face to show off your features."

When she flipped to the next page, Lexi gasped at the stunning, simple dress on the page. It hugged the model's body to the waist before falling to trail on the ground behind her. The lacy design was simple, the scalloped neck enticing, and the simple gold chains around the middle, eye-catching.

"You like this one?" Amaris asked.

"It's beautiful."

"And simple on you is the best option. You're far too beautiful for anything more."

A blush burned Lexi's cheeks as she bowed her head. "That's very kind of you."

"It's the truth," Amaris said as she closed the notebook and turned her brilliant smile on Lexi. "As soon as you have a date, we'll get to work on the dress."

"I'm looking forward to it. You're extremely talented."

Amaris looked up at Lexi from under her thick lashes. "Thank you."

As Amaris hurried over to put her sketch pad down, Lexi found herself hoping she got the chance to set a date. She and Cole hadn't really discussed their wedding; they were both too focused on surviving this "celebratory" ball.

She lifted her head to stare out the window at the Gloaming. She could see the rolling fields and some newly built homes from her position. The echoing sounds of hammers hitting nails reverberated across the land.

"I heard it's going to be a big ball," one of the women said as she stepped back to survey her handiwork on Lexi's dress.

"How exciting," another murmured.

Lexi didn't find anything exciting about any of this. Ever since reading the invitation, she felt like a frog that had jumped into the frying pan.

The Lord had commanded one of his dragons to eat Cole's father and killed hundreds of pixies to prove a vicious point. Now they were going to walk into Dragonia, where they would have to pretend to be happy the murderous bastard was throwing them a party.

She was *not* a good actress.

And it didn't help that she could feel the darkness and anger churning incessantly inside Cole. The shadows moved and responded to him, even when he wasn't paying attention to them.

She wasn't the only one on edge about this ball; he was too. The shadows were using that as their opportunity to grow stronger and become more a part of him. She was terrified they would one day take him over.

The only thing she could do was hope the Lord didn't try something. Cole would call on the shadows then. He'd draw them in, and they would latch on and dig their way deeper into him.

But she highly doubted this ball was going to go through without something horrible happening. The Lord had been looking for an excuse to go after them. Their engagement, and the traitor or *traitors* in the Gloaming, had handed it to him.

Both she and Cole believed Becca was reporting back to him. She hated Lexi and wanted Cole for herself. She also craved power and would do whatever it took to get it, even betray her king.

The problem was they had no proof it was her or anyone else. So, for now, that traitor would remain amongst them, at least until the Lord had them killed or thrown in his dungeon.

Stop it! she commanded herself.

If this all went wrong, she *would* get them out of there by opening a portal. No one would expect it, so no one would try to stop her, and as Cole said, it became easier every time she did it.

She'd become a pro at opening them and could do so in mere seconds. They would escape Dragonia if things went wrong.

Lexi played with her ring as she stared out the window. She recalled how happy she was that day by the waterfall. How ecstatic she was to one day become Cole's wife.

He'd always talked about it, always stated it was a given they would marry, but having the ring presented to her had made it a reality.

Seeing that ring slide onto her finger had been the happiest day of her life, especially after all the struggles she'd gone through before then. And all the battles he'd gone through with the shadows and trying to keep the lycan at bay.

"Is everything okay?" Amaris asked when Lexi sighed.

"Of course," Lexi murmured.

"We're almost done."

Normally, Lexi would have been relieved to hear this. It meant she wouldn't have to keep standing here, as still as possible, while these women fussed over her. She'd never been one for dresses, even though she loved how they felt when she walked in them.

But now, she dreaded when they finished because that meant they were one step closer to attending the ball. Her skin prickled as if a ghost had slipped inside her dress and pressed against her skin.

"Great," Lexi said.

The confused look on Amaris's face said she wasn't completely buying it, but she returned to work.

CHAPTER FORTY

"COME WITH ME," Cole said to Niall as they finished working on the fae homes for the day.

The remaining homes should all be standing within the next few days. Cole hoped something didn't destroy them as soon as they were completed.

Cole glanced at the palace in the distance in the hopes of spotting his fiancée; then, he recalled that Lexi had remained at the manor today. Now that they'd finished her dress, she planned to spend extra time training with Kaylia and the others.

He hated that she continued to push herself so hard, but he'd noticed Kaylia was tempering their training time together. She didn't push Lexi but let her guide herself. And when Lexi tried too hard, Kaylia walked her back or ended their sessions.

The crone must have come to the same conclusion as him; Lexi pushing herself to a breaking point wasn't going to do any of them any good. It would be best if his mate realized that too.

As much as he hated to admit it, he was starting to like Kaylia. She was still cold toward Del, Brokk, and Sahira, but she was good with Lexi, kind to her, and it was obvious she'd come to care for her.

He didn't fear she would do anything to put Lexi at risk anymore. The woman was determined to take down the Lord, but she also wanted to keep Lexi safe and alive.

Did he completely trust her?

No, but there were few he completely trusted. He had come to consider her an ally. Her knowledge, as well as her ability to keep Lexi from pushing herself too much, was good for Lexi.

Neither he nor Niall spoke as they rode back to the palace and dismounted by the steps. Cole led the way inside and up the stairs to his rooms.

He opened the door to his sitting room and stepped aside as he gestured for Niall to enter ahead of him. When he did, Cole followed him inside and closed the door behind them.

Cole waved a hand at one of the chairs in the room. "Make yourself comfortable."

He poured them some whiskey as Niall settled into one of the chairs. Cole handed Niall his glass, and he walked over to stand by one of the windows. As he gazed down at the nearly completed homes and healing land, he sipped his drink.

"The ball is tomorrow," Cole said.

"I'm aware."

And Niall didn't sound happy about it. They hadn't discussed it, but he was sure Niall suspected the same as him—this ball was not going to end well.

"Who in the Gloaming do you trust?" Cole asked.

"Besides you and Brokk?"

"Yes."

"Completely?"

"Yes."

"No one."

Cole felt much the same way, but he'd hoped Niall would have a different answer. "If things go badly at the ball, the Lord is going to come for the Gloaming."

"I think that's his intention."

Cole glanced at the head of his guard. There was a reason Niall had risen to his position and a reason he survived the war; he was far from a dumb man.

"He wants me under his thumb," Cole said. "He plans to prove to everyone who attends this shit show that he has the king of the Gloaming right where he wants him. He's going to make it clear to all the leaders of the realms that they have no chance against him."

"Everyone knows this realm is one of the strongest... if not *the* strongest outside of Dragonia."

That was true, or at least it was before the rebellion killed more dark fae, ruined their homes, and destroyed their land. Now, the Gloaming was hurting, as were its residents.

If his father hadn't stockpiled so much food, they might also face a famine issue, but they should have plenty of time to replant the land before anyone went hungry. And he would make sure to start refilling their larders as the new crops came in.

Even after the rebellion and the number of troops they lost during the war, they were still a powerful species. The only realm that might be stronger than them was the Lunar realm, but the lycans were often too busy fighting each other to band together enough to become a problem.

If the lycans ever got on the same side of things, they would be a fierce enemy or ally. But they all enjoyed fighting each other too much for that to happen any time soon.

His uncle Maverick had a firm handle on his pack, but his was one of many in the Lunar realm. Even with as strong an alpha as Maverick was, some of his wolves rebelled during the war.

A couple of Maverick's pack members had challenged his position as alpha since the war. They saw the defection of some of his pack as a sign of weakness. They all regretted their decision.

His uncle had told Cole he'd been invited to the ball and congratulated him on his engagement. He requested to meet in person, but Cole didn't have time.

He'd sent a crow back explaining this and told his uncle he

would see him at the ball. His uncle sent back a simple reply. *See you then.*

In the other realms, the witches and warlocks were strong, but they didn't have the army of the dark fae. The war decimated the fae military, and they lost more during the rebellion, but it was still larger than most and well trained.

But its smaller size was one of the many reasons the Lord felt Cole couldn't stand up to him. Lexi was another one.

When he felt the shadows rising inside him, he turned away from Niall. He trusted the man with his life. More than that, he trusted Niall with *Lexi's* life, but there were some secrets he still wasn't ready to share, and the shadows were one of them.

CHAPTER FORTY-ONE

"IF THINGS GO WRONG, we're going to have to get as many dark fae out of the Gloaming as possible," Cole said.

"Should we evacuate them now?" Niall asked.

"No. If the Lord hears of that, he'll make us all pay for it, and there is someone here telling him things. If we try to remove any dark fae, he'll know about it and retaliate."

"Do you have any suspects?"

"One," Cole said. "But there could be dozens… if not more."

"Most of the dark fae residing in this area are still working to put the homes together. If something happens at the ball, they'll be in the field. And if nothing happens until tomorrow night, then I'll have the men stay with me in the field."

"Good idea. Tell them I want them to finish building the homes. We're so close it shouldn't be a problem, and that will keep most of the residents together."

"And I'll have the king's guard there to protect the civilians if it becomes necessary."

"That will work," Cole said.

"But how will I know when it's time to get them out?"

"I'll make sure you do," Cole said.

Lexi could get them out of Dragonia; no one would see that coming, so he should be able to return to the Gloaming pretty fast.

"But if something goes wrong, when the first dragon shows up, start evacuating," Cole said.

"I hope we don't have to deal with one of those things," Niall muttered and finished his whiskey.

"Or more than one."

Niall winced and rose to refill his glass. He held the decanter toward Cole, who shook his head.

"What about those in the outer lands like Underhill?" Niall asked as he returned to his chair.

"If I can beat the Lord back to the Gloaming, we should be able to get word to them to get out. The Lord doesn't know the other areas of this realm well, and the dragons can't fly there as fast as we can open a portal to reach them. There was that one dragon who went to Underhill and would know how to return, but if I can get there before that dragon, they should be safe. I could always send out word to the outer lands to be ready to flee."

"But that could bring down the Lord's wrath if the traitor hears about it and reports back to him."

"It could also save lives."

"It could, but I would advise against it."

"So would I," Cole murmured.

He had to weigh how many lives would be lost if the Lord continued to rule, compared to how many they would save if they succeeded in taking him down.

"Where do we send the dark fae if we do have to evacuate?" Niall asked.

"Tell them to scatter and go somewhere they believe is safe. If we all meet at the same place, then whoever is reporting to the Lord will inform him where everyone is. We can't have that. If they're going to live, they have to run."

"He'll hunt them all like he hunted Orin and Varo."

Cole turned to look out the window again. Yet another secret he kept from Niall... he didn't know that his brothers still lived. Cole wouldn't jeopardize Niall's life by revealing that secret to him, at least not now.

He suspected Niall would soon learn it.

"He will," Cole confirmed.

"What about the rebels still in the dungeon?"

Cole considered leaving them there, but if the Lord discovered they were there and didn't immediately kill them, he might add them to his army.

"We'll behead them," Cole said. "Have them brought out now."

"I'll see to it," Niall replied.

Though he didn't want to see it, Cole remained until the last of the prisoners was dead.

CHAPTER FORTY-TWO

"I THINK that's enough for today," Kaylia said.

Lexi continued to glare at her palm as it consistently failed to throw fire or weave magic. Even if it made no sense, she was starting to hate the thing.

"I'm not done," Lexi protested.

"We've done all we can for today. It's time to rest."

Lexi shifted her glare to Kaylia as the crone rose, stretched her arms over her head, and leaned back. She yawned as she turned to study the land stretching out around them.

"I can do this," Lexi insisted.

"I know you can, but it's time for a break."

"The ball is tomorrow."

"I know."

"I'm not prepared."

Kaylia's silvery blonde hair swayed around her knees as she looked over her shoulder at Lexi. "You could spend all your time between now and the ball trying to awaken your fire and magic and still not succeed. You need a break."

"But—"

"I'm far older than you; I know when it's time to rest. If you keep going like this, you're going to burn yourself out, and that won't do anyone any good, especially if things go wrong tomorrow and you have to flee Dragonia. Trust me, the best preparation you can do for tomorrow is to take it easy and sleep as much as possible."

"There's no way I'm going to sleep tonight."

"You probably won't get a lot, but a little is better than none."

"What if I refuse to go back?"

"Then I'll have Brokk come and drag you out of here."

"The one time you want to work with him *would* be to team up against me," Lexi muttered.

Kaylia chuckled. "Are you ready to go?"

Lexi sighed and pushed herself up from the ground. Kaylia may be calling it an early day, but that didn't mean she couldn't work on more self-defense training with Brokk and her dad.

She recalled a question she'd been meaning to ask Kaylia as she wiped the dirt from her ass. "I was wondering something about the arach."

"What about them?"

"Do they have a fated loved one like the lycans have mates and vampires have consorts?"

"No," Kaylia said. "They loved deeply, as immortals do, but they don't have fated mates."

"I see," Lexi murmured.

"That makes your love for Cole more frightening, doesn't it?"

It made no sense, but for some reason, it did. "Why do you say that?"

"Because if it was some biological reaction you were having to him, and that's what initially attracted you to him, you could always blame that for losing your heart and mind if it all goes wrong. But if it's just you, then *you* decided to love someone you could lose. Love is terrifying in that way. All those who love know they could one day end up with a broken heart, yet they still choose to love and to one day bear that suffering."

"Nothing is going to go wrong."

Kaylia's smile was sad as she gave a small nod. "No, it won't."

But Lexi heard the doubt in her voice. How could Kaylia not doubt it? How could *she* not doubt it? They were going to the Lord's ball tomorrow, and even if they survived unscathed, the Lord would remain breathing down their necks and waiting for a chance to pounce.

And as soon as they were ready to take the Lord on, another war would unfold. As much as she tried to deny it, there was one solid truth about the futures of everyone involved in this...

Not all of them would survive.

"Every love story ends in heartbreak," Kaylia said. "It's inevitable. Even immortals die."

"So, you think it's better not to love?"

"Absolutely not. I would gladly take that shattering of my heart to experience the wondrous joy of love."

"Have you ever been in love?"

Sorrow flared in Kaylia's eyes before she looked away. Lexi wished she could take the question back.

"I'm sorry, it's none of my business," she blurted.

"No, it's fine." Kaylia gave a dismissive wave of her hand, but it couldn't cover her sadness. "I was in love once with an *amazing* man. He was the best I've ever met, and I lost him."

Lexi didn't ask what happened to him. The anguish in Kaylia's eyes and voice, her retreat to the crone realm, and the fact she still considered her ex a good man all spoke of death. No one called the guy who cheated on them and ran away with an incubus a good man.

"I'm sorry," Lexi said.

Kaylia lifted one shoulder in a half-hearted shrug. "It was many years ago, but I still miss him every day. His name was Fabian."

Lexi bit her lip against asking any more questions and upsetting the woman she'd grown to consider a friend. However, Kaylia seemed to want to talk about him, and she couldn't resist learning more about the woman who had mostly remained an enigma since arriving.

"Was he an immortal?" Lexi asked.

"Yes, he was a warlock," Kaylia confirmed. "We met at a mutual friend's Samhain party. It wasn't love at first sight, but we got along well, and over time, it grew into something more. Something powerful and profound."

Lexi was shocked by the tears in Kaylia's eyes before she blinked them away. Her heart ached for the woman and her loss.

"He was the love of my life," Kaylia murmured.

"Did you marry him?" Lexi asked.

"We were engaged when he died."

"Wh-what happened?"

Kaylia's face hardened, and her tears dried as her eyes met Lexi's. A simmering fury emanated from them.

"A vampire murdered him," she stated.

"Oh." Lexi's hand flew to her throat as understanding dawned. All witches hated vampires; that was no secret, but Kaylia's antipathy toward them had always seemed more intense than normal. And now she understood why. "I'm so sorry."

Kaylia closed her eyes and lifted her face to the sun. "It was many years ago."

But it obviously still tormented her. Without thinking, Lexi crossed to Kaylia and hugged her. At first, the witch didn't respond, but then she relaxed against Lexi and hugged her back.

"You know what, I think you're right," Lexi said. "It is time to call it a day. I'm not going to learn anything earth-shattering by tomorrow. How about we head back and have a couple of drinks?"

Kaylia smiled as she stepped out of Lexi's embrace. "That sounds fantastic."

CHAPTER FORTY-THREE

"ARE YOU SURE ABOUT THIS?" Orin asked.

He adjusted the chains Cole wore so they fell across the shoulders of his black fae tunic. The black belt, with its silver buckles, cinched the tunic at his waist. Black, formfitting pants and a black cloak completed the outfit.

Cole couldn't remember the last time it was just him and his brother in a room... or the last time they hadn't been at each other's throats. Instead, as Orin adjusted the chains again, Cole sensed his apprehension.

When Orin reached to fiddle with the chains once more, Cole seized his hands and moved them away. "Afraid of losing me?"

Orin snorted. "I'm more afraid of losing our only chance at defeating that fucker."

Cole laughed. "Deny it all you want, but you know you'd miss me."

Orin scowled as Cole glanced around Lexi's empty room. She was getting dressed in Sahira's room, and he hoped things were going well for them.

"I'm *not* sure about this," he admitted. "But I don't have a choice."

Orin grunted, and his jaw muscle ticked in rhythm with his heart. "I know you don't," he finally admitted.

Orin ran his hands over Cole's shoulders, smoothing out the material there, before smiling. "I guess that's the best we're going to do. The unfortunate reality is you're nowhere near as handsome as me."

"Only you think so," Cole replied.

"I know so. That lycan blood ruined you."

Cole chuckled as he slapped Orin on the back hard enough to stagger him forward. "Sorry," he said. "Sometimes lycan blood forgets its strength."

Orin glowered at him, but a knock on the door silenced his words before he could reply.

"Come in," Cole beckoned.

The door opened, and Brokk poked his head inside. "How's it going in here?"

"We're all set," Cole replied.

"I've tried my best," Orin said as he sauntered toward the door, "but he's still ugly."

"You wish you looked this good," Cole called after him.

Orin waved a hand dismissively back at him before walking out the door. He didn't fool Cole; his brother would never admit it, but he was nervous.

"Is Lexi ready?" Cole asked Brokk.

"Sahira said it would only be a few more minutes."

"Okay."

Cole strode toward the door. He followed Brokk downstairs and into the library, where Del sat in a chair with his elbows on his knees. He clasped his bent head between his hands as he tugged at his hair and tapped one foot.

Kaylia drummed her fingers against the fireplace mantle as she stared at the door. The nervous tic was the first time Cole had ever seen her reveal any kind of anxiety.

Though she remained distant with most of them, she liked

Lexi. The two of them were half-drunk and laughing as they sat on the back porch when he returned to the manor last night.

He didn't know who he was more surprised to find in that condition; Kaylia, who was so rigid, or Lexi, who relentlessly pushed herself every day. But he'd been happy to see them having fun, especially Lexi, who leapt up to hug him, tripped over a chair, and nearly faceplanted.

Her laughter was pure music to his ears after watching his prisoners die. He embraced her and they kissed before he retreated to find Sahira, Del, and Brokk in the kitchen. Orin was nowhere to be seen, but that wasn't new.

"What's going on out there?" he asked the others.

"We don't know, but we're enjoying their laughter," Del replied.

"They came back from the outer realm, grabbed some rum, and went to the porch," Brokk said.

"It's probably not great for Lexi to get drunk, but we didn't have the heart to stop it," Sahira said.

Neither did he. An hour later, when Lexi and Kaylia joined them for dinner, they were still giggling and happy.

And now, as he watched Kaylia's fingers moving faster and faster against the stone, he realized she was as anxious as the rest of them about this day.

"I'm not sure this is a good idea," Kaylia said.

"*No* one thinks this is a good idea," Cole replied. "If you have any better suggestions, I'm all ears."

"I don't," she admitted. "I just hate this."

Those words summed up his feelings about it too.

Kaylia resumed drumming her fingers against the mantle as she focused on the books across from her.

A step in the hall turned his head toward it a second before Lexi glided into view with Sahira at her side. His heart battered his ribs as she entered the library.

He could only stand and stare as she stopped in the doorway.

The dress fit her curves in all the right ways. It emphasized the swell of her lush breasts and small waist before falling into a full skirt.

The pale-yellow color emphasized the golden hue of her skin, the hint of her freckles, and the simple pearl necklace she wore. Sahira had pulled her hair into a twist, but tendrils of it fell to frame her face.

She didn't wear any makeup to hide the freckles on the bridge of her slender nose, but Sahira had added a touch of black around her eyes. That black made the green of them stand out more than normal.

"Wow," Brokk breathed.

When Cole shot him a look, Brokk took a quick step away as he held his hands up. "Uh... wow... that's a beautiful dress," he stammered.

Orin and Varo appeared behind Sahira and Lexi. Orin had been about to bite into an apple but froze when he saw them. Varo smiled as he strode forward to clasp Lexi's hands.

"You look beautiful, sister of mine," Varo said.

A small flush crept up Lexi's neck and into her cheeks as she smiled at him. "Thank you."

Cole broke out of his paralysis and swept across the room toward her. As Varo released her, Cole claimed her hands, and Lexi beamed up at him.

"You're stunning," he said, his voice hoarse with the emotion choking him.

She looked gorgeous, and he might be leading her to her death. Her eyes flickered toward the walls, and her smile faltered as the shadows swayed.

"Don't," she said.

He smiled at her as he reined in the shadows, but he wouldn't keep them caged today. He would set them free if it became necessary and damn the consequences.

"We're going to be fine." She let go of his hands to brush her hand down his chest. "You're looking pretty good yourself."

He stroked her cheek with his knuckles as he contemplated running with her. What did it matter if thousands died as long as *she* lived? And if he went to the Gloaming first, he could order them all to evacuate before the Lord attacked.

He wouldn't have much time before the Lord received word of his orders, and he would be tearing apart the lives of his followers and making them marks for the Lord when he might not have to, but she would live.

They would hunt them, but he could keep her safe.

They could run.

CHAPTER FORTY-FOUR

LEXI MUST HAVE SEEN something on his face as she said, "We can't run."

"We can. I'll keep you safe; I won't let him get to you."

"And you can keep me safe in Dragonia too. But we saw what he did to the pixies; do you think he'd be less merciful to the Gloaming, or the witches' realm, or the lycans' realm? He could go after all of them too. We never know what he's going to do, and we can't throw everyone else to the wolf to save ourselves."

"He wouldn't go after them too," Sahira said.

"But he might," Lexi insisted. "And he could destroy them all before they got a chance to fight. He doesn't kill everyone now because they pay taxes and bow down to him. He loves controlling them, but we're all puppets in his game, and he'd be more than happy to cut our strings."

"If this goes badly, he'll destroy them all anyway," Orin said.

"But that won't happen because of *us*. If this goes badly, it will be *his* fault. But if we run now, it will be *ours*."

"He won't go after so many," Brokk said. "He still needs followers, even if he'd prefer them all dead. He gets the most joy from torturing and killing; he can't do that if all his followers are dead."

"There's the bright side we've all been searching for," Orin said.

Del rose from where he sat, and his gaze fastened on Lexi while he spoke. "When you were a baby, all I wanted was to keep you safe. As you grew, Sahira and I knew that, no matter what we did in this life, the most important thing was keeping you alive."

Lexi's hands tightened around Cole's, and her chin rose. Cole recognized the look as the one she got when she was about to fight for something, but then Del kept talking.

"Maybe we didn't always do things the right way, but I'm very proud of the woman you've become. It doesn't matter what anybody else says; you know what you have to do today."

Lexi gulped, and tears pooled in her eyes before she blinked them away. "We have to go."

Del gave a brief bow of his head. "You have to go. You have to know if there are answers in Dragonia for you, and you can't run away and leave others to suffer. If you ascend that throne, you can't sit on it and look into the faces of those you left behind."

Cole had always admired Del's insights and steadfast demeanor. He despised them now.

Lexi released his hands and walked over to embrace her father. They clung to each other before Del pulled away.

"You've grown into such a beautiful young woman," Del said. "And I don't just mean on the outside. You're more beautiful on the inside."

"The inside is all because of you and Sahira," Lexi told him.

This time, Del had to wipe tears from his eyes. "I love you."

"I love you too." Lexi rested her palm against Del's cheek and rose to kiss the other one. "Dad."

Cole had to look away as a pang of longing pierced through his heart. He'd barely had time to grieve his father, a man he'd loved deeply. Seeing these two together was a blessing, but it also reminded him of the hole in his life.

When he glanced at his brothers, he discovered them focused on anything but Del and Lexi. It didn't matter that Varo and Orin had stood against their father. They'd also loved him dearly.

Lexi pulled away from Del and walked over to hug Sahira. The two of them embraced before saying I love you and breaking apart. When Cole held out his hand to Lexi, she returned to him.

"Be ready in case something goes wrong," he told the others. "You might be better off going to the prison realm now. It will be safer for you there."

"You know nothing about that realm," Brokk said. "You've never been there and wouldn't be able to find it."

"You could leave a portal open for us."

"And if trouble follows you here?" Orin inquired. "You could need help."

"We'll wait here for you," Varo said. "But we'll be ready to go if it becomes necessary."

"Okay," Cole relented; he couldn't force them to leave.

"Bye, everyone," Lexi said and gave a small wave as Cole opened a portal before them.

"Be safe!" Kaylia called as they stepped into the portal.

CHAPTER FORTY-FIVE

LEXI STEPPED out of the portal and into an area closer to the human city. She'd seen the smoke from the ruined city from her home, but she'd never ventured close to it until the Lord's men came to take her to Dragonia.

That was the only other time she'd ever entered the realm that should have been her home, but she had no powers then, and it wasn't a fun visit. This one wasn't going to be fun either.

The burnt-out ruins of the city had always made her uneasy. The people who straggled from it, searching for something better, had broken her heart, and she often gave them what little food they could spare.

But some people still resided within the crumbled walls and buildings. Their lives were far from the ones they once held, and most of their shiny skyscrapers fell beneath the dragons' wrath.

The people who continued to make their home in the city amazed and unnerved her. She had no idea what kind of a person could survive what they had and still forge a life in this barren, forsaken place.

They were either incredibly brave and strong or lunatics. Or, most likely, a combination of all three.

If she ever managed to reclaim the throne that belonged to her ancestors, she would make sure these people knew they would never have to fear the dragons again.

Cole led her toward a brick wall with charred marks on it. Most of the wall had toppled and was little more than a pile of rubble, but a few sections remained standing. Rats squeaked and scurried out of their way as Cole kicked aside some of the bricks. They were the only living things anywhere near them.

Lifting her skirt, Lexi climbed carefully over the rubble toward a still-standing section of wall. In the center of it, something shimmered. No, not shimmered; it was more like the bricks *wavered* like hot air rising from the asphalt in July.

The bricks in the wavering center looked exactly like those surrounding them, but that wavering was there. She'd never seen anything like it before. It certainly hadn't been there when the Lord's men brought her here.

When she'd been here with them, and they'd led her toward this section of wall, she'd been certain she was going to walk straight into the wall. She'd braced herself for the impact.

Instead, they'd walked straight into it, and the wall absorbed them. It took her a few seconds to realize the wall had been hiding a portal, and they were now inside it.

"What is that wavering?" she whispered.

"It's the portal," he said.

"I've never seen it before."

"It's spelled," Cole said. "It's usually what the few permanently open portals look like to an immortal, and only an immortal can see it."

"I've been to this area of the city before; I've seen this wall and been through this portal, but I've still never seen it before."

"Sahira's potion must have tamped down your ability to do so."

"What if a human accidentally finds it?"

"If they do, then they'll most likely die as soon as they enter

Dragonia. Before the Lord revealed to humans that immortals exist, some of them stumbled upon this and other open portals.

"It's risky to leave a portal permanently open like this. But since only an arach can open a portal in and out of Dragonia, the arach set these up so immortals who needed to enter the realm could do so."

"It's *extremely* risky to put one in the human realm," Lexi said. "They have no idea what they're encountering. They must have been so scared."

"Some managed to escape again. That's probably how their legends about immortals were born. Come on," Cole said.

He linked his arm through hers and clasped her hand as they strode through the wavering section of the brick wall.

Keep your shield in place, she told herself as the portal enveloped them.

CHAPTER FORTY-SIX

WHEN THEY EXITED THE PORTAL, the wondrous beauty of Dragonia greeted her. She'd only ever been to the realm once before, but the memory of that terrifying encounter with the Lord still haunted her dreams.

As the sun streamed over them, Lexi cast a nervous glance down at her bare arms, but they didn't glow, and she didn't see any silver markings.

One fear down, a thousand more to go before this is over.

But at least she didn't give away what she was by stepping into the realm. Some of the tension in her chest eased, and she couldn't stop herself from grinning at Cole. He squeezed her hand as he smiled back.

Straightening her shoulders, she lifted her chin. She would not fail here today. She would keep her shield in place, and one day, she would reclaim this land. She *would* make it a happy place again.

But then, she didn't know if it was *ever* a happy, beautiful place. She assumed it was with its towering mountains, rolling green fields, the golden towers of the palace, and purple sky, but she couldn't be positive.

If anything, over the past millennia, the land and immortals here had endured some *very* unhappy years. Once the Arach turned on and destroyed each other, Dragonia became a miserable, bloody place to reside.

In all the realms, the immortals lived under the rule of a leader corrupted by the power of a throne that didn't belong to him.

She liked to think that before the arach destroyed themselves, Dragonia had been a place of beauty and wonder. But it couldn't have been all great if the arach fought so much.

It doesn't matter if it was once a happy place or not; I will make it so when we take down the Lord.

The guards stationed outside the portal were all focused on them. They all held swords or staffs, but none lifted a weapon against them. In fact, they all shifted uneasily and glanced away from Cole's penetrating stare.

"King Colburn," one of them greeted. "It's a pleasure to have you back in our realm."

The man looked like it was anything but a pleasure as he stared over Cole's shoulder while speaking.

"It's a pleasure to be back," Cole replied with an aplomb that almost made Lexi believe this was all going to go well.

Almost, but she wasn't an idiot.

When a shadow sweeping across the land blocked out the sun, Lexi tilted her head back as a green dragon soared into view. The hair on her nape and arms rose on end as something inside her reacted to its power and beauty.

Yearning clawed at her insides in a way it never had when she'd seen the formidable creatures before, but she couldn't shake it, and she didn't want to. She longed to be up there, sweeping over the land with the dragon.

For all she knew, the dragons *never* allowed that, not even with the arach who once lived so freely amongst them. It would probably eat her if she tried to climb onto its back, but she itched to go to it and touch it.

The dragon didn't look at her or tip its wing; it showed no reaction to her presence in their realm, *her* realm, but the reaction in her body was undeniable.

"The Lord will be happy to see you," the man continued. "All of the other guests have already arrived."

Cole stiffened a little but showed no other sign that the man's words irritated him.

"We'll be happy to see the Lord too," Cole replied.

"This way," the man said.

As he started toward the golden palace, set up high on a mountain, they followed him. The man turned his head to speak over his shoulder. "Congratulations on your engagement."

"Thank you," Cole said.

"Thank you," Lexi murmured.

They followed the guard into the bailey and through the outdoor market area. They passed immortals with hunched shoulders, dirty clothes, and shadows under their eyes. Though they were trying to sell their wares, they barely waved their merchandise in the air, and they didn't shout about its abilities.

Lexi lifted her skirt as they hiked the dirt path leading up the hill and toward the rock bridge spanning the river. The river ran far below the palace, and as they climbed higher, it became nothing more than a ribbon of blue as the rush of water over rocks faded away.

She tried to imagine what it would be like to live in a place so beautiful and grand, but she couldn't see herself here. She didn't fit into this world. But she would have to figure out how to fit because this was *hers*.

There was no denying the growing feeling of possessiveness inside her. This was her realm, her land, and *her* dragons.

CHAPTER FORTY-SEVEN

SHE STARED at the back of the man in front of them as they arrived at the bridge. Trying not to fidget with her skirt or necklace, she searched for something to distract herself from what lay ahead of them.

"I'm not a very good dancer," she told Cole.

"It's a good thing you'll have me to lead the way then. And I've danced with you before; you were amazing."

"You're biased."

His laughter drew the guard's attention. The man frowned at them before turning and stalking onward.

She did her best not to let her alarm show, but tension crept across her shoulders.

If it all goes wrong, we can open a portal out of here.

What if you can't get one to open here?

She buried that niggling doubt. It wouldn't do her any good; it was far too late for them to turn back now, and it *had* to work. She was an arach. They were the only ones who possessed the ability.

She tried not to think about the possibility that one of the last arachs to reside here might have magically stripped the ability from all the others.

No, Kaylia said that was very unlikely, and they would need your name, so just stop! You're here. There's no turning back. Work on controlling what you can, like your shield.

Lexi focused on her shield, but it was still firmly intact. She didn't feel so much as a tiny crack in it, and she was doing great at keeping it in place without having to remain focused on it.

As they stepped onto the bridge, pebbles broke free of the rocky formation and tumbled into the river below. She hated being on the rickety structure, but she hated it more when they walked beneath the silver portcullis and through the open, golden gates shaped like dragons.

The sound of music and laughter drifted to them as the guard led them down a hall before taking a left. Lexi glanced up at Cole to discover his jaw tensed and his shoulders rigid.

She'd only ever been to the throne room before, and that was in the opposite direction of where they were headed now. When the guard took another left, the music and laughter grew louder, but now she heard the clink of glasses and silverware too.

A set of open, double doors came into view at the end of the hall. Through the doors, she could see immortals gliding across the floor, opening their arms in greeting to each other and swiping glasses from the trays of the servants passing by.

They all looked like they were having a good time, but they drank their alcohol too fast, talked too loudly, and smiled too brightly for it to be real.

Lexi braced for the worst, but her breath was stolen from her when they stepped into one of the most lavish, beautiful rooms she'd ever seen. Her mouth parted, and her head tipped back as she tried to take it all in.

After what Cole had told her about the Lord's throne room and the bloody fountain, she hadn't known what would greet them at the ball. She hadn't expected such beauty in a palace that harbored such horrors.

A golden, domed ceiling arched far above their heads and

reflected the light of the giant chandelier dangling above them. It was so large it took up a quarter of the ceiling. The thousands of diamonds encompassing the light fixture reflected hundreds of rainbow colors across the dome, walls, and white, marble floor.

Those rainbow colors came from the light spilling through the stained-glass windows lining the bottom of the dome. Dozens of dragons, wolves, crows, cats, horses, phoenixes, and more comprised the multicolored panes of those spectacular windows.

The walls of the room mostly consisted of floor-to-ceiling windows and sliding glass doors that opened onto what looked like a courtyard or garden beyond. She hoped it wasn't the dead garden with the blood fountain Cole told her about, but she couldn't tell.

The room was mostly bare of furniture, but some chairs and love seats lined the walls for the dancers who required a break. No one sat on the cream-colored furniture with its fluffy, inviting-looking cushions.

The four musicians sat on stools in a corner of the room; one played the cello, another the flute, and the third a lute, while the fourth sang. The woman singing had a mesmerizing voice that wove a haunting melody throughout the room.

Lexi was so awed by the beauty around her that it took a minute to realize all the immortals were turning toward them. Some of their smiles faltered; more than a few looked terrified, while hope filled the eyes of others.

She wasn't sure if their terror or hope unnerved her more.

Sitting at the far end of the room, high up on a black dais that stood out sharply from the room's color, the Lord sat on his throne. He must have had it moved from the throne room for him.

When the monster spotted them, he slapped his hands against the arms of his chair and started to beam. "Silence!" he commanded.

The musicians immediately stopped playing, but the fading cords of their music hung in the air for a few more seconds. Lexi found herself gazing into the wide eyes of a troubadour clutching his lute to his chest as he silenced the vibrating strings of his instrument.

Looking into that man's eyes, Lexi saw her future staring back at her.

This was a game, and the pawns had arrived.

And it was going to be bad. Really, *really* bad.

CHAPTER FORTY-EIGHT

"COME FORWARD! COME FORWARD!" the Lord called as he beckoned to them.

Cole plastered on a smile and looked down to see Lexi had done the same. Except, unlike the radiant smiles she bestowed on others when she was truly happy, this one didn't light up her eyes.

Her hand clenched around his as the crowd parted to give them a clear path to the Lord. To the man who had slaughtered countless pixies to sate his bloodlust. Revulsion and loathing built within Cole as they started toward the sick prick.

He spotted Circe, a powerful witch and coalition member, as they moved. Her skin was far paler than normal. Her black hair hung in ringlets to her shoulders, and black eyeliner emphasized her doe-brown eyes. She didn't acknowledge him as he passed, but her lips compressed slightly.

It had been a couple of months since the coalition last met, but their shared hatred of the Lord united the group. The coalition had plotted to take the Lord down from inside his ranks during the war, and they failed.

That failure led to the death of countless innocents and was the reason they were all in this room. It weighed heavy on his shoulders as they approached the Lord.

If he'd made other choices, if maybe he'd joined the rebels, if they *all* had, would things have been different?

At the time, he'd been certain espionage was the way to destroy this asshole, but he'd been wrong. And now, he would never know if he'd made a mistake.

No, it couldn't have been a mistake. He wouldn't have met Lexi if he'd done things differently, and they could both be dead. At least now, they were still alive to fight, and they had each other.

And a secret weapon stood at his side; he planned to keep it that way. He'd trusted the coalition completely before, but not with this. Not with *Lexi*.

And as he passed Circe, he spotted Talon, a warlock on the coalition. He'd always been their most timid member. Now, he stood with his shoulders back and his chin raised as if he were the one walking toward an uncertain future.

Talon's shoulder-length blond hair curled at the ends, and his murky blue eyes reminded Cole of a storm-tossed sea when they met his. At one time, Talon would have been the first to look away, but now he held Cole's gaze.

It was as if the once-timid warlock was now trying to give Cole the strength to get through this.

A commotion in the crowd drew Cole's attention to his Uncle Maverick elbowing his way toward the front. It was easy to follow his progress through the mass as Maverick stood almost a full head over everyone else. At six foot nine, he was two inches taller than Cole and broader through the shoulders.

The immortals who saw him coming scampered out of his way, but others were too engrossed with Lexi and Cole to move. Maverick shoved those unsuspecting souls out of the way until he stood at the edge of the makeshift aisle.

His dark, wavy brown hair framed his broad face, and apprehension filled his chestnut-brown eyes. His lips clamped together as his nostrils flared.

Cole suspected most of those in this room hadn't expected them to show. It was obvious Maverick wished they hadn't. Cole was his only living family member; he'd been exceptionally close with his sister, Cole's mother, and a constant presence and strength in Cole's life over the years.

He'd die to protect his sister's child. Cole would make sure that didn't happen.

The only coalition members missing were Brokk, his father, and Del. It was the reunion he'd never wanted... at least not in this place.

But more than the coalition crowded this room. There were far more immortals than he'd expected, and they were all from some of the most prominent families throughout the realm. He'd fought beside a few of them during the war, but most bought their way out of the battle.

He stiffened when he spotted Becca amid the crowd, standing beside Finn. Though he didn't see them now, he assumed the rest of the dark fae council was here too.

The only immortals he didn't see here were the light fae, but no one wanted to see them after they refused to participate in the war. He suspected the only reason the Lord hadn't killed them all yet was that they paid an exorbitant amount of taxes and were shitty fighters. They would have been useless in the war.

Behind all the guests and lining the walls were the Lord's guards. It was the first ball Cole had ever attended where fully armed guards outnumbered the guests and stood like sentinels throughout the room. It certainly put a damper on the mood.

But then, all the laughter they heard on their way here was all pretend. Most of the guests had sweat beading the brows of their too pale faces, and no one spoke or smiled as they walked past.

When they drew closer to the Lord, the dragon hidden by the curtain behind the dais lifted its head. The small intake of Lexi's breath was the only reaction she gave to the creature's sudden emergence.

Gasps filled the room as the rest of the immortals became aware of the dragon's presence. The Lord had been keeping this little secret tucked up his sleeve; he laughed at the reaction of the others, but he never took his eyes off Lexi and Cole.

The dragon stared out at them from golden eyes with slitted pupils that revealed no hint of emotion. Its red scales brought to mind the dragon who entered the Gloaming, but he couldn't see how big it was.

When it lifted its head a little higher, it revealed the flecks of yellow under its neck. They traveled toward its belly before vanishing, but he knew it was the same creature.

This beast was not the one who killed his father; he'd killed that one, but he still despised its brethren. The dragon returned his loathing as it eyed him like a cat preparing to pounce.

Cole was more than ready for it, but he hoped it didn't happen. If Lexi did have a connection to the dragons, then he'd prefer not to slaughter one in front of her. And if she somehow did bond with them, he would learn to tolerate them.

However, he'd always hate the murderous beasts who destroyed his father, ravaged the mortal realm, and kept most immortals living in fear.

And then, the curtains swayed and another dragon head emerged. A harsh intake of breaths filled the air, and the Lord chuckled. The beast yawned as it brought its front legs forward and settled its blue head onto them.

It was smaller than the other one, and its scales shimmered with dozens of different hues of blue. It revealed all its massive, razor-sharp teeth when it yawned, but Cole suspected it was nowhere near as relaxed as it acted.

For one thing, all of its three-foot-long talons hadn't retracted and remained on full display.

The red dragon continued to watch them as they stopped before the steps leading up to the Lord. So far, neither dragon had shown any special interest in Lexi.

A fact that both calmed and troubled him.

If the dragons didn't pay her any special attention, they could get through this without the Lord learning what she was. But if the dragons *didn't* react or acknowledge her, then they could be wrong about her having some sway over them.

CHAPTER FORTY-NINE

"You've arrived, finally!" the Lord declared as he slapped his hands off the ends of the throne and grinned at them. "We've been waiting for you!"

"Our invite said to arrive at four," Cole replied.

"Of course it did! This is a party for *you* after all. I planned to surprise you with all the guests excited to celebrate your upcoming nuptials. If you had arrived first, it would be a lot less fun."

The Lord had certainly succeeded in surprising him with the amount of immortals in attendance. And after seeing that most of them were the elite of their realms, he didn't doubt the Lord was making a point.

He'd made some of the most powerful immortals in many of the realms drop everything to be here. Cole suspected that not a single immortal had turned down their invite.

"And don't you look beautiful," the Lord said to Lexi.

"Thank you," she murmured.

"How did you both enjoy my presents?" he asked. "I was so eager for Cole to receive them once I saw how much he liked pixies."

A murmur of curiosity ran through the crowd, but Cole would never satisfy it.

"It was quite a surprise," Cole said diplomatically.

"It was beautiful," Lexi murmured.

"Not so beautiful as you. Malakai was very upset when he learned of your engagement. Isn't that true, Malakai?" the Lord said and shifted his attention to the crowd.

Cole's upper and lower fangs lengthened at the mention of that bastard and the realization he was here. He should have expected the Lord to invite Malakai too. That made things more fun for him.

It took a great deal of effort, but Cole managed to retract his fangs again as Lexi's nails dug into his arm. Cole rested his other hand over hers as he turned to discover Malakai standing at the front of the crowd.

Malakai's face was as cold as stone, and hatred shone in his eyes when they met Cole's. Despite wanting nothing more than to tear out Malakai's throat, Cole smiled at the piece of shit.

It only made things more fun for *him* when red sparked through Malakai's eyes before fading away.

"But, as I told him," the Lord continued, "sometimes these things don't work out, and you did ask her first. However, who knows what the future holds; he could always have a chance later."

Cole's shoulders went back as a whisper ran through the crowd, and some of them shifted uneasily. No immortals treated marriage so flippantly. Cole didn't know of anyone who remarried after losing a spouse. They went on, they had other lovers, but they never said those vows again.

A small tremor ran through Lexi before she steadied herself, and her chin rose a little. Then the Lord laughed before slapping his knee.

"Of course, that would never happen to the two of you," he said. "You're so happy and *so* in love."

He said love like it was the most disgusting word he'd ever

uttered. And to this monster, who could never understand the concept of love, it probably was.

If Cole harbored any hope they might make it through this event unscathed, it vanished with that word.

The Lord sat back on his throne as he spoke. "And all of these fine nobles are here to celebrate your love."

"And we truly appreciate it," Cole said. "It is an unexpected, blessed event to have so many here to celebrate our upcoming nuptials and our love."

The slight narrowing of the Lord's eyes told Cole he wasn't buying the bullshit Cole shoveled, but Cole had to utter the basic niceties. They both knew it.

"It's my pleasure!" the Lord cried. "It has been far too many years since I've hosted a ball, what with the war and all, but now my enemies are defeated, your brothers and father—" He smiled at Cole, who ground his teeth together until he swore he cracked a few. "—are dead, and the good times will once again rule in this land."

"Of course, my Lord," Cole murmured.

"Musicians, play!" the Lord commanded.

The silence stretched for so long the Lord's head spun toward the minstrels. One of them released a squeak before hitting the cords of his cello with too much force. The resulting sound was far from pleasant.

The Lord laughed while everyone else in the room winced. The rest of the musicians started playing, but no one in the room moved. Lifting his hands, the Lord clapped loudly.

"Drinks! Food! Bring it all forth. Everyone, return to dancing!" the Lord commanded.

The Lord's bellow reverberated off the golden walls and rattled the windows. At first, the others were slow to move, but they rushed to find a partner when the blue dragon lifted its head.

This ball had turned the most powerful leaders of the Shadow Realms into the Lord's puppets. He could command them to do whatever he wanted, and they all would as long as the dragons and guards watched their every move.

He was exerting his power over them as he not-so-subtly reminded them who was in charge. In their realms, they were the elite, but they would always be at his mercy and under his thumb, no matter where they resided.

It was a move meant to keep these leaders meek, but it could also backfire. There was far too much pride in this room for many of these immortals to take being pushed around like this well.

The Lord leaned forward and rested his hands on his knees to study Lexi and Cole. "This party is for you. Go, have fun! Eat, drink, and be merry."

For tomorrow we die.

The Lord didn't say those words, but they ran through Cole's head.

However, he didn't think the Lord would wait until tomorrow to make his move.

CHAPTER FIFTY

THE NEXT FEW hours passed in a tense blur. Lexi sipped champagne and picked at the food carried by harried servers who rushed from one end of the room to the other.

When one of them accidentally dropped a tray of champagne, a musician screeched their bow across their strings, and everyone else in the room jumped. Before the servant could clean it up, a couple of guards grabbed him by the arms, lifted him off the ground, and carried him from the room.

When Lexi took a step toward them to intervene, Cole clasped her elbow and pulled her back. He kept his fake smile lodged firmly in place.

"Cole," Lexi whispered.

Releasing her elbow, he rested his hand in the small of her back and steered her away as other servants rushed to clean up the mess. Their hands quivered as they picked up the larger pieces of glass and set them on the tray while another hovered nearby with a broom.

Tears streaked the cheeks of one of the musicians while they played. At first, Lexi thought they knew the servant who was removed, but then she saw the streaks of red coating the instrument's strings.

Bile burned her throat as the woman's bloody fingers continued to glide across the top of her cello while her bow slid across its strings. And then the woman vanished from view as immortals danced across the floor.

Cole led her over to his uncle standing near the doors with two glasses of champagne in his hands. The two of them hadn't been far from each other since she and Cole arrived.

Maverick drank one, set the glass on a passing tray, and grabbed another before downing his other drink.

"How long have the musicians been playing?" Lexi inquired.

"We all arrived at noon," Maverick answered. "And they were already playing then."

"So at least seven hours," she said.

And the Lord didn't have any intention of letting them stop soon.

"From what I've seen, they've only taken the small break they were granted when you arrived," Maverick replied and downed another glass of champagne.

He'd consumed more alcohol than she'd ever seen anyone drink, but his gait remained steady, his eyes were clear, and his words didn't slur. She was curious if he had a hollow leg or something.

However, he was the largest man she'd ever seen. It would probably take a *whole* lot to get him drunk and fill him up, but despite his overbearing appearance, and the lycans' reputation for being brusque, he was kind to her.

She liked his robust laugh and the way his eyes twinkled when he saw Cole, even though there was little joy here. He couldn't hide his love for his nephew; that only made her like him more.

When she turned to face the dancers, her eyes traveled back to the dragons behind the Lord's throne. The blue one was now awake and watchful while the red one dozed.

Lexi's fingers twitched as she imagined walking up and resting her hand on one of their noses. She was desperate to touch one, but she liked her hand far too much to risk it.

Besides, they'd shown no interest in her while she had to keep reminding herself to look away from them. Just because she felt a new, strong pull to them didn't mean they returned it.

A striking woman in a blue dress distracted her from the dragons as she stopped to offer her congratulations. Lexi sipped her champagne while Cole and Maverick made small talk with the woman.

They knew the woman, so she let them handle it. By now, she was pretty sure they'd talked to everyone in the room as they offered their congratulations, and she could barely remember any of them.

There weren't as many immortals here as the ball Cole's father held where she first met him, but after hours of hearing so many new names, she forgot them almost as soon as the immortal turned away. If she ever claimed the arach throne, she would need cheat sheets to help her remember everyone.

Becca and Malakai didn't come to congratulate them, and for that, she was glad. She was more than happy to keep her distance from them.

As the evening progressed and more food and drinks circulated, she expected the immortals in the room to start relaxing. If anything, the tension ratcheted up.

Another one of the musicians started crying as his blood stained the strings of his lute. Her heart ached for them.

She twirled her glass between her fingers as she considered asking the Lord to give them a break. After all, it was a party in her honor, but she imagined he would only use it against her, or worse... the musicians.

As much as she hated it, silence was her best option. If the Lord knew how much this bothered her, he would relish that knowledge.

As the moon rose and its softer radiance replaced the sun, vampires arrived. There weren't many of them, but the arrival of night made it possible for them to be here without bursting into flame.

Deep lines etched the Lord's forehead and the corners of his pinched mouth as he leaned forward. His knuckles turned white on the ends of his throne, and his eyes burned a more vibrant shade of red.

The displeasure he exuded was nearly palpable. And as his displeasure mounted, so did the tension in the room.

The fake laughter ebbed, the smiles became more grim than happy, and more than a few immortals tugged at the collars of their shirts and dresses. It was impossible to pretend to have fun when a murderous psychopath was glowering down at them.

"He's going to lose it soon," Maverick murmured.

"He is," Cole agreed.

"You'll be his target, nephew."

"I know."

"What is your plan?"

"To survive."

It took everything Lexi had not to tug at the collar of her dress as beads of sweat slid down her nape. The temperature of the room hadn't changed and suddenly felt suffocating. She wouldn't let the Lord see her discomfort, though.

They were like a bunch of unhappy sardines all crammed into the room as they jittered around the floor. Thankfully, they didn't smell like sardines, but they weren't much better as the aromas of sweat, body odor, and perfume permeated the air.

Her stomach churned, a dull throb started in her temples, and everything in her screamed it was time to run.

"Cole," she whispered.

He slid his arm around her waist and drew her closer. "It's going to be okay."

Maverick set his empty glass on a passing tray, but for the first time, he didn't grab a fresh one.

"Silence!" the Lord roared.

The musicians did their best to quiet their instruments immediately. One of them sobbed with relief as she slumped forward. When the Lord's narrowed eyes swung toward her, the woman realized she'd drawn his attention and sat up in her chair.

The blood dripping from her fingers made a soft plop on the floor that was too loud in the hushed room. Lexi wasn't sure any of the immortals dared to breathe. She didn't until her lungs burned, and then she barely sucked in a breath.

"I'm so glad everyone is enjoying the celebration!" the Lord declared. "It's what I envisioned when I planned this."

Either the man was delusional and truly believed everyone was having fun, or he was fucking with them even more. He was so twisted she couldn't decide which it was.

"It's time for more dancing!"

Lexi gulped as the musicians all visibly paled. One looked about to say something, but then he clamped his trembling lips together.

"Music!" the Lord declared and clapped his hands. "*Everyone*, dance!"

The last thing Lexi—and she suspected everyone else in this room—felt like doing was dancing. But she took Cole's hand, and he spun her around before drawing her into his arms.

Maverick grasped a witch and gave her a small dip as the music started again. All around Lexi, immortals moved like wooden figurines as they marched more than danced to the music.

No one pretended to laugh anymore, and the few remaining smiles reminded Lexi of the Joker's painted on one. When the Lord beckoned to someone, the hair on Lexi's nape rose as Malakai emerged from the crowd and ascended the stairs to speak with the madman.

Turning away from the Lord and Malakai, Lexi rested her head on Cole's chest. She listened to the soothing, reassuring beat of his heart as she tried to ignore the ache in her feet and exhaustion creeping over her.

No matter how tired she got, she had to keep her shield in place. She couldn't allow it to come down here, with all the moonlight spilling through the windows behind the guards and the stained glass in the ceiling.

How long did the Lord plan to make them dance like this? Until they all dropped? What would he do to the first ones who went down?

She tried not to think about it, but the musicians would probably give out before anyone else. When that happened, there was no way she would stand by and watch the Lord punish them after torturing them like this.

She already hated herself for not intervening now. She hated *all* of this.

Cole's hand flattened against her back when the Lord gave a loud clap and declared. "It's time to switch partners!"

CHAPTER FIFTY-ONE

COLE REMAINED UNMOVING when the Lord announced this. His eyes met the burning red ones of the *fucker* on the throne while he strained to contain the lycan and shadows seeking to break free of him.

He couldn't stomach the idea of parting from Lexi and allowing *others* to touch her.

"Everyone must switch!" the Lord commanded; he never took his eyes from Cole's. "It's more fun that way."

Lexi's fingers dug into his back before she released him and started to step away. She didn't get far before he pulled her back. The Lord was angling to put her and Malakai together, and he would not allow it.

"Cole," she whispered as she tried to pull away. "Cole, he's testing you."

She was right, but his hands remained locked on her. "I don't care."

When she rested her hand on his cheek and nudged his face toward her, he finally looked away from the Lord. He focused on the beautiful green of her eyes and the distress in them.

"We have to do this," she whispered.

"I'll take her, nephew," Maverick said and extended one of his large hands toward them.

The lycan inside him stirred, and its hackles went up. His fangs elongated as his knuckles popped and the bones in his hands shifted toward the change. He'd rather have her with Maverick than Malakai, but he couldn't let her go.

"It's okay," Lexi assured him. "I'll stay close to you."

"And I won't get too close to her," Maverick promised. "It's better me than someone else in this room."

Reluctantly, Cole eased his grip on Lexi before finally releasing her. Her eyes held his as she took Maverick's hand. Cole's jaw popped as his fangs and chin lengthened.

Cole reined the lycan in with momentous effort, but the shadows churned inside him. They battered his insides like bats emerging from a cave. And if he let them, they would take flight and sweep across the room.

But then, he would give away what he was becoming, put Lexi in jeopardy, and possibly be slaughtered before he caused any real damage. The shadows were malevolent, but he had no idea how much destruction they could unleash.

It might not be enough to take down anyone in this room, though he doubted that was true. However, he wasn't going to test their capacity for destruction in a room full of immortals, the Lord's guards, and dragons.

That would be a good way to get him and Lexi killed.

"Play!" the Lord shouted at the musicians. "Everybody dance!"

The music started again, but it was nowhere near as good as when they arrived. The musicians were doing their best, but they missed notes, played the wrong strains, and their voices cracked as they took turns singing.

Lexi held Cole's gaze as she stood almost a foot away from Maverick with her hands in his uncle's, but her attention shifted to his uncle when the music started. Dancers moved and swayed all around him, but he couldn't tear his eyes away from Lexi.

Maverick said something, and she smiled before glancing uneasily at him. Cole wouldn't attack his uncle; never before had he considered doing such a thing, but seeing her in the arms of another, even in the arms of a man he trusted, was one of the worst things he'd ever endured.

Someone touched his arm, and he looked down to discover Becca standing beside him with a sly smile on her face as she held her hand out to him. Cole glanced up at Lexi, who couldn't hide the flash of fury in her eyes.

When she looked from Becca to him, the unhappiness in her gaze was like a knife to his heart. She didn't want to see him in the arms of his ex-lover and a woman Lexi believed to be in love with him.

And she shouldn't have to see it. Hate filled him as he looked to the Lord again, who leaned forward on his throne to watch them raptly.

If Becca was the one running back to the Lord and telling him everything, then the Lord must know how badly Becca wanted power and *him*. Like Malakai, she was here to test Cole's restraint and the strength of his relationship with Lexi.

Becca must mistakenly believe she was safe here because she was the Lord's informant. Cole was not so foolish to think such a thing. The Lord might be using her for information about him and the Gloaming, but he would have no problem killing her tonight.

"Would you care to dance, my king?" Becca inquired.

"No."

He looked away from her to follow Lexi and Maverick as they danced in a slow circle only a few feet away from them.

"Dance, Cole!" the Lord shouted across the room.

Lexi lifted her chin, and her movements became more wooden, but she gave no other sign that the Lord's words bothered her.

Cole's fingers dug into his palms, peeling back his skin and spilling his blood.

And now the games really begin.

Becca smirked as she held her hand out again, but there was no way in hell he was touching her.

Turning away, he searched for another immortal without a partner. He spotted a small witch trying to blend into the wall.

Cole stalked toward her and held out his hand. The marks on his palm had healed, but he wiped his blood on his pants before holding out his hand to her again.

"Would you like to dance?"

When her eyes darted around the room, he understood her nervousness of him. He barely recognized his voice as he maintained a thin hold on his control.

His refusal of Becca was bound to annoy the Lord, but he wasn't going to give her one second of satisfaction by thinking she could force him into something.

The witch glanced nervously around, but he'd alerted the Lord she was there, and she couldn't keep hiding. She probably hated him for it; he didn't care.

Reluctantly, she placed her trembling hand in his. Cole led her across the floor until he was once again close to Maverick and Lexi.

"Cole," Lexi whispered, her voice filled with worry.

She stepped toward him, but the Lord's next words froze her.

"I love to see everyone so happy and dancing!" He boomed across the room. "I could watch this for days."

Lexi's eyes widened, and Maverick released a low growl that caused Cole to snap, "*Not* around her."

The glimmer of silver in Maverick's eyes when they met his nearly set Cole's wolf free. His involuntary snarl caused the witch to recoil from him, and he released her as he prepared to battle his uncle, a man he'd *never* considered fighting.

But there was no way he was going to let a lycan who was showing signs of breaking anywhere near Lexi. Maverick's eyes narrowed as his alpha wolf responded to Cole's.

Then, his uncle released Lexi as he regained control of his

wolf. They didn't stop dancing together, but they didn't touch while moving around the dance floor.

Most of the others in the room ravenously watched while they waited to see what would happen. As they waited to see how far the Lord could push the newly crowned king of the dark fae before he snapped.

And once he snapped, the Lord would have no choice but to put him in his place or destroy him. Cole suspected the Lord wasn't done toying with him yet, so he doubted death was on the table, but he would torment him as much as possible before death became the only option.

Cole didn't reclaim the witch's hand as he continued to move with her in a close circle to Lexi and Maverick. Over the witch's head, he spotted Becca glaring at him as she danced with a warlock.

His rebuke of her, in front of so many others, might be the thing that pushed her away for good. When he gave her a grim smile in return, she stuck her nose in the air and turned haughtily away.

If he discovered she *was* the one reporting everything back to the Lord, she wouldn't survive to see tomorrow.

CHAPTER FIFTY-TWO

WHEN THE SONG ENDED, the Lord called out, "Switch!"

Cole went to reclaim Lexi, but the Lord's voice carried over the crowd. "King Colburn, let others have a chance to know your fiancée. It's only fair they also get the joy of her company since she's spent so little time in the Shadow Realms."

His shoulder blades popped and cracked as the change started to come over him. The shadows snarled as they sought to break free, and his claws lengthened.

"Cole, no," Lexi whispered.

Her hand on his arm helped calm the wolf, but the shadows still battered against his insides like a trapped bird seeking to flee its cage. He wouldn't let them win, he wouldn't set them free, but for the first time, he was as eager for blood as they were.

Cole scowled at the warlock, who stepped forward and held his hand out to Lexi. When the man saw Cole's face, he backed away.

"Cole, please."

The pleading tone in Lexi's voice dampened some of his blood-lust, but not all of it, as his claws retracted and his joints and bones settled back into place.

"Cole," Maverick cautioned. "If you lose it, he's going to make an example of you. The Lord will use you to show everyone here that he can beat down one of the most powerful men in all the realms. He'll imprison you or kill you. *Don't* let him push you over the edge."

"You've never found your mate. You don't know what it's like to watch her with *others*."

"I have not been so fortunate, but nothing can break your bond to her. *Nothing*."

Cole's gaze fell to the marks he'd left on Lexi's shoulder. The chains of her dress hid most of his bite, but a faint silver glow shone beneath the moonlight streaming into the room. The silver wasn't from her arach markings but *his*.

No, no one could break their bond, but he still didn't want her being passed from man to man so the Lord could fuck with him.

"He's not going to stop tonight. Don't you see that? He's going to push until I finally break," Cole said.

Maverick stepped closer and rested his hand on Cole's shoulder. "Listen to me. You have to keep your *shit* together, or this night will end with our blood splattering these walls. He doesn't want you dead. You would be dead already if that were the case."

"No, he just wants to humiliate me and abuse *her*."

He barely recognized the voice coming out of him. It was his but mottled and disjointed. It was more than his vocal cords fighting the change. It was like when he was in the crone realm and fighting against the shadows breaking free, but they kept coming out as they deepened their hold on him and tried to take over.

Cole tried to control his temper, but the shadows on the wall near him shifted closer. He didn't think anyone else noticed. They were all too ensconced in their misery to pay attention to the shadows surrounding them, but if he didn't get himself under control, someone was bound to notice.

"Keep dancing!" the Lord commanded.

"Cole?" Lexi asked.

He could only manage a small nod. When a vampire held his hand out to her, she waved it away but started dancing.

The vampire glanced nervously at Cole before falling into step with her. The vamp wisely didn't try to take her hand again.

"Keep it together," Maverick said before he claimed the hand of the witch Cole had danced with.

Becca didn't approach him again, but her eyes bored into his back as a hand extended to him through the crowd. He claimed the hand of the siren before releasing it.

He barely acknowledged the woman as they danced, and other than that first, brief contact, they didn't touch again.

As the song started to wind down, the siren rose onto her toes to whisper in his ear. "Do not die here tonight."

Cole didn't get a chance to reply before she slipped into the crowd, and he claimed a lycan woman as his next partner. He searched the throng for the siren, but she was gone.

Was she another possible ally or someone who wanted to see his torture drawn out for weeks and months instead of one night?

The sirens weren't known for their kindness, but their thirst for blood was renowned.

A growing mass of immortals had started to separate him from Lexi, so he steered the woman toward where she danced with his uncle again. Cole had no idea how Maverick maneuvered back to her, but he appreciated his uncle looking after her.

If Maverick had any idea of what she truly was, he'd probably pick her up and flee while cursing Cole for bringing her here. When Lexi's eyes met his, she smiled at him, but she couldn't hide her growing exhaustion.

The tendrils of hair framing her face stuck to her skin, and her face was starting to redden. He would have to do something about this before she became too tired.

"Switch!" the Lord bellowed before the song ended.

The crowd swept between him and Lexi again, creating a divide he despised as another woman approached him. She was an exhausted witch who looked like she would prefer to be sleeping on the floor rather than standing across from him.

When she started to dance, some of the innate grace of an immortal abandoned her as her toe caught on the floor, and she staggered into Cole's arms. He grabbed her before she went down.

Adjusting his hold on her, Cole looked to Lexi as Malakai emerged from the crowd and extended his hand to her. Taking a step back, Lexi's face scrunched in disgust.

Cole all but shoved the poor woman away from him before storming toward them. This was *not* going to happen.

"Dance with him, honey!" the Lord called out. "He's one of my most loyal followers, and I won't have him refused something as simple as a dance."

This is it!

This was what the entire evening had been building to; this moment, this time, and this tipping point.

CHAPTER FIFTY-THREE

LEXI'S SKIN crawled as she glanced from Malakai to the Lord. The malicious, fevered gleam in the Lord's eyes told her he was enjoying every second of this.

The cruel, amused gleam in Malakai's brown eyes told her that no matter what decision she made, she would regret it. The idea of touching him almost had her spewing champagne all over his shiny black shoes.

He looked handsome in his tuxedo and his dark brown hair slicked back from his face. But then, he *was* handsome on the outside; his insides were what made him putrid.

"Come now, Elexiandra, you wouldn't deny an old friend a dance," Malakai said.

"We were never friends," she retorted.

"I recall things differently."

She was sure he did in that rotten mind of his, but she knew the truth. They'd never been friends. They never played together or talked or laughed. He'd been the neighbor's son, the one she always tried to avoid.

"This is *not* going to happen," Cole vowed from beside her.

She'd known he arrived before he spoke. The wrath emanating

from him reverberated against her skin and sent prickles of unease throughout her body.

He'd been maintaining his calm, but this might be what pushed him over the edge.

No, she realized when she saw the vibrant silver of his eyes, there was no *might*. This *would* unravel him.

Then, she noticed the shadows on the walls creeping closer. The moonlight and the torches on the walls created plenty of shadows within the room. And now those shadows hovered in the corners, hid beneath the occupants' feet, and danced across the ceiling.

She had to keep him from calling on those shadows while they were here. They had two secrets on their side that could save them, and she hated giving up either of them, but her secret would get them out of this place if this became ugly.

If she had to reveal herself, then so be it, but Cole could get away from this place with his secret still intact.

Malakai smirked at Cole. "I hate to disagree, but it *is* going to happen. The Lord commanded it."

"Let them dance, King Colburn," the Lord called out in a singsong voice.

Cole's gaze remained on Malakai as he replied to the Lord's command. "I understand, my Lord, but my fiancée does not wish to dance with this man."

"I don't care what your fiancée wants," the Lord said. "She's a mere woman, and a half human at that. Her opinion doesn't matter here, and frankly, neither does *yours*."

A collective murmur ran through the crowd as some immortals started edging away from them. Lexi didn't blame them. They'd be a whole lot smarter if they all fled this room, but that might trigger the dragons.

"Allow them to dance, or I'll put her in my dungeon, and you will have to *earn* her back."

When Cole's head rose and gasps sounded around the room,

Lexi's hand shot out and seized his arm. She could only imagine all the horrible things Cole would have to do to *earn* her back, and she couldn't think about what condition she'd emerge in by the time this freak finished with her.

With her heart hammering in her ears, Lexi became aware the music had stopped, and everyone was waiting to see if the dark fae king would bend or break.

Lexi couldn't let him break. Her fingers dug into Cole's arm as she silently pleaded for him to look at her. Finally, his eyes met hers. She tried to convey her desperation as she stared at him.

"It's okay," she said. "It's only one dance. It's okay."

It was far from okay, but she'd spend the rest of the night dancing with Malakai, and all of tomorrow showering, if it got them through this.

Maverick stepped closer and rested his hand on Cole's shoulder. "Let them dance, nephew."

"You don't know what he did to her," Cole said.

A small line formed between Maverick's brows as his eyes briefly met Lexi's. She gave a small nod. She hoped it conveyed to him that she would do this no matter *what* Malakai had done to her.

"No, I don't, but she's fine with a dance," Maverick replied. "And we're all here right now; he can't do anything to her."

Lexi wished that were true, but she had a bad feeling it wasn't.

"His touching her is going to hurt her," Cole retorted. "She should *never* have to experience his hands on her again."

Maverick winced as if he felt Cole's torment, and maybe he did; the lycans were part beast after all, and beasts sensed things that no others could.

"He can't hurt me anymore," Lexi said. "His touch means nothing because *he* is nothing to me."

Until she said it, she hadn't realized it was true. When Malakai first approached her, the idea of touching him, dancing with him, or being anywhere near him almost made her run screaming. But now, she realized how little and insignificant he was.

She turned back to Malakai and, lifting her chin, met his eyes. "He's a nobody who clawed his way into being a kept pet by destroying others."

Rage burned in Malakai's eyes as she smiled and continued speaking. "He's a coward, and the only damage he can inflict is on those weaker than him." She met Cole's eyes again. "But I'm not weaker than him, and I never was."

Anguish and fury warred across Cole's face as he caught her hand and slid his fingers between hers. "You don't have to do this."

"But I do," she said. "He should know how little he means to everyone here."

Cole's gaze shifted from her to Malakai. "Just remember, you're a dead man walking. This is all borrowed time before I kill you."

Some of Malakai's color drained from his face before he smiled; it didn't hide his uneasiness. Lexi smiled at the truth within those words and squeezed Cole's hand before releasing it.

CHAPTER FIFTY-FOUR

Turning to Malakai, she kept her face impassive as she clasped the tips of the fingers he'd extended to her. His lips skimmed back before he snatched hold of her hand.

Somehow, Lexi managed to keep herself from reacting as his grip ground her bones together. If she showed any reaction to the pain he inflicted, Cole would be on him in an instant, and chaos would ensue.

She kept her distance from Malakai as he led her into the center of the dance floor. When he tried to put his hand on her waist, she pulled it away and threw it down as the music started again.

"It's not going to be a close dance," she told him.

Thinking he'd managed to upset her, he grinned, and Lexi smiled coolly in return. Her smile rattled him enough that he frowned as the music started again.

At first, they moved awkwardly around the floor together, but they slowly found a rhythm. Lexi pretended she was dancing with Cole as she stared at him. No one else danced with them, so it was easy to keep her focus on him.

The silver of his eyes burned as he stood with his hands fisted and his gaze on Malakai. Maverick stood beside him, with his hand on Cole's chest. He said something Lexi couldn't hear, but it did nothing to relax his nephew.

Maverick kept Cole from pouncing on them, but the shadows on the wall behind them shifted unnaturally and dipped toward Cole.

"You think I'm weak," Malakai sneered, drawing her attention back to him. "But *he's* the weak one. I would *never* allow this to happen. If our roles were reversed, I never would have allowed him to touch you tonight."

Lexi laughed. She was instigating him; she should just shut up and smile and get through this dance, but she couldn't let him talk about Cole that way.

"But your roles would never be reversed," she told him. "I *want* to fuck him. I *relish* it, and it's so good I *crave* it, but I'd kill you before I ever let you inside me."

Rage flared in his eyes, and she saw again how much he *despised* her. His determination to have her wasn't about love or desire. This was her punishment for rebuking him; he would come after her again and again, but it wasn't just because he sought to have her for himself.

He intended to make her pay.

She planned to do the same to him.

"And let's face it, when the time finally comes for him to go after you, he *is* going to kill you. There's no doubt about that. You don't stand a chance, and everyone in this room knows it... *including you*."

Malakai laughed before stepping closer. Though the sensation of his chest brushing against hers made her nauseous, Lexi refused to back away.

"You've got so many things wrong, Elexiandra. I don't have to worry about your little dog because the Lord will keep him in check, and once I fuck you, *no* one else ever will again. You'll be too broken for such a thing by the time I finish with you."

"You could *never* break me, you pathetic excuse for a man."

His hand clamped down so fiercely on hers that she nearly cried out, but she bit her lip and kept her phony smile plastered in place.

Cole can't know. Cole can't know. Keep up your shield and keep up pretenses.

Unexpectedly, Malakai spun her away before jerking her back. She caught herself before crashing into his chest and staggered back, but he wasn't finished.

Before she could fully regain her balance, his hand settled on her lower back and pulled her closer. Lexi almost kicked him in the nuts so hard his unborn children felt it, but the Lord's gaze burrowing into her back stopped her.

If she kicked him, *she* would be the one to start something. This whole time, she'd been so concerned about Cole that she never considered *she* might unravel too.

Focusing on her breathing and maintaining her calm, she stared at Malakai's chest as she willed herself to get through the rest of this dance.

And then, Malakai's hand descended from the small of her back... to her ass.

CHAPTER FIFTY-FIVE

LEXI SMOTHERED A SQUEAK AS A SOUND, unlike anything she'd ever heard before, rumbled across the room. At first, she thought one of the dragons had roused from its pretense of slumber and was about to eat them.

Then she realized that though it sounded like the noise was coming from all around her, it was really coming from her right. A chill slid down Lexi's back, and goose bumps broke out on her flesh as her head turned toward Cole.

When her eyes met his, she knew shit was about to hit the fan.

～

THE SECOND MALAKAI'S hand settled on Lexi's ass, Maverick sighed in resignation. He didn't want Cole fighting here; it could get everyone in the room killed, but he had to acknowledge what Malakai did was an insult no lycan could let go.

Malakai was seeking a reaction from Cole, but the one he was about to receive was one he never could have seen coming. Maverick's hand slid away from Cole's chest, and he fell into step beside Cole as he stalked across the room toward them.

The shadows twisted around him, and their power thrummed through his veins. They wanted blood, and so did *he*.

Malakai's laughter echoed across the room as the Lord's voice boomed out. "There will be no fighting here!"

Cole ignored the Lord as he commanded, "Let her go."

Malakai laughed louder, and though the music stopped, he spun Lexi away and started to draw her close again. She jerked her hand out of his.

"No more," she said.

"I will decide when there is to be no more!" the Lord shouted. "Resume dancing."

"No," Cole growled as Malakai reached for Lexi.

She pulled her hand away again and stepped back as the shadows within Cole rippled and the ones on the wall and floor slinked toward him. Startled cries filled the air as the shadows crept across the room toward Cole.

Some immortals danced away from the shadows as they picked up speed, but others remained frozen in place. He didn't know if the Lord was unaware of the change in the room, but he seemed oblivious as he remained focused on Lexi.

And it was then Cole realized this entire event was because of *her*. The Lord wanted *her*. He didn't need an excuse to take her from him, but it was much more fun to push them until they broke and to have witnesses here to see it.

The Lord intended to take her, use her against him, and twist him until he broke. He wanted to hear Cole beg for her return to him, but he never would because he would *never* get his hands on her.

"What is happening?" Maverick muttered as the shadows gathered like storm clouds around Cole.

He didn't know if the others realized the change in the room was because of *him* or if they believed the Lord was doing this. If Malakai didn't get away from her, they would all learn the truth soon, and he didn't care.

Cole held his hand out to Lexi. She stared nervously at it before glancing at the Lord. Cole refused to look at the madman on the throne; the only thing that mattered was *her*.

"Take my hand," he commanded.

"Cole—" Maverick started to say but stopped when Lexi stretched her hand toward his.

Before they touched, Malakai seized her arm and pulled her back toward him.

"This is my dance," he said to Cole. "If I were you, I'd learn my place, dog."

And that was the final snapping point. With a snarl, Cole lurched for Malakai as the vamp slammed Lexi against his chest and clasped her throat. Cole came to an abrupt halt when she sucked in a startled gasp that broke off as Malakai's hand tightened.

No one else in the room moved, but the thunderous beats of their hearts pounded in his ears. Immortals were not an easy bunch to frighten, but the shadows thrived on it as their terror crackled against his skin.

Malakai's fingers dug into her throat, and the Lord laughed. "Let them finish their dance, King Colburn."

"You just brought yourself closer to death," Cole told Malakai. "You're still breathing now, but you're already dead."

For a second, the smug expression on his face faltered, and then he started laughing.

"I'm not the one in danger here," Malakai said.

When the Lord beckoned to them, the guards edged closer. Both dragons had slipped beyond the curtains to sit beside the throne. Cole didn't care about any of them as his attention remained on Malakai.

Lexi stood on her tiptoes as she gazed at him with wide eyes. The increasing redness of her face proved she wasn't getting enough air.

"Let her go," Cole commanded in a voice he didn't recognize.

CHAPTER FIFTY-SIX

LEXI CONTEMPLATED ELBOWING Malakai in the ribs and stomping on his foot. However, she couldn't decide if it was better to break free or maintain Malakai's mistaken belief she was weaker than him.

She doubted it would happen, but there was still a very small chance they might make it out of here with all their secrets intact. The Lord, and most of those in the room, probably hadn't fully grasped what was happening with the shadows, but if Cole continued to unravel, they would.

The Lord's men lifted their spears and unsheathed their swords as they came closer. She couldn't see the dragons, but she didn't doubt they were ready to start eating.

When her eyes met Cole's again, she saw the shadows creeping into the whites of them. For a second, all she could see were those eyes as they became disembodied from the rest of him.

Closing her eyes, Lexi concentrated on slowing the rapid beat of her heart and calming herself as she breathed in tiny, shallow breaths of air. Lack of oxygen was making thinking difficult.

She had to do something; she had to figure *some*thing out.

"Let her go," Cole said again in that strange, guttural voice.

Lexi realized it didn't matter what she did, Cole would go after Malakai, and he would do it tonight. Malakai had pushed him too far.

Having Malakai holding her prisoner didn't help the situation, and if she didn't breathe soon, she would pass out. That would be the *worst* thing to happen. If she were unconscious, she couldn't open a portal out of here.

From the second they received their invitation, she'd known this night was going to turn into a nightmare. But she'd been foolish enough to maintain some hope that escaping, completely unscathed, was a possibility.

That hope was gone. Now, she just prayed they made it out of here with their lives.

Drawing on the training Cole, her dad, and Brokk had put her through, she clasped her hands together and bashed her elbow into Malakai's ribs. The explosion of air he released blew her hair forward and would have made her smile, but it was impossible to smile when this was all so awful.

While Malakai was still distracted by her jab to his ribs, she stomped on his foot. In response, his head came forward enough that she could swing her head back and hit him with it.

Something gave way with a loud crack, and a wash of something hot spilled down her neck. The coppery aroma on the air alerted her it was blood as Malakai released her to grab his face.

"Bitch!" he exclaimed in a voice muffled by his hands as the Lord's laughter boomed through the room.

Gasping in air, Lexi lunged forward, her hand extended toward Cole. But before she could get to him, another hand caught in her hair.

She couldn't hold back her cry of pain as strands of her hair ripped free, and her head jerked back. As Malakai pulled her back toward him, a roar like that of an approaching train filled the room.

This time, there was no doubt where the sound came from as Cole surged forward. But as he was coming, a flash of silver glinted past Lexi's eyes a second before something cold pricked her throat as Malakai's other arm cinched around her waist.

She tried to look down at the dagger Malakai held against her neck, but all she succeeded in doing was having her eyes cross. Cole froze, and the joints in his hands popped as his claws extended into lethal points.

When he took a small step toward them, the blade dug deeper, and a trickle of warm blood slid down her throat to stain the collar of her dress. Lexi ran through the possible ways to free herself, but every scenario ended up with her throat most likely being slit.

He wouldn't be able to cut her head off, but what would happen if she was seriously wounded? Would her shield fail as her body turned its attention to healing? Would she still be able to open a portal?

Everyone in the room was as still as statues as they all focused on them. A bead of sweat trickled down Lexi's temple to the corner of her eye.

It tickled her skin and irritated her eye, but she resisted her impulse to wipe it away. After what she'd done to him, Malakai would slit her throat before he realized she was only wiping away sweat.

He was far too jittery to react sanely right now. His hand was steady on the dagger, but his body trembled against hers.

She understood his fear as shadows seeped out of Cole to darken the room around him.

CHAPTER FIFTY-SEVEN

BREAKING THE HUSH, murmurs of uncertainty spread through the crowd. Some of the immortals edged toward the open doors as the shadows on the walls and floor slid toward Cole.

As the air around Cole swelled with darkness, the blade bit deeper into Lexi's neck. She bit her lip to keep from crying out, but the sting of it made her wince.

"What is going on?" Maverick asked.

"I don't know," Malakai said. "But whatever it is, it had better stop soon, or I'm going to kill her."

"That is enough!" the Lord thundered across the room. "Whatever you are doing, stop it now."

But one look at Cole told Lexi he had no intention of stopping this. Whatever he was about to unleash would make Hell look like a vacation spot.

∾

"COLE," Maverick murmured from beside him. "What are you doing?"

Cole didn't bother to answer his uncle; his attention remained riveted on Malakai and the blade against Lexi's throat. This man had deserved to die so many times before, but tonight, he would finally meet that fate.

He wouldn't walk out of this hall after hurting Lexi. He'd spilled her blood, and because of that, Cole would see this room *drenched* in Malakai's.

The vamp had a very limited number of breaths left, and they were rapidly dwindling to zero. The shadows swelled within him as more gathered around Malakai.

The shadows seeping out of him begged to be set free. Whereas he couldn't stop Malakai while he held Lexi, the shadows could. He thrived on that knowledge as he smiled at Malakai.

He'd meant to keep the shadows hidden from the Lord, but that wasn't going to happen. Everyone in this room knew something was happening; none of them were quite sure what, but they knew it was *him*.

His secret was out, and now it was time to play.

"Cole," Maverick said again.

"I'm going to kill him," Cole stated. "If you want to make it out of here alive, then stay close to me."

"Shit."

"I said *stop!*" the Lord yelled, but he was nothing to Cole now.

It was all about Malakai as he kept the blade against Lexi's throat while he edged further away. When Cole met Lexi's eyes, the love and terror radiating from them warmed the ice flowing through his veins, but it also unleashed something lethal in him.

Through his connection to the shadows, he pulled them closer to Malakai. Like hornets knocked free of their nest, the shadows swarmed Malakai. They darkened his legs and torso before rising to his arms.

"Stop it!" Malakai hissed. "I'll kill her. I swear I will."

His hand tightened on the blade. Cole had no doubt he was about to slice into Lexi's throat, but before he could, a shadow swooped down from above, enclosed on Malakai's wrist, and ripped it away from Lexi's throat.

Malakai shouted as the dagger hit the floor and spun across the room. The immortals closest to the blade danced away from it like it was a poisonous scorpion.

More shadows wrapped around Malakai, encircling him like a boa constrictor on its prey. They tore his hand free of Lexi's waist and pried his arm back into an unnatural angle that finally gave way with a snap.

As Lexi staggered free of Malakai's hold, Cole roared as he charged across the distance separating them. He grasped her arms, pulling her further away as he turned her toward his uncle.

Maverick grabbed her. Once she was safe, Cole raced toward Malakai and leapt into the air. With the power of the shadows building around him, he came down with his fist aimed at Malakai's face.

His punch slammed into the vampire and knocked him off his feet. He hit the floor on his back, and Cole came down on top of him.

Kicking and screaming, Malakai thrashed against the shadows embracing him in a cocoon of death. Cole relished Malakai's screams as he battered the vamp's face again and again.

"I said stop it!" the Lord shouted. And then, like a toddler denied their toy, his shouts became shorter and more incessant. "Stop it! Stop it! Stop it!"

But nothing would stop Cole. He'd been denied this moment for too long, and now that it was finally here, he would ensure Malakai's death. And the magic of Dragonia assured that the vampire wouldn't be able to teleport away from him this time.

The shadows continued to rip and pull at Malakai as Cole battered him. They tore away an arm and a leg as Malakai's screams became muffled by the blood pooling in his mouth.

Not only did the power of the shadows swarm inside Cole, but so did something malicious and cruel. It was something far more brutal than anything he'd ever experienced before, but he thrived on it.

Malakai's teeth gave way, as did his jaw, beneath the onslaught of Cole's punches. He hammered the vampire long after the screaming stopped. He beat him until nothing remained but a broken pile of shattered bone and bloody fragments that would never again walk this earth or touch *his* mate.

Like some kind of morbid jigsaw puzzle, Malakai's extremities littered the ground around him as Cole lifted his gaze to focus on the man sitting on the throne across the room from him. The blood dripping from his hair and onto the marble floor was the only sound in the room.

The Lord had stopped looking amused, annoyed, or gloating. If the Lord stood up to run, Cole wouldn't have been surprised to discover he'd shit himself as the shadows continued to weave through the air around Cole.

Despite satisfying some of their bloodlust, the shadows craved more as they waited to kill again. Malakai's brutal death hadn't quenched their thirst for blood. Instead, it teased it with the possibilities of what they could do, and they were thirsty for *so much more*.

And so was Cole. He was more than happy to let them continue their murderous spree as he smiled at the Lord.

"Kill him!" the Lord bellowed and thrust a finger at Cole. "KILL HIM!"

CHAPTER FIFTY-EIGHT

TOO STUNNED BY what they'd just witnessed, the guards remained unmoving as the Lord's command filled the room. *None* of the immortals had moved since Cole unleashed the shadows with ruthless brutality that left Lexi speechless.

Staring at the torn and battered remains of Malakai, Lexi pressed a hand against her mouth to keep the bile in her throat suppressed. She *hated* Malakai; many times, she would have beaten him to death herself, but this….

Well, she had no idea what *this* was. The shadows had helped Cole *tear him apart*. Pieces of him littered the once pristine floor; she was sure the bloodstain would never come out, and his head…

Well, there was no head anymore. It was nothing more than mush and gore. And some of it was dripping off Cole. It soaked his clothes and slid down his face and hair, but he seemed oblivious to it.

Like leaves skittering across the ground on a cool, fall day, the shadows danced around him. The shadows had no eyes, but she felt them watching everyone in this room.

Including her.

Beside her, Maverick remained as still as stone. The arm he'd put in front of her when she tried to get back to Cole remained there, but she could probably push it away without any resistance.

"Cole," she whispered in a voice barely more than a croak.

Even though she'd shown the first sign of life, no one else moved. She didn't know if it was the terror of Cole, the Lord, or shock that still held them immobile, but they didn't run as they probably should.

Lexi clasped her hands in front of her as her eyes bored into Cole's back. She needed to see his eyes and know that he was still there because she greatly feared something else had taken his place.

Had the shadows, that became a part of him during the trials, taken over? Was he now a pod person like in one of those old sci-fi movies she sometimes watched with her dad?

Then, she realized it didn't matter. The shadows could try to take him from her, but she would never allow it. He was *her* Cole, and she would always love him. She wouldn't let the darkness destroy him.

Besides, Cole was too strong and good for anything to take him over. He would *not* allow it to happen.

But even as she tried to reassure herself of this, she couldn't deny the horror of what they'd all witnessed, and he still hadn't looked at her.

"Are you okay?" Maverick demanded.

A few immortals winced at the harsh tone of his voice. He'd spoken normally, but the volume was too loud in this room of unnatural silence.

It took Lexi a few seconds to realize he was talking to *her*. She blinked as she tipped her head back to look at him. His silver eyes were full of concern as he lowered his arm to reach for her, but when a low, unnatural hiss filled the room, his hand fell away.

Lexi was startled to realize the *shadows* had made that sound. How could shadows make noise?

Then she realized it was pointless to question such things when they'd just drawn and quartered Malakai. This was the Shadow Realms; anything and everything could happen here.

"KILL HIM!" the Lord bellowed again, and this time, his command snapped others into motion.

While the guards remained hesitant, many guests turned and fled toward the doors. And the dragons came for them, but there was something different about the dragons... something *off.*

They didn't rush forward as if they were eager to destroy, or at least the red one didn't. The blue one roared as it lumbered toward them while the red one remained behind.

Screams filled the air as more immortals fled. Cole remained kneeling, with one fist on the ground, in the middle of Malakai's soupy remains.

The floor beneath her quaked with each of the dragon's thunderous footfalls. The chandelier overhead clinked as it swayed so much the diamonds in it dinged together.

With a surge of power and strength, the red dragon shot forward too. It half flew, half ran across the floor to pursue the blue one.

Now that they were out in the open, Lexi could see their full size. The red one was twice as big as the blue one, and for a crazy second, she thought it might be trying to stop the blue one.

With the approach of the dragons, the guards became braver. They raised their weapons and charged toward Cole. Even with the shadows on their side, it was too many coming at once, they were all too well-armed, and those beasts would eat him alive.

"No!" Lexi screamed and ran toward Cole.

CHAPTER FIFTY-NINE

MAVERICK FELL in beside her as one of the windows shattered. She didn't know if that meant more guards were trying to get into the room or more dragons. Or perhaps, some of the crowd was trying to flee through the windows.

Some immortals remained unmoving as she raced past them. They were either too stunned to move or too excited for more blood to realize they were in jeopardy.

Cole finally moved as he leaned forward. He tore something away from Malakai before shoving it in his pocket.

The red dragon had caught up to the blue, and they were nearly to Cole when he stood. One of the guards reached Cole first and swung his blade at him. It whistled as it sliced through the air toward Cole's neck.

When Cole ducked, the blade crashed into the marble floor.

"Stop them!" the Lord screamed and pointed at her and Maverick.

Some of the guards split away and came toward them. Their maniacal grins were entirely out of place with all the bloodshed sure to follow.

No!

Lexi couldn't be separated from Cole. The shadows might help them destroy many of these guards and possibly one of the dragons, but a portal was their only hope of surviving this.

And she couldn't open it when she wasn't with Cole.

When one of the guards grabbed for her, something inside her broke. A rush of terror, desperation, and *love* washed through her… so much love for her family, herself, and Cole. She couldn't lose any of them.

The guard grabbed her arm as she flung up her hand, and fire erupted from her palm. When her flames scorched the man's face, he reeled back, screaming as his hair and clothes caught fire.

So astonished by what she'd done and the suffering she inflicted, Lexi froze. Maverick cursed under his breath but didn't stop running. The dragons stopped, though.

They skidded to a halt a few feet away from Cole. The blue one recoiled, and the red one hit it with its head, shoving it further back.

Grasping her arm, Maverick spun away from the next guard rushing toward her as a shadow snapped out from Cole. It knocked back the other guards charging toward them. Cole's back remained to her, but the shadows knew where to go and what to do.

The Lord rose from the throne as some shadows seeped away from Cole and toward him. The blue dragon had recovered and lunged at Cole.

Its razor-sharp teeth clamped down on air as it only missed Cole by a foot. The only thing that saved Cole from becoming its meal was a shadow lashing out to bash the dragon across its snout.

There were so many of them closing in, swarming around them. Guards were everywhere, lunging and trying to break through the shadows and Cole and Maverick's defense.

The dragons looming over them could easily kill them. The twang of bowstrings releasing their arrows filled the air.

"No!" Lexi screamed as her defenses crumbled.

The moonlight streaming through the windows caught on her

fingers as they stretched for Cole. The tips of them blazed to golden life as the silver, scale-like markings formed across her skin.

It came in slow motion, and as she reached for Cole, the glow spread from her hand to her arms and up across her face.

But though it came slowly, by the time she grasped Cole's arm, it nearly encompassed her. Her fingers gripped his forearm as the dragons recoiled like she was some kind of poisonous frog.

And maybe she was poisonous to them; maybe that was how the arach controlled them, but she was *not* sticking around to find out.

"Maverick!" she shouted.

Her fingers grazed his arm, but she missed him. He was close, though, and it had to be enough for him to follow them through.

Lexi didn't see what happened next as she pictured the library in her manor and a portal opened in the floor before them. Throwing herself forward, she clung to Cole as she fell into the hole.

Twisting, Cole's silver eyes met hers, but when his gaze locked on hers, the cruelty in them eased.

Maverick tumbled in behind them... so did some of the guards.

The roar of a dragon echoed around the portal. As Cole's arms encircled her, Lexi prayed the portal was too small for the dragons to follow.

CHAPTER SIXTY

"WHAT WAS THAT?" the Lord yelled. When no one answered him, he screamed the words again so loudly and violently that spittle flew from his mouth. "*WHAT WAS THAT?*"

Alina knew exactly what *that* was; she'd seen it before, more times than she could recall, but she'd never thought to see it again. In all her life, only a handful of things ever shocked her.

This time defeated all the others. Something she'd never believed could ever happen again had just occurred.

She'd felt something recently, a tug she hadn't felt in years, but it faded soon after it arose. She wrote it off as a longing for the way things were... for a time when an imposter didn't control the throne.

At the time, she'd cursed herself for her sentimentality, but she couldn't deny what she'd witnessed. She couldn't deny what that woman was.

Not only was that woman the rightful heir to this realm, but she was with *that* man, the murderer of dragons... *the Shadow Reaver.*

His control over the shadows meant she couldn't kill him, no matter how badly she wanted to. Doryu knew this too, but that hadn't stopped him from trying.

She'd wanted to stop Doryu, she'd chased him down, but that monster had killed Doryu's sister. His mind knew the Shadow Reaver was off-limits, but his heart called for vengeance. However, he couldn't lose control again.

"Arach," someone in the crowd whispered.

Alina turned her head to see a beautiful woman standing to the right of her. Her black hair hung in ringlets to her shoulders, and shock filled her brown eyes. She was the woman who'd spoken.

"What did you say?" the Lord demanded.

The woman continued to gaze at the spot on the floor where the portal had opened. She didn't speak again, and Alina could tell she regretted having said anything.

"How did that... that *girl* open a portal in here?" the Lord shouted.

Those closest to the woman had to have heard what she said, but no one replied. Instead, they remained unmoving with their lips clamped together.

Alina didn't know how the Lord wasn't grasping what happened here. The woman *shot fire* from her hands, bore the mark of the dragon, and had opened a portal in Dragonia.

There was only one species of immortal who could do those things, and everyone in this room knew it. Was he so far gone in his madness, or was he simply too dumbfounded to think clearly?

Either way, his inability to think clearly didn't bode well for the future of Dragonia or any of the other realms.

And then, the stupid man with the rotten mind finally came to the same conclusion Alina was certain *everyone* else in this room had already ascertained.

"How can an arach possibly be alive?" the Lord shouted.

If he expected a reply, he didn't get one, but Alina doubted anyone in this room had an answer for him. She certainly didn't.

"Go to the human realm and find her!" the Lord screamed. "If you can bring her to me alive, then do so, but I'll happily take her head on a stake too. And I want the Gloaming destroyed. King Colburn will pay for this."

A loud gasp went through what remained of the crowd before they quieted again. Alina didn't know why any of them remained.

Maybe the bloodshed kept them here. Or perhaps they were hoping to see the Lord go down tonight and believed the king of the dark fae stood a chance of killing him, but at least thirty of the guests remained in the grand ballroom.

Not the king of the dark fae, she reminded herself. *Or at least not* just *the king. He's also the Shadow Reaver.*

And as she stared at the bloody remains of the idiot vampire, she knew *why*.

"Go!" the Lord shouted at her and Doryu and thrust his finger at the large, open ballroom doors. He pointed to the guards next. "Go! And take more with you! Take enough to destroy *everything*!"

Guards raced from the room and toward the portals that would take them to the Gloaming and the human realm. It would take the guards a while to get there; Alina would be much faster about it.

Arach weren't the only ones who could open portals in and out of Dragonia. They had to obey the Lord, but there were some things not even *he* could command them to do.

Alina released a warning shriek at Doryu, who bowed his head in shame. Certain Doryu wouldn't allow emotion to rule him again, she unfurled her wings and pushed off her hind feet as she opened a portal near the ceiling and went through.

CHAPTER SIXTY-ONE

COLE SAW the end of the portal coming and realized Lexi had opened it in the library ceiling. Twisting through the air, he met Maverick's eyes as they plunged out of the portal. Cole kept Lexi cradled protectively against him as he turned to get his legs under him.

"Incoming!" Cole yelled as they plunged from the portal.

He bent his knees as he hit the floor and threw himself forward. His shoulder took the brunt of the impact. As soon as he hit, he rolled across the ground before his uncle crashed into them.

Lexi curled protectively against him as she clutched his shirt and tucked her chin under his head. After everything that happened, he did *not* want to release her, but the guards would be here soon.

Letting her go, he rolled to his feet and tore his cape free. He turned as Maverick landed on the balls of his feet. His uncle's fingers rested on the ground before he sprang forward and rolled toward Kaylia.

"Not him!" Cole shouted when Kaylia started waving her hands. "Anyone after him, though."

Maverick bounced to his feet and grinned at the crone. Lexi

closed the portal with a wave of her hand, but not before nearly a dozen guards tumbled through it. Some of them landed on their feet, others hit on their backs, and three of them crashed into the others.

As soon as the guards hit the ground, Orin, Maverick, and Del pounced. Brokk threw their father's sheathed sword to Cole before plunging into the fray. Cole caught it in one hand and unsheathed it before swinging the scabbard over his shoulder.

Cole ducked back as one of the guards swung a sword at him. The blade sliced into one of the chair arms and embedded there. The guard placed his foot against the chair to yank it free, but Cole sliced the foolish man's head off before he succeeded.

Maverick lunged forward and seized the shirt of a guard running toward Brokk. The man's feet flew out from under him before he hit the floor with a solid thud.

"It's Orin!" one of the guards blurted.

Orin grinned at the man as he weaved his sword through the air in a leisurely, measured dance that hid the lethality of his movements.

"You're… you're dead!" the same guard sputtered in disbelief. "I saw your body!"

Orin continued to swing the blade back and forth as he released it with one hand to pat himself down. "I'm *dead*? I sure feel pretty alive."

The guard's eyes shot from him to Cole before going to the doorway. It was impossible to tell if the man wanted to bolt to save his ass or if he was desperate to reveal this to the Lord, but he wouldn't get the chance.

"I think it's you who's going to be dead," Orin said as he lunged forward.

The guard didn't have time to block the move before the sword plunged into his throat. Orin sliced upward as Brokk took out the legs of another. Del finished him off with a swift decapitation.

Kaylia weaved a spell that erected a barrier between her and another guard as she bent to lift the sword from a dead man. The guard battered the air between them as Kaylia plunged a blade into his belly. Apparently, the barrier only kept one of them from getting at the other.

Cole smiled grimly and positioned himself in front of Lexi as two guards charged at them.

～

LEXI JUMPED BACK as one of the guards pointed a sword at her. From the corner of her eye, a flash of motion blurred across her vision as a shadow lashed out. It smashed into the guard's wrist and knocked the sword from his hand.

The guy didn't move as he gawked at them. Lexi used his confusion to her advantage as she lunged forward and claimed the sword.

Someone shouted in pain; she hoped it wasn't one of her friends as the scent of blood permeated the room. The place she loved so much and often saw as her refuge had become a place of death; she'd be amazed if any of it remained standing after this night.

The guard looked from her to Cole and back again as Sahira and Varo skidded into the library's doorway. They only took a second to ascertain what was happening before Varo charged across the room.

Wrapping his arms around one of the guards closing in on Cole, Varo tackled the man to the ground. But two more were already coming at them again.

The shadows dancing around Cole didn't dissuade the guards, and Cole didn't release them. She suspected it was because he preferred that *she* didn't see that kind of carnage again.

When the guard Cole disarmed lifted another discarded sword from the ground and started toward her, Lexi lifted her blade. The guard laughed and darted to the side.

Lexi followed his movement, but before she could resume her stance, he switched back to the other side. He came at her again.

Since she'd stopped taking Sahira's potion, her strength and speed had increased, and Lexi had gotten better at wielding heavier, more cumbersome weapons, but she still wasn't as good with a sword as she was with a dagger or throwing stars.

Because of that, and the guard's unexpected move, she barely had time to adjust before he knocked her sword to the side and was on her. Lexi swung up with her elbow and hit him under the chin as his fingers caught in her dress.

The gold chains on her shoulder tore away beneath his hooked fingers and gave way. They clinked and clattered as they bounced across the floor.

When Lexi drove her fist into his face, his head shot back, and she pulled her sword out from under where his blade had pinned it to the floor. Without thinking, she plunged it into his belly.

She grimaced at the sensation of the blade slicing through flesh, tearing through organs, and lodging in his spine. Her stomach twisted with nausea as the man grunted. He clutched the blade as agony contorted his features.

She'd never stabbed anyone before. She understood it was necessary and would do whatever it took to save herself and the others, but it didn't mean she had to like it.

Lexi started to pull the sword free as shadows encircled his head. They muffled the man's startled screams; his arms flailed as he tried to beat them away but only succeeded in hitting himself as his hands went through the shadows.

Torn away from her sword, the shadows ripped the man backward and slammed him into the floor. More shadows encompassed him until they entombed him like a mummy.

Then they drew together. Lexi winced as his bones cracked and his muffled screams grew louder before the crushing force of the shadows silenced them.

CHAPTER SIXTY-TWO

When the guard finally stopped screaming, Lexi realized he was the last of the Lord's men to fall. No one else in the room moved as a strained hush descended. They simply stood and stared at the man's crushed remains before their attention shifted to Cole.

When Cole lifted his head and looked at her, Lexi saw the uncertainty in his eyes. Her fingers stretched toward him as she sought to comfort and connect with him, but her hand froze between them when a dragon's bellow shook the walls.

Rage replaced Cole's apprehension as all their heads turned toward the windows. The glass rattled, and shouts rained across the land as another roar sounded.

"They're here," Lexi breathed.

"Orin, Brokk, and Varo, take Lexi and the others to the prison realm," Cole commanded. "I'll meet you there."

"Where are you going?" Lexi demanded.

"I have to get to the Gloaming. I have to warn them that the Lord is going to attack."

"The Lord's men are probably already there," Orin said.

"I know, but I have to go."

"I'm going with you," Brokk said.

"No, stay with Lexi."

"You don't know what the prison realm looks like; you won't be able to find it without me. And you're not going into another battle in the Gloaming alone."

"Fine." Cole dipped a hand into his pocket, pulled something out, and tossed it to her dad. "You deserve this far more than its previous owner."

When her dad caught it, the lanterns in the room glinted off the sun medallion the Lord had given Malakai. His blood still stained the red amulet and golden chain that allowed the vampire to walk outside during the day.

"How?" her dad asked as he slid it over his head.

"Malakai is no longer an issue," Cole replied.

Her dad smiled as the amulet settled into place against his chest. His smile vanished when the scent of smoke wafted into the room.

"They're going to burn it down," Kaylia said.

Sorrow clogged Lexi's throat, but she couldn't give in to it. Later, she could grieve the loss of her home, but survival came first.

"I'm assuming you have to get to the Lunar realm," Cole said to his uncle.

"I evacuated my pack before going to the ball, or most of them anyway," Maverick said. "Some remained behind to give the impression my pack was still there. As soon as they see the Lord's men or a dragon, they'll evacuate too.

"If he attacks the other packs, then so be it; there's nothing I can do for them. I'll meet up with my pack later. Until then, I'm staying with her." Maverick thrust a finger at Lexi. "After seeing what she is, she's going to need all the protection she can get."

"Good," Cole said. "What about you?" he asked Kaylia.

"The Lord still has no idea I'm involved with you. As long as he doesn't see me with you, the crones and witches will remain safe. For now, I'm staying with Lexi too."

"Thank you."

Kaylia nodded, and Cole strode over to clasp Lexi's cheeks; he tenderly kissed her forehead and lips.

"I'll come with you," she said as she grasped his wrists.

"No. I need you somewhere safe, and I have to save as many of the dark fae as possible. Hopefully, Niall has already started to evacuate them."

She was desperate to stay with him, but he would only fight her on it, and the longer he remained here, the more innocents in the Gloaming would die. Releasing his wrists, she stepped back and blinked away her tears.

"Go," she whispered. "But you better come back to me."

"Always."

Then, he opened a portal, and she watched as he and Brokk vanished.

CHAPTER SIXTY-THREE

"LET'S GO!" Orin shouted as her dad opened a portal.

Another roar quaked the house as the scent of smoke grew stronger.

Had the Lord's soldiers already set the manor on fire? Or had the dragons set fire to it?

But that wasn't right. If the dragons had unleashed their fury on the manor, it wouldn't be standing anymore.

"Let's go!" Orin shouted again.

She started toward the portal but stopped when she recalled, "The harrow stone!"

"Forget it!" her father yelled as a window in another room shattered.

But she couldn't forget it. That stone was powerful, and it belonged to *her*. She couldn't leave it here, where it could fall into the wrong hands.

And if the Lord somehow learned they possessed the stone, they would know of Kaylia's involvement. He would also probably realize the bodies Cole had given him weren't Orin and Varo. Other than her dad, that was the last secret weapon they had.

"I'm not leaving it," she said.

She sprinted for the doorway, but Sahira had already run for the kitchen.

"We have to go!" Orin shouted after them, and another window shattered.

Are they coming inside?

Lexi couldn't let that possibility slow her down. She had to get the stone and get out of here.

Sahira already had the safe open when Lexi arrived in the kitchen. She'd removed her two Books of Shadows and shoved them down her shirt. They were lumpy beneath the material but tucked safely away.

Her aunt also removed a couple of potions, but didn't reach for the stone. Lexi didn't know if it would still burn anyone else who touched it, but her aunt wasn't taking the chance.

Stepping away from the safe, Sahira lifted Shade, her cat familiar, from the ground. She cradled the feline against her chest as Lexi reached into the safe.

The stone warmed against her palm as she removed it. She went to slip it into her pocket before recalling she didn't have any pockets.

"Here." Sahira rushed over to one of the cabinets and flung open the door. She pulled out a small pouch and returned to Lexi. "Put it in here, and I'll carry it."

Lexi wasn't sure the pouch would be enough protection for Sahira to hold the stone again, but she didn't have any other choice. She dropped the stone into the pouch and pulled the strings closed.

The voices grew louder outside before the window over the sink shattered. Lexi bit back a scream as a glass bottle with a flaming rag stuffed into it was tossed inside. The glass exploded, and flames erupted across the floor.

Sahira snatched the pouch from her hand and shoved it in her pocket as the flames ate the floor and surged toward the ceiling. The crackle of the fire increased, and the smoke grew thicker. The flames wouldn't affect her, but they could kill every person in this room.

Then, over the crackle of the fire, a loud bang reverberated from the barn.

"They wouldn't," she breathed.

"Lexi, no!" Sahira cried when she ran around the flames and raced for the broken window.

She pulled back a corner of the curtain to reveal flames licking up the side of her home to fill the window. Beyond the fire, dozens of the Lord's men spread out across the yard. They filled the space in between her and the stables.

One of them walked toward the barn with a torch in hand.

～

COLE EXITED the portal in the spot he and Niall had agreed upon before going to the ball. He was maybe seconds ahead of the Lord's men and the dragons, but when he stepped out of the portal, everything remained serene.

As promised, many of the fae were eating at the banquet Cole had ordered for them. Fires crackled as his men sat around them, talking and singing, but their peaceful night was over.

When Niall turned toward him, his jaw dropped. Cole didn't have to look down to know what Niall saw. The blood coating his clothes adhered them to him in a sticky goo that would only get worse before the night was over.

"Everybody out of the Gloaming!" he shouted. "We're about to be attacked!"

Silence descended as all their heads turned toward him. Some of them looked around, but with no imminent threat coming for them, no one, other than Niall, moved.

Niall jumped to his feet and opened a portal. As he did so, the dark fae closest to him looked up but still didn't move.

The portal went to an outer realm they'd agreed upon earlier.

From there, the fae would each have to find their way in the realms. He couldn't tell them all to stay somewhere together.

There was a traitor amongst their people telling the Lord things. If Cole told them all to stay in the same place, that traitor would get word to the Lord about their location, and he *would* destroy them all.

The dark fae would be hunted as the enemy until they took down the Lord, but he couldn't do anything about that now. He would make sure they could all come out of hiding and return to the Gloaming as soon as possible.

He was failing as their king, but he would *not* fail them completely.

"Once you get to the outer realm, find somewhere else to go and *hide*," Cole told them as the confused fae continued to stare at Niall's portal. "Don't tell anyone where you're going. There is a traitor in the Gloaming. Be sure you can trust those you reveal things to. Stay safe and stay on the move. We will one day reclaim the Gloaming, but you have to go!"

"Reclaim from who?" a man blurted.

In response, the scream of a dragon pierced the night a second before the monstrous creature soared over the land. It released a wave of fire as it swooped down on them.

The dark fae threw aside their food and drinks as they screamed and leapt to their feet. Many of them raced for the portal as another dragon soared into view.

"Run! Go!" Brokk shouted.

He recognized the second dragon as the big red beast who had entered the Gloaming and flown to Underhill before. It was also the one who'd sat behind the Lord's throne.

He suspected it was one of the Lord's most favored pets. Because of that, Cole would do everything he could to destroy it.

"Go!" Cole bellowed.

Some of the fae opened their own portals and fled the realm, while others continued to run into Niall's. The red beast scanned the land but didn't unleash its fire on them.

It swung to the side as the Lord's men came over the top of one of the hills. They stood, silhouetted against the glow of the moons before they lifted their swords and released a battle cry before rushing down the hill.

Another dragon appeared, but the fae's screams faded as their numbers lessened. Cole looked to the palace, but the helots had to have seen what was happening. They all would have fled by now.

"I have to go to Underhill and the other areas of the Gloaming before the dragons do," Cole said to Niall. "I also have to get to Torigon."

"I'm coming with you," Niall said. "I'm in this until the end."

Cole nodded before opening a portal leading into the stable. When he looked back, the red dragon had turned toward them and was coming fast.

Cole didn't look back as he entered the portal with Niall and Brokk.

CHAPTER SIXTY-FOUR

LEXI RACED through the tunnels beneath the manor and toward the stable as Orin, complaining the entire time, followed. Her dad ran beside her. Behind him, Maverick, Varo, Kaylia, and Sahira sprinted through the tunnels.

"This is the dumbest thing anyone has ever considered doing," Orin grumbled.

"No, that would be anyone who has done *you*," Sahira retorted.

"All of them left happier than when they came."

"I doubt they came."

"Look at you with all the jokes!" Orin retorted.

Lexi would have laughed if every rapid beat of her heart wasn't screaming at her to *go faster!*

"You're risking your life for horses!" Orin exclaimed.

He would never understand they were more than horses to her. They were also her friends, and she'd be damned if she left them to die in such a horrible way.

"You might think it's dumb, but it's happening," Lexi told him.

"Don't you have anything to say, Del?" Orin demanded.

"Fuck off," Del replied, and Maverick laughed.

Lexi skidded to a halt at the stairs leading up to the barn's feed room. No light crept around the edges of the door, but she'd never seen any before either. She also didn't know if any smoke would get through.

When her dad built these tunnels, he did a fantastic job ensuring they were completely secure and well hidden. But she also didn't know if someone above would see them emerging.

That man had been heading toward the barn with a torch; she assumed it was to set the building on fire, but maybe they had entered the stables instead. Either way, she had to know what was happening with the horses.

Grasping her skirt, she cursed the dress she once loved so much as she grabbed one of the rungs. Before she could start to climb, her dad caught her wrist to halt her.

"I'll go first," he said.

Unwilling to waste time arguing with him, Lexi stepped aside. He climbed the steps and rested his hand against the hidden door above.

With deft fingers, he found the latch and undid the lock. Lexi held her breath as the door opened an inch or two.

He rested his hands against the bottom and pushed it upward. It didn't make a sound as it revealed more of the tack room, and smoke crept into the tunnel.

One of the horses kicked the wall, another thudded against their door, but they hadn't started screaming... yet.

"Assholes," Orin bit out.

Apparently, he was against saving the horses, but he didn't like the idea of anyone setting them on fire either.

She waited for someone to attack, but nothing happened as her dad stuck his head further out. When he pushed it all the way open, the crackle of flames drifted down to her.

Lexi had seen and heard so many revolting things from the Lord and his men recently, but she still couldn't believe these bastards had set the barn on fire with the horses *inside*. That took a special kind of cruelty, one she couldn't begin to fathom.

She would torch anyone who tried to hurt someone here or who tried to stop them from saving the animals. It didn't matter that she didn't like inflicting pain on others; they deserved it.

Her dad crept further up the stairs and disappeared into the feed room. Before Lexi could follow him, Orin nudged her out of the way and swiftly ascended. She scowled at his back before lifting her skirt, shooting Maverick a glare when he tried to go next, and following them up the stairs.

Once inside the barn, she crept to the feed room door as her father slipped into the shedrow. The horses whinnied and pranced nervously in their stalls; one of them kicked the wall again, and another banged at their water buckets as the smoke grew thicker.

When she stepped out of the room, she saw why as flames consumed the side of the barn. The fire surged toward the hayloft, where it would gain more fuel to feed its ravenous appetite.

They didn't have long before the fire fully engulfed the barn, and while she could withstand the flames, none of the others could. The only thing they had going for them was they were the only ones in the barn.

Maverick appeared at her side, and she looked back as Varo emerged from the tunnels.

"Let's be quick about this," her dad said.

Running behind him and Orin, Lexi flung open the first stall door. She released her skirt; she didn't care if it was completely ruined but hoped she didn't trip over the damn thing.

She dashed inside as smoke grew thicker in the air. The horses weren't completely panicking yet, but they would soon, and they'd be a lot more hazardous to rescue once they were.

The horse stood at the back of the stall with its head down in the straw. Grasping its halter, she led it out of the stall as her dad, Orin, and Maverick emerged with the other animals.

When Orin started for the back door with his horse, Lexi stopped him. "That leads to the paddock. If we turn them loose out there, the guards can still get at them, and the dragons will probably eat them. They have to go out the front doors. That's the only chance they have to survive."

"Have you lost your mind?" Orin demanded.

Maybe she had, but the only thing she could think about was getting these horses out of this barn and free of this fire.

"Let's take them with us to the prison realm," Varo suggested.

"Good idea," her dad said as Orin muttered something about horse shit in his halls.

"You're a miserable prick," Maverick told him.

Orin shrugged, but with a wave of his hand, he opened a portal before him. He slapped the animal's rump and sent it racing toward the portal.

Lexi sent hers through next. Her dad and Maverick were about to send theirs through when something cracked overhead, and a large beam crashed into the ground.

Flames shot toward them as an echoing crash filled the air, and the whole building shook. Her dad's horse veered away from the portal while Maverick's reared. Its front legs kicked at the air as it screamed, and another flaming beam fell to the earth before it.

Maverick managed to keep hold of Cricket, but the buckle on her halter broke when she jerked to the side. Cricket slipped free of the broken halter and joined Darby. They both charged toward the closed door before spinning and bolting back toward them.

Their panic only fueled Lexi's as another beam crashed to the ground. She coughed as the thickening smoke burned her throat and lungs. Varo and Maverick closed the open doors before either of them could return to their stalls.

"We have to go!" Orin shouted.

He grasped Lexi's hand and started pulling her toward the portal. For once, her father agreed with him as he took her elbow and rushed her forward.

"No!" she yelled. "I can withstand the flames. You go! I'll get them out of here!"

Sahira and Kaylia stood in the doorway of the feed room.

Shade remained nestled in Sahira's arms; his tail twitched as he watched them.

Kaylia broke away, and jogging over to the main door, she grasped it. If she opened that door, the horses might run out. Right now, they were avoiding the portal as the heat of the fire increased.

Lexi could barely see more than a few feet in front of her as she tore her arms away from Orin and her dad. Wiping the sweat from her forehead, she whistled for the horses. Cricket turned toward her, but Darby was too terrified to react.

"Open the door!" Lexi shouted.

She sprinted toward Kaylia. It was her last hope of getting the animals to safety. They *had* to take it. She couldn't stand to watch them burn in this barn or to abandon them to the fire.

"Get in the portal!" she shouted at Sahira as she ran past her aunt.

"Lexi, no!" Sahira shouted after her, but Lexi didn't stop as Cricket's hoofbeats followed her down the shedrow.

Drawn by the sound and movement of his friend, Darby fell in behind Cricket. When Kaylia pulled the door open, Lexi skidded to a halt as she inhaled gulps of the fresh air beyond.

Darby and Cricket shot out the door, drawing the attention of the Lord's men. Many of them turned toward her, some of them shouted and pointed, and then a green dragon soared into view.

A burst of dragon fire seared the earth as it came straight at her.

CHAPTER SIXTY-FIVE

None of the stable boys were present when Cole, Brokk, and Niall entered the barn. They'd probably all gone scrambling for their parents the second the dragons arrived, or at least he hoped they had.

The three of them opened the stall doors as they ran through the stables. Most of the horses wandered out on their own, but they pulled a few of the more frightened ones from their stalls and sent them running for the doors.

When they finished, Brokk opened a portal to the prison realm and sent his horse, Aspri, through while Cole led Torigon to it. He patted Torigon on the back before sending the horse through.

Cole was about to open a portal to Underhill when dozens of the Lord's guards poured into the stable as shadows swept across the ceiling, coming toward him. He didn't have time for these assholes.

Either the men hadn't been in the ballroom to see what happened, or they mistakenly believed they could get to Cole and the others before he destroyed them. As he drew the shadows toward him, their power swelled inside, and their darkness seeped in to touch his soul.

That touch spread out to corrupt his soul, but he didn't care. He welcomed their power and wrath because it fueled *his* power and wrath. The more he drew on them, the more like them he became, and he was starting to *like* it.

The shadows gave him the ability to take down his enemies, and he gave them blood. It was a good, symbiotic relationship.

A part of him knew they were corrupting him, but he welcomed the corruption.

When he unleashed the shadows on the guards, he smiled at their screams and tasted their blood in the air before he turned back to his brother and Niall.

Niall looked on in horror while an almost resolved look had settled over Brokk's face. He ignored both of them as he opened the portal to Underhill.

"Go," Cole commanded.

Niall closed his mouth, and with a glance back at the men, whose screams were fading, he walked into the portal; Brokk followed.

Cole watched as the guards fell silent. When the shadows pulled back to reveal the destruction they'd wrought, he smiled.

∾

LUNGING TO THE SIDE, Lexi yanked the door away from Kaylia, but the flame hit her before she could get it closed. It blew her hair back and scorched her dress.

The heat of it warmed her skin but didn't melt it away. The fire died off, and the smoke parted; as the moonlight touched her skin, it began to glow. When the silver markings spread over her arms, she realized she'd forgotten to erect her shield.

The dragon landed and ran a few steps toward her before skidding to a halt twenty feet away. Dirt flew up around its talons as its wings folded against its back.

When Lexi met its golden eyes, she swore shock resonated

there before the creature released a bellow that blew her hair back as much as its fire had. However, this bellow sounded more upset than furious.

The creature bowed its neck until its chin rested flat against the ground. There was something almost yearning about the dragon's golden eyes. It called to her, but before she could think on it too much or go to the beast, like she longed to do, Kaylia slammed the door shut.

"Go!" her dad yelled as he grabbed her arm and spun her away from the door; he pushed her toward the portal. "Go!"

With the spell of the dragon's stare broken, Lexi stumbled toward the portal and into it. She staggered forward as reality descended in a heart-crushing wave. A sob lodged in her throat as grief for the home and land she loved so dearly struck her.

When she exited the portal, she found herself staring into a gray hall of locked cells. A bunch of loud whistles and some pretty lewd comments alerted her that she was naked.

"Here," Maverick said in his gruff voice.

She looked down to discover his jacket dangling from one of his fingers. She took it from him and hastily shrugged it on. Wearing Cole's clothes made her feel like a child; wearing Maverick's made her feel like a toddler.

The sleeves fell way past her wrists to dangle comically. She tried to roll them but gave up when they kept falling. The tears blurring her vision didn't help, and she wiped them angrily away as her dad draped his arm around her shoulders.

He pulled her close as Orin led the way down the hall. Lexi cringed when prisoners started pleading for their freedom from behind the cell doors. She huddled deeper into Maverick's jacket as the desperate words followed them down the hall.

"Get her away from them," her dad snarled at Orin.

Orin didn't look back as he turned a corner and entered another hall. Tucker and Sunny stood at the end of the hall; when they saw her, they lifted their heads and nickered before trotting toward her.

Lexi stopped to pet their velvety noses. She buried her face in their necks, hugging one and then the other as she inhaled the familiar, much-loved scent of horse beneath the smoke.

She couldn't think of Darby and Cricket, still out there, alone and frightened. They'd saved these two, and she might be able to find them. When she finally pulled away from Tucker and Sunny, they turned and trotted down the hall again.

"I'll have someone come and find them in a bit. They can't get into any trouble before then," Orin said as he started walking again. "They'll be fed and put somewhere safe."

"Thank you," Lexi murmured.

She glanced at the barren walls as they walked. Though doors were closed to it, they weren't cells, and she was grateful for that.

"Where are we going?" Maverick inquired.

"Our quarters are downstairs. We have extra rooms there."

"What about Cole?" Lexi asked.

"I'm sure he'll be here soon," Sahira said as she rubbed Shade's head. The cat didn't look happy at all, but he purred for her.

"Of course he will," Varo said as he touched Lexi's arm.

Lexi smiled, but her concern was growing. Not only was she worried about Cole's safety, but she was also concerned about what was going on *with* him. What would happen if he called more shadows to him and allowed them to kill again?

Each time they responded to him, she sensed their hold on him solidifying, and she *hated* it. What happened at the ball was brutal, but it was also cruel, and she'd never known Cole to take pleasure in cruelty.

She tried to tell herself it was because Cole had been planning to kill Malakai for months, but she feared it was more than that. She worried he was beginning to enjoy the power and destruction of the shadows.

CHAPTER SIXTY-SIX

"WHO ARE YOU, BY THE WAY?" Maverick asked Kaylia before turning to her dad. "And when the *fuck* did you come back to life?"

Her dad chuckled. "It's been a long time, Mav. We have a lot to catch up on."

"Obviously," Maverick retorted before turning to Kaylia. "And you are?"

"I'm Kaylia. Who are you?"

Maverick puffed out his chest as he smiled. "I assumed my reputation would precede me, but obviously not. I'm Maverick. Cole's uncle."

Kaylia's eyes were assessing as they ran over him. "Lycan."

Maverick returned her assessing look. "Witch."

"Crone."

"So… you're an old witch."

"That I am. Which also means I'm more powerful."

"I have no doubt, but then, I'm an old lycan."

"Maybe she can teach you some new tricks," Orin suggested and laughed.

If looks could have killed, Maverick and Kaylia would have

stabbed him a thousand times over, but Orin didn't notice as he kept his back to them.

They descended a flight of stairs, and Orin led down another before turning a corner. Another row of doors came into view, but some were open, while the others remained closed.

"Here we are," Orin said.

Lexi tugged nervously at Maverick's jacket as they passed the doors. It concealed most of her as it fell to mid thigh, but she still felt exposed beneath the material.

"Do you have any extra clothes somewhere?" she asked Orin.

"There are some women here who are about your size," he said. "I'll find something for you."

"Thank you."

"The open doors are available rooms," Orin said. "They're all identical, and none of them are fancy."

Lexi didn't care about fancy. All she wanted was a shower to scrub the smoke scent from her, some clothes, and Cole... if Cole still existed.

An uneasy feeling settled into the pit of her stomach as the possibility something other than Cole might return sank in. Seeming to sense the direction of her thoughts, her father squeezed her shoulder.

"It's going to be okay," he assured her.

She wanted to tell him there was *no* way he could be sure of that, but he hadn't witnessed what she saw in Dragonia. If he had seen that, he might not think it would be okay.

Although, he *did* witness the brutality Cole unleashed at the manor. They'd all seen what the shadows could do, but had they noticed how much Cole *enjoyed* it?

When she first met Cole, he had nightmares over the acts he committed and witnessed during the war. That man had committed violence, but he hadn't relished it.

That wasn't the same man before her today.

"I'm going to take this room," she murmured.

She hugged her dad and kissed his cheek before ducking out from under his arm and into the first room with an open door.

She glanced back at Maverick as she pulled the jacket tighter. "Thank you for this; I'll get it back to you as soon as I can."

"No rush," he replied. "Once Cole's back, we all have to talk."

"We will," she agreed before looking to Varo and Orin. "Is there somewhere I can shower?"

They both pointed to a room across the hall from her. "Right in there," Orin said.

Lexi said goodnight to everyone and darted across the hall. She shut the door, stripped out of her jacket, pulled the pins from her hair, and stepped beneath the showerhead jutting out of the concrete wall.

She used a forgotten shampoo bottle to scrub her hair and body before reluctantly leaving the water behind.

Since a towel wasn't hiding behind the toilet, there was nowhere for one to be, she slid Maverick's jacket back on. Her nose wrinkled when the potent scent of smoke filled her nostrils, but it was better than being nude.

She gathered her pins, opened the door, strode across the hall to the room she'd claimed, and closed the door. A torch burned on the wall beside the bed; it was the only thing with any warmth in the room.

Concrete walls, a small bed with no frame, and a single closet made her feel like *she* was in a cell. She almost flung the door back open, but she'd had enough of dealing with anyone else today and simply required some time to herself.

Sinking onto the bed, which was more comfortable than she'd expected, she shrugged out of Maverick's jacket and tossed it over the metal chair in the corner. She dropped her pins in the trash.

Wrapping the blanket around her shoulders, she buried herself in it as she settled in to wait.

CHAPTER SIXTY-SEVEN

A THIRST for blood pounded through Cole's veins, swelled his muscles, and throbbed in his temples. Every beat of his heart called for more death.

Blood coated the front of him; it stuck his hair to his face, clung to his beard, and plastered his clothes to him. The last time he was this covered in blood, it was his father's, and it had repulsed him. Now, he barely noticed it as he stepped out of the portal behind Brokk.

Lexi's strawberry scent instantly filled his nostrils, and his racing pulse eased as his bloodlust ebbed. That sweet aroma calmed the shadows' unquenchable vengeance, and they settled down as they eased away from him.

For the first time since he beat Malakai to death, the blood coating him was unacceptable and abhorrent. She'd seen him at the ball and the manor, but she couldn't see him like this again.

As soon as they exited the portal, Orin turned a corner and strode toward them. The apprehension on his face made his cheekbones sharper. His black eyes stood out more starkly against the pallor of his skin.

Varo emerged behind him, and the second his eyes landed on

Cole, he blanched. Cole kept his shoulders back as he walked toward them. He could act as if he didn't have a care in the world, but he was aware something wasn't right with him.

The shadows were changing him; he couldn't deny it, but he also couldn't turn away from the power they gave him. They would help him protect Lexi, which was *the* most important thing.

"Where is she?" he demanded.

"She's in her room," Orin said.

"She's really upset," Varo said. "They lit her home and barn on fire... with the horses still inside."

"Did she see that?"

"Yes, that's why we risked our asses to save them and why we now have two of them running around this place," Orin said.

"Make that four," Brokk said. "Torigon and Aspri are here too."

Orin looked to Cole and shook his head. "You two tender-hearted morons are perfect for each other." Then his gaze raked Cole, and he winced a little. "Or... maybe one of you isn't so tenderhearted anymore."

Cole's eyebrows shot up as he briefly envisioned tearing his brother's heart out. In response, the shadows stirred. Varo and Orin paled a little further but didn't back away.

"You better control those things," Orin said.

"What do you think I'm doing?" Cole demanded through his clenched teeth. "You let Lexi go into a burning barn?"

"In case you forgot, Cole, your fiancée is a bit stubborn and doesn't like to listen to reason," Orin retorted. "Believe me, if it were up to me, it would *not* have happened, but I was outvoted. Besides, she was the only one who was safe in that barn. It was the rest of us who would have crisp fried."

Cole's fingers dug into his palms as he took a slow breath before releasing it. He had to calm down. He wouldn't have been able to stop Lexi either; he shouldn't expect them to do so.

"Did you save all of them?" he asked.

"Two of them panicked too much and had to be set free; whether they survived or not, I don't know. I wasn't sticking around to find out, especially once the dragon arrived and released its fire, but we all survived."

"Good to know. What happened after that?"

"Well, your fiancée took the brunt of the fire," Orin said. "She lost all her clothes, but the rest of her remained intact."

Cole's hands fisted again. If she'd been anyone else, the dragon fire would have killed her, but she was far from anyone else.

"Others saw her?" he growled.

No one answered him, which was the wisest choice. It was irrational to be annoyed by this, but the lycan was not pleased that others had seen *his* mate naked.

He took another deep breath, drawing her scent into his lungs and holding it there as he allowed it to soothe him.

"Okay," he said through his teeth.

"And then the dragon landed, put its head on the ground, and looked at her," Orin continued.

"It was truly amazing," Varo whispered. "It looked like it was sorry for what it did."

Cole glanced at Orin, the more cynical of his brothers. He simply couldn't believe a dragon would be remorseful about anything.

"It's true," Orin confirmed. "It was amazing and scary and strange."

Hearing Orin admitting to anything being scary was new for Cole. It must have been a spectacle to see if Orin was impressed. "I'm sorry I missed it."

"She has a connection to the dragons; we have to find out how much of one," Orin said.

Cole chose to ignore him; he wasn't in the mood to figure it out. "Is she okay?"

"She'll be better once you're with her," Varo said.

"I can't go to her looking like this."

"There's a shower in the bathroom on this floor," Orin said. "I'll take you there."

"I'll get you some clothes," Varo offered.

"Have you seen Torigon?" he asked.

"No," Orin said. "But he can't get out of the building, so I'm sure he's fine."

"How is the Gloaming?" Varo asked.

"On fire," Cole replied. "But I think we got most, if not everyone, out safely."

"If anyone remains, it's because of their own doing," Niall said. "I thought you two were dead."

"Many do, and that was the plan," Orin said.

"You have more lives than a cat," Niall replied. "I'm not sure that's a good thing."

Orin and Niall had never gotten along, but Orin wasn't exactly Mr. Personality.

"Oh, good, another immortal who likes to pick on poor little me," Orin retorted. "This way."

"How is it possible Lexi withstood dragon fire?" Niall asked.

Cole fell in beside his brother as they walked down the hall. "I'll explain everything to you soon," he said to Niall.

"I'm looking forward to it."

Orin led them to a small room with craggy rock walls, a sink, toilet, and a shower set into the back wall. There was no curtain or door to cover the shower; it was simply a faucet sticking out of the wall with a drain below it.

"I'll find you some clothes," Varo said and left.

"You can show Brokk and Niall to their rooms," Cole said to Orin. "I'll be here."

"Fine," Orin said. "There's some soap on the sink."

"Thanks," Cole muttered.

"Leave your clothes on the floor. I'll have them burned."

When Cole didn't reply, Orin jerked his head at Brokk and Niall before disappearing from the doorway. It took a while for

Cole to peel his clothes off; he tossed them into the corner when he finished.

He lifted the bar of soap from the sink, crossed over to the shower, and turned on the water. He hadn't bothered to close the door, and he didn't care who saw him in there.

Using the soap, he scrubbed the blood from his skin and hair and watched as the red water flowed down the drain. Every time he believed there couldn't be any more blood, more came off him until finally, after what seemed like hours, the water ran clear.

Even still, he remained beneath the hot spray, with his head bowed and his thoughts a tumbled mess as the shadows called for more blood.

But he couldn't give them more. He had nothing left to give.

Now that the adrenaline rush of the fight was gone, the screams were getting louder in his head. He flexed his fingers as he felt Malakai's bones breaking again.

Cole would never regret killing that bastard. He would gladly beat him to death again, but he didn't like how out of control he was when it happened.

Lexi's arrival in his life had rattled the dark fae will he'd exerted over his life. She'd awakened the lycan part of him, stirred its protective instincts, and made it take control in a way it never had before he encountered his mate.

The shadows had shaken his restraint further, and though he relished the rush they gave, he despised their hold on him. He wasn't entirely sure who had more control anymore; himself or the shadows.

CHAPTER SIXTY-EIGHT

COLE TURNED the water off and stepped out from beneath the spray as Varo returned with clothes and a towel. He tossed the towel to Cole and set the clothes on the sink.

"Are you okay?" Varo asked.

Cole almost said he was fine, but he'd never been able to lie to his youngest brother. "No."

"How bad is it?" Varo asked.

"I don't know."

It killed him to admit that as he lifted his head to meet Varo's troubled eyes.

"Can you control this, Cole?"

"I have no other choice."

"That's not an answer."

"That's because I don't have an answer. Why did you choose Orin and our brothers over Father?"

It was a question he'd pondered since the beginning of their divide. Varo didn't enjoy the battle or seek power, unlike his other hotheaded brothers. It would have been best if he stayed out of the war, something their father could have arranged for him.

"They needed me more," Varo replied.

"What?"

Varo looked past Cole to the mirror over the sink. "Father had you and Brokk and the others. He had reasonable people surrounding him; he was a reasonable, considerate, and kind man. He would never do anything foolish, and if, for some reason, he lost his way, he had you and Brokk to help him through it. Orin and our brothers didn't have that."

"So, you became it for them?"

"I did my best to try to be it for them. It didn't always work."

"You sacrificed yourself to be their conscience?"

"I don't see it as a sacrifice."

"Father could have kept you from the war."

"I know, but I stopped letting you fight my battles for me centuries ago, and I wasn't going to let Father do it for me either. Our brothers needed me."

"I can see the toll the war has taken on you."

"Yes, but it was worth it. Orin is still alive; without me, he wouldn't be, and you must admit you're grateful for that."

"I am, but not at the cost of you or your relationship with Father."

"Father understood."

"Did he?"

"Yes. He knew why I went; he may not have liked it, but he understood."

Cole bent his head into his hands and rubbed at his face. He understood Varo's reason, but he didn't like it either.

"Does Orin know this?" he asked.

"I'm sure he suspects. He's an asshole, but he's not stupid."

"Very true," Cole muttered and turned away from his youngest brother.

Learning Varo's reason for leaving their father was annoying him enough that he could feel the shadows slipping closer. He dried himself and tugged on clothes that were too small for him.

He almost ripped the clingy material back off, but he had to appear as normal as possible when he saw Lexi. But if that was going to happen, he had to go somewhere to settle down first.

"Is there somewhere quiet I can go?" he asked Varo. And once he got there, these fucking clothes were coming off.

"Don't you want to see Lexi?"

"Not while I'm in this state. I need to go somewhere to regain control of myself first."

"She can help you do that."

"Most likely, but she can't see me like this… again."

"Cole—"

"She already saw far too much in that ballroom and the library. She can't see any more of me as a monster. I *won't* allow it."

Varo sighed and jerked his head toward the doorway. "I know of a place. Follow me."

$$\sim$$

VARO LED him through the prison and toward the stairs leading to one of the balconies overlooking the realm. He didn't take him to the balcony with the whipping wind he loved, because it was so loud there that it often drowned out his thoughts.

Cole had requested quiet, and he could give him that. He took him to the other side of the prison and the stairs leading to the balcony protected from the wind.

Varo pulled it open when they arrived at the door and gestured for Cole to ascend.

"It's a long climb, but that will probably help to calm you. It's peaceful up there. I prefer the other side where the wind and the noise cleanse me, but it's loud. If you think you might prefer it too, I can take you there instead."

"No," Cole said. "This is perfect. I'll be back later."

Varo watched Cole ascend the stairs. Though there was something sad and defeated about him, he kept his shoulders back and chin high while he climbed.

Despite having no reason to draw them to him, the shadows in the hall turned as if they were going to follow but remained where they were. There were many things in Varo's lengthy life that he'd hated seeing, but watching Cole climb those steps, and the shadows reacting to him, was in the top ten.

Refusing to plunge his brother into darkness, Varo left the door open and turned away. Cole hadn't wanted to go to Lexi, but that didn't mean Varo couldn't bring her to him.

Because, if there was one thing he was certain about, it was that she could help with this.

CHAPTER SIXTY-NINE

When a knock sounded on the door, Lexi's head lifted, and her heart soared. But then, it crashed. Cole wouldn't knock.

Rising, she discarded the blanket and pulled Maverick's jacket around her. She felt a little more prepared to deal with someone in the jacket than in a blanket, especially since it was probably Orin with clothes for her.

She opened the door, and her eyebrows rose when she discovered Varo there. She liked Cole's youngest brother, but they hadn't had much contact with each other. He was the last immortal she expected to see on the other side of the door.

He held some clothes out to her. "Cole is back."

Ignoring the clothes, Lexi stepped forward to search the hall but didn't see him. Uncertainty twisted in her belly as she looked back to Varo. She bit her lip when she discovered his eyes haunted in a way she'd never seen before.

"What happened?" she whispered.

"He needs you."

"Is he okay?"

Varo nudged her with the clothes. "He will be. Get dressed."

Lexi almost threw the clothes aside. She didn't care about them. "Take me to him."

"It's best if he doesn't see you wearing his uncle's jacket. You know how a lycan can be."

Lexi grunted. She hated that he was right, and she would have to waste time dressing, but he was.

Closing the door, she shed Maverick's jacket and yanked on the brown pants and black fae tunic with green piping. Her hands trembled as she dressed.

Where was Cole? What had happened that stopped him from coming to her immediately?

There were no socks or shoes, and she was fine with that. She'd already wasted too much time dressing in the first place.

Flinging the door open, she almost walked into Varo, hovering on the other side. She snatched Maverick's jacket off the floor and handed it to him.

"This shouldn't be in our room when Cole enters it," she said.

She was being optimistic about him coming with her when she had no idea what was keeping him away now.

"I'll make sure it gets back to its owner," Varo promised. "This way."

Varo took the jacket from her and started down the hall. The cool stone floor chilled her feet as she hurried to keep up with him.

"Where is he?" she asked.

"He wanted to be alone, so I escorted him to a place."

Lexi's step faltered for a second. "And you don't think that's best for him?"

"No, I don't. Do you?"

"No."

Whatever was happening with Cole, she didn't think it was best he was alone. Whenever he was alone, he tended to beat himself up about things that weren't his fault.

With what happened at the ball and the fall of the Gloaming, she suspected he was kicking the shit out of himself, and she hated it. When her pace increased, so did Varo's as they wound through the prison.

Once, they turned a corner, and Lexi chuckled as Torigon came into view. The horse was going in the opposite direction, trotting along behind Sunny.

Then, they took a few more turns and climbed a set of stairs until they arrived at an open doorway. Lexi peered at the stairs until they faded into the darkness.

Varo waved a hand at the shadowed doorway. "He's up there. It's a long climb."

"I don't care," Lexi said. "Thank you."

She didn't look back as she entered the stairwell and started jogging up the stairs. She didn't know how far she'd climbed before her legs and lungs burned with every step, but when she looked back, only a pinpoint of light remained behind her.

Ahead of her was only shadows and more stairs. Still, she didn't slow but instead pushed herself faster while her body protested every step.

She was practically wheezing and had a stitch in her side when she finally reached the thick metal door at the top. She must have climbed a thousand feet.

Bending over, she placed a hand against her side and took a deep breath to settle her racing heart and growing anxiety. She'd been so determined to find Cole, she hadn't considered what would happen once she got here.

She had no idea what lay beyond this door, but she knew what she'd seen in the ballroom and her manor. Knew the violence and blood he unleashed with such savagery.

But that wasn't *her* Cole, and no matter what happened earlier, he would always be *hers*. When she could breathe better and her side no longer felt like a dagger was stabbing her ribs, she grasped the door handle, turned it, and pushed it open.

Taking a deep breath, she squared her shoulders and stepped onto a large, stone balcony at least fifty feet wide and long. The moon's rays, hanging heavily above the prison, shone off the stone's surface. They illuminated the night as they reflected all around her.

She'd forgotten to put her shield back up, and when she started to glow, she resolutely erected it as she searched for Cole. But all she saw was darkness and shadows hanging heavily over the balcony.

Maybe he left here without Varo knowing.

She was about to turn away and run back down to see if he'd gone to their room, but movement in the corner of her eye caught her attention. Frowning, she studied the heavy shadows there as she tried to make sense of what she saw.

Her breath exploded out of her when she realized the darkness in the corner was *him*.

CHAPTER SEVENTY

SHE COULDN'T SEE Cole through the twisting and turning shadows, but he was there. They only acted like that when he was around.

Amid all that darkness was the man she loved with all her heart and soul.

Terrified of going any closer to that rolling ball of shadows, Lexi's feet remained locked in place. Her mind screamed at her to run, but she was more afraid of leaving him.

He needed her. She could help him.

She wasn't sure how, but she *could* help him.

It took every ounce of courage and strength she had to approach him. As she did, some of the shadows swiveled toward her. They rose to tower over her like a genie escaping its bottle and seeking to destroy.

She glowered at them as she refused to let them intimidate her.

"Varo shouldn't have brought you here," Cole growled.

She didn't recognize his voice. It was worse than when they were at the ball. It was more guttural, angrier, and she would swear it was more than just *his* voice coming out of him.

Goose bumps broke out on her arms as she stopped at the edge of the shadows. They dipped to hover before her; there were no eyes, but she sensed them eyeing her in the ravenous way a wolf watches a rabbit.

But Cole was *her* wolf, and she wouldn't allow him, or these things, to scare her.

"Yes, he should have," she said.

The shadows parted enough to reveal Cole's broad back. Sometimes, because he was so gentle and caring with her, she forgot how large he was. But seeing the corded muscles of his back bunched as if preparing for a fight, she couldn't stop herself from remembering what he'd done to Malakai with such ease.

However, even with these malevolent shadows surrounding him, he would *never* harm her.

"I'm not going anywhere," she told him.

His head turned until he looked at her over his shoulder, but he didn't face her. She wasn't sure if he could see her through the shadows, but he most likely sensed her distress or smelled it. Lycans were known for their keen sense of smell and hyped-up senses.

"I'm not afraid of you," she stated.

"Your scent says differently."

"That's because I'm afraid of losing you, but you won't hurt me."

He didn't move, and neither did the shadows as they hovered around her. She wasn't sure he breathed as his hands fisted and the corded muscles of his arms stood out starkly.

"You should leave here; I'm not sure what I am anymore," he said.

"I know what you are, and I know *who* you are, and that's what matters to me."

"I'm a monster."

"No, you're not."

"You didn't see all of what I did."

"I saw enough to know you could never be a monster. The

shadows are changing you"—she had to admit it, they all did—"
but you won't lose yourself to them. Neither of us will allow it."

The shadows hissed and darted toward her, but when she didn't
move, they recoiled and retreated to his back as they spread out
like wings from his spine. She imagined this was what Lucifer
looked like, in the pits of Hell, with his blackened, broken wings
spread around him.

After seeing what the shadows could do, she wouldn't be
astonished to learn he could also use them to fly. The possibility
was as awing as it was terrifying.

WHAT IF HE decided to fly away from her?

She didn't doubt that if he left now, she might never get him
back.

LIFTING HER CHIN, she walked straight into the shadows. Instead of
trying to stop her or pushing her away, they parted for her.

She hadn't expected them to do so, but as she continued toward
Cole, they moved out of her way. When she stopped behind him,
the blackness swelled around his back.

"You're wrong," he said in a voice more his own. "I *am*
becoming a monster."

She wrapped her arms around his waist and rested her cheek
against his bare back. "If you are, then we'll become one together."

The shadows either dissipated or moved away from her skin;
she couldn't tell which, but it didn't matter as they no longer
floated between them. When Cole shuddered against her, she
pressed closer as she sensed his need for more.

She tenderly kissed his back as she hugged him closer. Like
someone flipped a light on, the shadows vanished, and the two of
them were all that remained.

Despite the shadows being gone, she sensed the darkness lingering within Cole, even before seeing his eyes.

CHAPTER SEVENTY-ONE

LEXI COULDN'T BREATHE as the brilliant silver of his eyes met hers. But it wasn't the impossibly silver color that trapped the breath in her chest...

No, it was the black that had seeped in to encompass the whites of his eyes. It encircled his silver iris in an embrace of such impenetrable and unfathomable darkness, it sent an icy chill straight to her soul.

That black made the silver burn like a fire illuminated them and his eyes almost didn't seem to be a part of him anymore. She'd never imagined such a thing could be possible. It was as beautiful as it was disconcerting.

The shadows had woven their way into him, and they weren't going to let go any time soon, but that was fine, because she wasn't letting go either. And she *would* win.

Resting her hands against his chest, she rose on her toes and kissed him. His firm lips remained rigid against hers, but she loved the familiar taste of them.

When he didn't respond and stayed as still as stone, Lexi knew it was because he feared hurting her, but he was wrong. She trusted him completely and wished he'd do the same.

Sliding her hands up his chest, she draped them around his neck and flattened herself against his bare flesh. He'd showered recently as his hair was damp when she slid her fingers through it, but then, so was hers.

The soap he'd used was heavy on his skin, but his natural aroma of allspice sharpened as she teased his lips with her tongue. She loved that crisp, familiar scent as much as she loved him.

When she nipped at his lip and drew it a little way into her mouth, some of his rigidity eased. She used her tongue to lessen the sting of her bite, and he released a low, throaty growl that made her toes curl.

She hadn't started this kiss with desire in mind; she'd simply been seeking to connect with him, drive away the darkness, and assure herself he was still *hers*. But passion built rapidly inside her, and she felt an answering wave of it emanating from him. Not only did she need him, but he needed her too.

~

THE SHADOWS within Cole released their vise-like grasp as Lexi's love chased them further away. They slithered into the farthest recesses of his soul, retreated to the darkness where they belonged, and fled back into the night.

He would never again be separate from the shadows residing within him. But he could banish them for periods as he embraced Lexi.

Earlier, when he first arrived at this place, the shadows creeping through the night had found him. He hadn't called for them, but he'd felt them out there, and they responded by coming to him.

And when they did, he'd welcomed them. Unable to stand his clothes rubbing against his skin, he'd pulled them off and tossed them aside as the shadows entered and surrounded him.

Welcoming them was a slippery slope he might never ascend again, but they felt so *fucking right.*

But not even the shadows felt as right as Lexi. Now, all he wanted was *her.*

She was the light to his darkness, the stability to his growing instability, and the love he required to chase away the frenzy growing inside him. The shadows were becoming a festering, malignant entity he could neither deny nor accept, but with her by his side, he could master them.

Pulling her closer, he bent her a little backward as her breath warmed his lips, her breasts pressed against his chest, and her body melded to his in all the right ways. Nothing had ever fit him as perfectly as she did; nothing had ever amazed and captivated him as much as her.

And nothing ever would.

He relished the power the shadows gave him, but it was nothing compared to the rush of being with her. The shadows made him more powerful, but she made him capable of doing anything.

He would never get enough of this woman, his mate, and his reason for living. One day, she would be his wife and the mother of his children. She would stand by his side as, together, they returned all the realms to places where cruelty didn't reign.

Cole weaved his fingers through the damp, silken tresses of her hair as he cupped the back of her head and deepened the kiss. Her fingers dug into his nape as she gave a small mewl and ground her hips against his.

His first instinct was to lower her to the ground and take her, but stone surrounded them, and he couldn't hurt her. However, there was no way he would make it down the stairs and to whatever room Orin had given them without taking her first.

Grasping the bottom of her shirt, he tugged it off and tossed it aside before reclaiming her mouth. His hands slid down the supple skin of her lower back, tracing its enticing curve until they settled against her firm ass.

With a gentle squeeze, he held her closer before releasing her; he hooked his fingers into the waistband of her pants. He pushed them down her hips and thighs before she broke away to shove them down further.

She stepped gracefully out and, with her toe, kicked them aside. The moonlight spilling over her didn't bring out her glow or the silver markings, but it did emphasize the deep red of her hair and the striking green of her eyes.

As he gazed at her, his cock hardened until it throbbed with every beat of his heart. And when he was around her, that beat was a *lot* faster.

Stepping close again, she smiled as she ran a finger down the center of his chest. She bent her head to his skin and followed her finger with her tongue as she made her way steadily lower.

When she went to her knees before him, he nearly pulled her up again. The stone couldn't be comfortable, but she showed no sign of it bothering her.

"The stone. Your knees." The clipped sentences were all he could manage as anticipation raged inside him.

"I'm fine."

His hands settled on her shoulders to lift her, but when she gripped his shaft and her tongue caressed its head, he froze as pleasure radiated through him.

CHAPTER SEVENTY-TWO

Bracing his legs apart, Cole cupped the back of her head with one hand. He forgot all about the brutality and uncertainty of this day as she weaved her magic over him.

Her hands and mouth worked his dick while she tasted, teased, took him deeper, and pushed him to the brink of his restraint. When he was about to come, he grasped her arms to pull her away. She refused to budge.

"I'm going to come," he told her gruffly.

In response, her fingers sank into his ass, and she pulled him deeper into her mouth. Cole's fingers threaded in her hair, his head tipped back, and he lost himself to the exquisite wonder of her mouth and hands until he couldn't take anymore.

He groaned, and his hand tightened in her hair as he found his release. Lexi drank him down before pulling away.

When his eyes met hers, she smiled, wiped her mouth with the back of her hand, and lay back on the stone. Spreading her legs, she hooked her finger and beckoned to him with it. With the moonlight illuminating her lithe body, she was a gorgeous temptress, one he couldn't refuse.

"My turn," she said.

Cole knelt between her thighs, and grasping her legs, he pulled them further apart. He cupped her ass and lifted it into the air before bending his mouth to her core.

His erection never had a chance to soften as the taste of her hardened him again. Though he'd just found his release, he ached for more of her.

As he used his tongue and fingers to fuck her, he savored her sweetness. He would never forget her strawberry taste as it burned its way onto his tongue and became as much a part of him as the shadows it chased further away.

As long as she was his and her love could spark a light in his soul, he would be okay. During these moments with her, he could tell himself this, but when they were apart, the shadows whispered different truths to him.

And those truths told him that, no matter what, the shadows would win.

But now, the shadows were losing as her sounds of ecstasy filled his ears and drifted on the night. Her fingernails scratched the stones as her body arched off the rock. When she cried out, he drank in her orgasm.

A few seconds later, she collapsed onto the rocks. Sweat beaded her forehead, and her small gasps for breath caused her breasts to rise and fall in the most enticing of ways.

A smile curved her lush, swollen lips as her eyes fluttered open. Wrapping his arms around her, he braced his knees apart and lifted her off the rocks. She draped her arms around his neck as love shone from her eyes.

He pressed his hand flat against her back. "You're beautiful."

When she traced the tips of his pointed ears, he shuddered. She knew how much he enjoyed that.

"You're not so bad yourself," she told him.

He reclaimed her mouth, and their tongues entwined as he guided her hips down and lowered her onto his dick. The tight muscles of her sheath gripped him while she drew him deep inside her.

Neither of them moved as the beats of their hearts found a matching, frantic rhythm. He relished being a part of her while their hands roamed over each other.

Then, she rose a little over him before taking him deep again. She rode him slowly at first, in no rush, and neither was he as the tension built between them in an exquisitely sensuous dance.

When the power of their joining filled the air, the dark fae part of him feasted on it and the strength she gave him. As he fed, she sank her fangs into his throat. His hands clenched on her hips, and they moved faster as his blood eased another one of her hungers.

The lycan part of him howled to mark its mate again; unable to resist, he allowed his four fangs to lengthen before clamping them onto her shoulder. She cried out and released her bite on him as she bowed back in his arms.

Her hair tickled his hands; her hips thrust eagerly as her breathing grew faster until she came apart. He gladly followed her.

CHAPTER SEVENTY-THREE

LEXI STARED up at the inky black sky with only the big, full moon to illuminate it. She lay against Cole's side, with her head on his shoulder and his arm around her. He'd propped his other hand behind his head.

The stone beneath her was cool, and bits of it dug into her flesh, but the discomfort wasn't unpleasant enough for her to move. She was enjoying her time here, with him, far too much to leave.

Up here, above the prison and looking out over this bleak realm, it was just the two of them. They both needed that.

He was warm beneath her, solid, and for now, not tormented by the shadows inside him. She didn't kid herself into thinking that would last or they were gone for good.

They would come back.

And when they did, she would be here for him, and she would help chase them away again.

So, no matter how shitty everything else was or how uncomfortable the ground, she would enjoy every stolen moment she got with him, even if it included stone.

"Aren't there any stars in this realm?" she asked.

"It doesn't seem so, but every outer realm is different."

"Interesting," she murmured.

Lifting a piece of her hair, he ran it through his fingers as he played with it. She loved when he did that. She nestled closer and rested her hand on his chest as he twined some of her hair around his finger before releasing it.

"A dragon burned off my dress," she murmured.

He stiffened beneath her before chuckling. "That's not something you hear every day. But then, a dragon's fire would have turned anyone else to ash, so no one else could ever say it."

"Yet here I am."

"Here you are."

"It was a pretty dress."

"I'll get you another."

"I didn't love it enough to go through more fittings."

He laughed before nuzzling her temple and kissing her. "Understandable."

She studied the moon as it moved across the sky and recalled the blast of heat that burned her clothes away. It hadn't scared her; instead, it filled her with excitement as the fire whipped around her.

"The Lord's men set the stable on fire," she whispered.

"I heard." Cole ran her hair through his fingers. "You should have stayed away from the stable and fled here."

"It's funny you should say that when I saw Torigon here."

"I said you *shouldn't* have done it; I didn't say I don't understand *why* you did it."

It was her turn to laugh. "I'm going to say the same thing to you about Torigon."

"And it would be deserved." He paused. "I've failed as the dark fae king."

Lexi's heart ached for him, but she hated the blame he put on himself when he didn't deserve it. "You haven't failed. You got most of them safely out of the Gloaming."

"And now they're being hunted by the Lord and on the run."

"We'll figure out a way to help them."

He ran his fingers through her hair again. "We will."

"You're doing a good job, Cole. There's nothing you could have done differently against the Lord."

They stopped talking for a little while before he spoke again.

"The darkness and shadows are growing inside me."

Lexi's hand flattened on his chest; her eyes closed as she tried to deny his words. She wanted to deny it, but not only had she seen it, he was well aware of what he was and his abilities. He wouldn't say this if it weren't true.

"I know," she admitted in a whisper.

"The more I draw them into me, and the more I call on them, the deeper they dig into my soul."

"Then you're going to have to stop doing that."

It sounded so simple. It *was* an easy solution, but *nothing* was ever that simple.

Surviving the trials had put those shadows inside him. They were a part of him, like her heart was a part of her, and she could no more command it to stop beating than he could compel the shadows out of him.

"Do you think your father had the shadows?" she asked.

"No. At first, I wasn't sure if he might have or not, and he was a *very* controlled man, but even he couldn't have kept them hidden from everyone for centuries."

"Then why you? He went through the trials too."

"I don't know."

Lexi bit her lip as she tried to ignore the incessant anxiety pecking away at her insides.

"I can try not calling on the shadows, but there are going to be times when I need the shadows to help us fight," Cole said. "Without them, we wouldn't have survived the ballroom, and Malakai would still be alive. The only thing that keeps the shadows at bay and chases them away is you. I am the darkness, and you are the light."

"If that's true, then there is another truth to that statement."

"Which is?"

"Darkness can't exist without light and vice versa."

"True."

"And it doesn't matter what either of us are; I will *always* be here for you. I'm not going to let the shadows take you from me."

"Their power is very tempting."

She heard the reverence in his tone but also the fear and... *need.*

Stroking his chest, she recalled what he could do with those shadows and the violence they unleashed. They were scary, awing, and a force to reckon with. Few could withstand their wrath and survive.

Those shadows were an asset against the Lord, but she never wanted to see them again. Unfortunately, that wasn't an option. They would make their presence known again the next time there was a threat.

"I know it is," she said. "You *are* the Shadow Reaver."

Neither of them had been sure of it before, but she was now.

"I am."

"The prophecy—"

"Means nothing," he interrupted. "The Shadow Reaver exists, and none of us know what that means, but prophecies are useless things meant to frighten those who are foolish enough to believe them. I'm *not* going to lose you."

"Never," she vowed. "No matter what happens, *nothing* will ever tear us apart. Not the monster on the throne, not the shadows, and not whatever we discover I can do."

"Speaking of which, you released fire at the ball earlier."

"I did."

When she pushed herself off his chest to sit up, his fingers slid away from her hair. Turning her hand over before her, she recalled the love propelling her in the ballroom.

She thought about Cole's scent, her father laughing as he bounced her on his knee, and the way Sahira's eyes sparkled with love. As all those things coalesced, they formed a ball of love in her chest.

A fire ignited in her palm. From what she'd seen earlier, the small flames hovering there could become a stream as lethal, but not nearly as large, as what the dragons unleashed.

Closing her fingers around the fire, she snuffed it out and lifted her eyes to Cole's. He smiled as he stared at her hand before meeting her eyes.

"How did you figure out how to make it work?" he asked.

"Love." Swinging her leg over his hips, she pulled herself on top of him and planted her hands on his chest as she straddled him. "Love is the key to activating the fire."

He settled his hands on her hips. "Interesting, but isn't love the key to everything?"

"I like to think so. I want to see the manor tomorrow."

"It's not safe, Lexi, and there's probably nothing left to see."

"Maybe so, but I still want to go."

His fingers tightened on her hips as she wiggled back to glide along the length of his shaft.

"I have to see, and I'm assuming you plan to return to the Gloaming," she said.

"I have to go. It's my realm."

"Then we'll go together."

"You know how much I enjoy doing things together," he groaned as she shifted her hips to take him into her once more.

CHAPTER SEVENTY-FOUR

LEXI HELD a dagger and had a set of throwing stars strapped to her side as she and Cole stepped out of the portal and into the day. They emerged into the trees that made up the woods across from the manor. Cole had his sword in hand, prepared for whatever enemy might greet them.

But instead of something looking to kill them, they discovered the land was far quieter than normal. A few squirrels sat in the branches of the maples sweeping overhead, but they didn't run and play like they normally would. It was as if they were afraid movement could bring death, and they might be right.

The birds didn't sing, and the lake between them and the manor was perfectly still. Not even a small breeze disturbed its pristine surface.

Before leaving the prison realm, they hadn't told the others they were coming here or the Gloaming. Neither of them wanted to deal with the protests and arguments sure to follow their decision.

And it was better if they came alone. They were far less noticeable if they moved in smaller numbers than if everyone came with them; she was sure they all would have insisted on coming.

So, instead, they dressed on the balcony, returned to her room for her shoes, and left from there. They had taken a chance on emerging into this forest; they couldn't have been sure it was still standing, but the thick canopies of the trees offered their protection.

Staring across the lake, tears blurred Lexi's vision as she took in the rubble of the only home she'd ever known. Smoke still drifted from the ashes, but the only thing still standing amid the pile of stone that once comprised her home, was the chimney. It rose like a phoenix from the pile of ash and debris surrounding it, except, unlike the phoenix, there was no beauty here.

Her beloved library, room, and all her things were nothing but rubble. Her favorite ratty old pink bathrobe that she'd worn bare over the years, all Sahira's potions, their photos, and clothes were gone. Her favorite teddy bear from when she was a baby was no longer tucked safely inside her closet, where she often said hi to it when she opened the doors.

So many memories took place in that home. Most of them were good, but some were sad, shocking, and fear haunted a couple of them.

Through it all, the good far outweighed the bad. She'd dreamt of so many things while growing up here, traveled to many different worlds thanks to her books, imagination, and Sahira's stories.

She'd played on this shore and swung through the branches of the trees surrounding them. Lexi hadn't known, until recently, that her birth parents were buried beneath these maples, but it had always been a favorite place of hers.

Across the lake and to her left was the giant weeping willow she loved so much. She'd spent hours playing beneath its branches as a child, hidden from the world, and dreaming of pixies and dragons.

It was also where she discovered Orin and chose to save him. Her life had forever changed that day, and while there were plenty of times she'd prefer to choke him, she was glad she'd saved him.

This manor was where she learned her father was dead and later discovered he was alive. As she grew, she'd envisioned living here with her children and their papa and great-aunt Sahira. She'd pictured listening to them laugh as they ran around the lake.

When she fell in love with Cole, she'd *known* that they would never raise their children here, but they would visit often. She would sit and read to them as her father did with her so often over the years. And later, she would listen as they read to her.

It had all been so vivid in her mind, and it still was, but there was no home to bring those children to anymore.

It was all gone. Even the stables were nothing but ash.

All that remained were the memories.

But no, it wasn't all gone, she realized. To the far left of the ruins stood a horse. Cricket's tail swished back and forth, and her ears flicked as she munched on the lush grass near the shoreline.

The lazy dog that would often wander onto the manor's grounds lounged near the willow. She was glad to see it and Cricket remained unharmed.

"Where's Darby?" she murmured as she searched for the fourth horse.

He wouldn't have gone far. He might have in the beginning as he fled the chaos, but he probably would have returned by now to rejoin Cricket on the land so familiar to him.

She didn't want to think about what might have happened to him and chose to believe he'd run until he found somewhere safer with green pastures. It was a far prettier picture than to think he'd filled the belly of a dragon.

"I have to get Cricket," she said. "I can't leave her here."

Cole clasped her arm when she started toward the lake. "I'll form a portal closer to her, and we'll get her to enter it. If someone is hiding and watching nearby, they won't have a chance to get to us if we do it that way."

"Okay."

Cole closed the portal they'd exited from and opened another before him. Opening portals normally drained immortals, but it wasn't slowing him down.

"Does opening a portal drain you at all anymore?" she inquired and braced herself for the answer.

He was getting stronger, but he still had to have some weaknesses, somewhere... other than her.

"Not as much as it used to," he said.

She suspected that was as good as it was bad, but she kept it to herself. She was sure he was already aware this was another change in him.

Keeping her face composed, she hid her apprehension as they stepped into the portal. When they emerged a few seconds later, they were only a few feet away from Cricket.

Cricket's head shot up, and she danced back before stopping when she recognized Lexi. Her happy whinny filled the air, and she and Cole walked over to her.

Lexi grasped her broken halter and shifted her hold to keep it from slipping over Cricket's head. Cole opened another portal as a group of the Lord's guards emerged from beneath the leaves of the willow.

They had been hiding and waiting, though she didn't understand why they waited so long to emerge. Then, she glanced at Cole. They'd most likely been debating who scared them more... Cole or the Lord.

The Lord had won, but Lexi doubted it was by much.

"Shit," Lexi hissed as some of the men charged at them with swords raised while others planted themselves and lifted their bows.

Lexi's grip on Cricket's halter tightened as the twangs of arrows releasing resonated in the air. She spun in time to see an arrow soaring toward them.

She yanked forward on Cricket's halter, but the unexpected movement caused her to shy and jerk back. Unprepared for the move, Lexi's feet briefly left the ground before she was able to right herself.

But by then, it was too late. The arrow was about to pierce through Cricket's heart when a shadow leapt from the ground and tore it from the air.

Lexi's head spun toward Cole as darkness gathered around him and the shadows split before rising into the air around him. He'd saved Cricket, but at the expense of himself.

"Cole, no!" Lexi screamed.

She regained control of Cricket and ran toward the portal before plunging into it. She released the mare and watched as she galloped away. Cricket would have to find her way around the prison realm for now; she was sure someone would find and take care of her.

Leaping back out of the portal, she grabbed Cole's arm and yanked him toward her as one of the guards screamed. She didn't have to look to know what had made the man scream like that. Malakai made the same agonized cries when the shadows tore his limbs away.

The man's inhuman shrieks followed them into the portal.

∼

COLE EXITED the portal first and turned to Lexi. She didn't say anything as they returned to the prison realm. Cricket was still in the hallway when they emerged, but no one else was around.

Cricket turned her head to gaze at them before trotting down the hall, presumably in search of some food. Her hooves clapped against the rocky floor as she turned the corner and vanished.

"She'll be okay," Lexi murmured.

"Someone will find her, and if not, we'll catch her and put her somewhere safe when we return."

Lexi finally shifted her attention from where Cricket had

turned the corner and back to him. When her eyes met his, a flicker of fear ran through them before she buried it.

He hated that she worried about him so much, but he would do whatever it took to keep her safe, even if it meant giving away tiny pieces of his soul to the shadows.

But that might not be necessary. When he recalled how right she felt, the love that ignited her flames and drove away his darkness, he pushed the shadows further away.

"Are you okay?" she asked.

She couldn't hide the uncertainty in her voice, but he couldn't take it away, and he wouldn't change what happened. Those guards could have killed her, and they'd paid the price for trying to do so.

"I'm fine," he assured her.

And he meant it. He was nowhere near as unstable now as he was last night. Maybe the more he called on the shadows, the more symbiotic they would become.

"Do you still want to go to the Gloaming with me?" he asked.

"Of course."

Taking hold of her hand, he opened another portal, and, together, they entered it.

CHAPTER SEVENTY-FIVE

THE PORTAL COLE had created opened into a small cave he knew from his days as a kid in the Gloaming. It wasn't far from the backside of the palace but located in the woods most avoided... except by foolish children.

He'd ventured into the woods a few times as a kid and to this cave, but he'd never frequented the forest, and he hadn't returned to it after his last time here. That was when he finally learned his lesson about these woods.

As a child, when he entered the woods, it was on dares from his friends. It was considered a rite of passage to sneak into the forest, to this cave, and to collect a pink stone.

The stones were worthless, but most in this section of the Gloaming had one tucked away somewhere... even those parents who forbid their children from entering the woods.

That forbidding never worked.

As adults, the dark fae didn't enter the forest without large numbers of other fae to help see them safely through. As children, they were crazy enough to do it alone because they taunted each other with dares.

Many of the kids were lucky enough to survive, but not all

came out again. That should have been enough to scare the rest of them away; it never was.

Cole never lost his friends to the woods, but he knew of children and adults who entered them and never returned. Most were never seen again, not even their bodies.

These woods weren't something to be messed with, something he was reminded of as the whispers and moans of the forest creatures scurrying about came from outside the entrance only a few feet away.

None of those creatures were vegetarians.

On his final dare and trip into the woods, he encountered a rat the size of a man. With its nose twitching, the creature rose onto its hind legs, and its red eyes focused on him.

Its front teeth were the size of a toddler as they hung over its lower lip. Blood dripped from them, and even before it issued an eager screech, Cole could tell it intended to add *his* flesh to its already overly bloated, pinkish belly.

Unable to think past not being eaten, Cole didn't attempt to open a portal; he simply turned and sprinted as fast as he could toward the palace. His rapid breaths sounded harsh in his ears as briars and branches tore at his skin and clothes; the more they shredded his flesh, the more excited the thing chasing him became.

The ground quaked as it thundered after him. Trees cracked and broke as the creature bounced off them. Its foot-long claws tore into the earth, propelling it faster as it squealed in anticipation. The sounds it made roused the other monsters in the woods.

His lungs had burned, he was certain death awaited him, but then, he burst free of the woods and into the sunlight of the Gloaming.

The thing must not have liked the sun or the idea of leaving the woods, because though Cole ran for at least another half a mile, it never pursued him past the trees. It took him a little while to realize the laughter of his friends, who had been waiting for him at the edge of the forest, was the only thing chasing him.

When he finally stopped, it took him another five minutes to catch his breath enough to tell the others what happened. Some of them paled at his description, others continued to laugh, but none of them ever entered the woods again.

He never believed he'd return to this place, but here he stood… with *Lexi*. They weren't far from the edge of the forest, but he'd never expected to bring her into it.

Even large contingents of dark fae, who traveled through the woods, didn't always make it. However, this was the safest place for them to remain undetected by the Lord's men and his dragons.

He didn't like her being in these woods, but he'd survived as a child, and the two of them were far more powerful now.

Not to mention… shadows filled these woods.

"Where are we?" Lexi whispered.

"The forest behind the palace."

She gulped. "Aren't there all kinds of creatures here?"

"Yes, and they're all deadly, but they never leave the trees, so if we can get to the edge of them, we can check on the Gloaming without being noticed."

"Solid reasoning," Lexi murmured as her eyes darted around. "Where are we *in* the woods?"

"A small cave about a hundred feet or so inside. When I was a kid, we used to dare each other to run to this cave and"—he reached overhead and plucked a pink stone from the ceiling before holding it out to her—"collect one of these to bring back."

A small smile tugged at Lexi's lips as she took the stone he offered her. "Such a reckless, childish thing to do. How many of you were eaten?"

"None while I was doing it, but many were lost over the years."

"How sad."

When she went to hand the stone back, he curved her hand around it. "It's yours. Everyone brave enough to enter these woods has one."

After Lexi slipped the stone into her pocket, he clasped her hand.

"It's not a far walk," he assured her. "Stay close to me, and we should make it through without any problems."

He'd tell her about his encounter with the giant rat later. Together, they stepped from the cave and into the woods.

~

Lexi's eyes darted around the forest as she tried to take in everything at once. She recalled when Cole was fighting against the rebels and she opened one of the doors in the palace to discover the woods on the other side.

That night, from within the trees, eyes the color of a rotting peach stared back at her. Those eyes scared her when they were a safe distance away, but now, she was in *their* domain.

From all around came the rustle of scurrying creatures. Their noises made the hair on her neck rise, but the silent ones unnerved her more.

And she suspected there were far more stealthy hunters in these trees than the noisy ones. Or... the noisy ones were covering for the others sneaking up on them now.

Her head swiveled as she searched the shadows but didn't see anything there. They'd never let her see them, though.

Taking a deep breath, she tried to calm the riotous beat of her heart as she focused forward. If something attacked them, she would *not* allow him to draw on the shadows to defeat it.

She focused on the heat of Cole's hand, his scent, and the way he made her skin come alive with a simple touch. Now that she'd learned how to activate her power, she felt the flame against her palm, waiting to break free.

She would torch anything that tried to hurt them.

They'd walked about fifty feet when something scuttling

through the bushes to her right spun her head in that direction. She glimpsed a flash of brown fur before it vanished.

When her lungs started to burn, she realized she'd stopped breathing and reminded herself to draw in air. It was tough to do when dozens of eyes burrowed into her back. They followed her every move as the unknown creatures of the Gloaming crept closer.

And then a horrifying possibility occurred to her...

What if they all attacked at once?

CHAPTER SEVENTY-SIX

THEN I'LL CRISP FRY their asses.

She didn't let herself consider that she'd just figured out *how* to use her fire and wasn't great at wielding it yet. She would do whatever was necessary to keep them safe and ensure Cole didn't have to use the shadows to aid them.

Something scooted behind a thick copse of bushes with thorns the size of her fingers. It didn't help that not only were there monsters hunting them, but this was by far the thickest forest she'd ever entered.

She couldn't see more than a few feet ahead of her as the massive tree trunks and copious bushes blocked her view. Overhead, only a few beams of the sun's rays pierced through the thick canopy of leaves.

When the wind blew through the trees, their swaying branches caused the shadows to dance across the earth. Not much light pierced through from above, but, like the plants, the shadows here thrived on darkness.

Despite the considerable amount of different plants, no flowers bloomed in these woods. The only color was the gray bark of the trees and the lush green of the plants. When she looked up, the leaves above were a brilliant green.

Sticks and dried, dead leaves littered the ground beneath her feet, but there was no moss or mushrooms. The forest floor was comprised only of debris, and... yep, that was a skeleton over there.

Lexi decided not to look too closely at the other sticks and debris sticking out of the ground. She doubted she would like what she discovered.

Cole edged around an enormous briar patch that would shred her clothes and skin if she tumbled into it. She warily eyed the lethal-looking thorns as she turned sideways to squeeze between them and a tree trunk so big she couldn't wrap her arms halfway around it.

A strange whirring sound started from somewhere in the woods. She'd never heard anything like it before; it reminded her of a mixer churning through batter. It was strange and out of place in a forest, but these woods were weird.

She sighed when she stepped out from the briars and could walk next to Cole again. She was starting to think they might get out of here without encountering anything.

Then, something dropped in front of her.

Lexi jumped as Cole's head shot up. She couldn't quite tell if the thing resembled a spider or monkey more. It possessed features similar to a monkey but dangled from a thick string and had more legs than any mammal.

She didn't take the time to count those legs as its mouth opened and two mandibles unfolded from inside. Lexi almost screamed when those hideous things revealed themselves.

Nothing this revolting and strange should exist in the world. Yet here it was, and it was *starving*. It wasn't much bigger than a small monkey, but she suspected it could devour her and Cole before happily searching out more prey.

When the shadows around them shifted and Cole's power

swelled on the air, Lexi recalled her vow not to let him use that ability. Drawing on her love for him, she flung her hand up, and a stream of fire erupted from it.

The flames hit the creature directly in its open, rotten-looking mouth. It screamed as fire consumed its thick, brown coat and reflected in its multiple, beady, black eyes.

As the creature turned and scurried up its string, fire licked at the air behind it. When the string broke, it fell to the ground and bounced away before going completely still.

The sudden hush of the woods was more unnerving than all the sounds before it. She could feel every eye in the forest focused on *them*. And they were *all* eager for more death… preferably hers and Cole's.

The hair on Lexi's nape rose as the forest remained silent. Her head tipped back, and she searched the leafy bowers above for more of those things. Nothing moved, but that didn't mean they couldn't be hiding there, stalking their prey.

"We're almost out of here," Cole told her. "Are you okay?"

"Fine," she whispered.

"Let's go."

He gave a small tug on her hand, and they started through the woods again, but this time, they walked a little faster. From behind, something released a high-pitch screech that broke the hush and made Lexi wince as it battered her eardrums.

Lexi glanced behind her, but if there was something there, she couldn't see it through the wall of vegetation. When Cole pulled her a little in front of him, she tried to edge back to stand at his side again, but he put a firm hand in her back and nudged her ahead.

She shot him an irritated look, but he kept his gaze focused ahead and purposely away from her. A muscle twitched in his cheek as his jaw locked. That steely look, more than the returning sounds of the forest, frightened her most.

If something attacked again, he would use the shadows against it.

Ahead of them, she searched for any sign they were near the edge of the woods. There was none. Noise came from all around them again, but this time, it was hiding something or trying to confuse them into making a mistake.

It would be so easy to get turned around in the forest, and it had been years since Cole was last here. They could be walking in circles right now, going in the completely wrong direction, or just on the edge of the wood. It was impossible to tell.

CHAPTER SEVENTY-SEVEN

YOU CAN OPEN A PORTAL. You're not lost here, and you're not stuck here.

She still wasn't used to having that ability, and Cole was far better at it than her. He could have them out of here in less than a second, but with all the noises coming from everywhere, it was easy to forget they weren't stuck here.

And it was easy to be trapped and killed here as the creatures waited for them to make a mistake. She swore the trees were creeping in on them, but that was impossible; they couldn't move.

Or could they? This was the Gloaming, after all.

"Can the trees move?" she whispered to Cole.

He chuckled as he replied. "No, not even these woods can pull that off."

"Good."

She was so busy searching for another threat, she didn't realize they were almost to the edge of the forest until Cole drew her against his side. She *finally* noticed a lightening in the trees, a glimpse at a brighter, better world, and something beyond the foliage.

Together, they stopped at the edge of the tree line. The forest noises died down as the sun warming her face eased the chill in her bones. She hadn't realized how cold she was until those rays hit her icy flesh.

Standing at the edge of the woods, still embraced by the darkness beneath the trees, but halfway back in the Gloaming, Lexi stifled a gasp. Her hand flew to her mouth as she took in the destruction.

The smoke rising from everywhere turned large sections of the pristine, blue sky into a murky gray. Around the palace, smoke spiraled from the fires still consuming the homes and land, but some of it also rose from the smoldering piles of ash.

She'd never been on the backside of the palace before, or at least she didn't think she had. It was easy to get lost, confused, and turned around inside. The palace liked to play games, and she suspected it enjoyed watching them bumbling around.

When she discovered the door to the woods, she swore it was on the side of the palace, to her right. Her heart sank when she saw the woods there and the black, charred remains of the jagged trees poking into the air.

Much of the woods in that section were gone. It was nothing more than a blackened stretch of land sandwiched between this section and another swath of dense, green forest a few thousand feet beyond it.

"Are we behind the palace?" she whispered just to make sure.

"Yes," Cole replied.

So that meant... to her left was the end of the barracks for the king's guard. The smoke rising from the front of the palace had to be from the homes they'd all worked so relentlessly to rebuild.

If any of those displaced fae decided to return to the Gloaming, they couldn't sleep in the guard's barracks again. All that remained of them was burnt lumber and smoke.

However, despite all the destruction surrounding it, the sharp peaks, numerous windows, and imposing air of the palace continued to tower over the land. Relief and joy swelled in her as she tipped her head back to take in all its wonder.

"How is it possible the palace survived?" she asked.

"Over its many thousands of years of existence, many protection spells have been weaved over it," Cole replied. "The palace has taken on a life of its own over the years. It has been built up and protected by magics created by fae who lived far longer than my father or me. I'm sure the Lord's men and the dragons tried to destroy it, but it would take more than them to do so."

"Did you expect to find it still standing?"

"No, but I'm not surprised either. And one day, I'll return to it."

A creak behind them turned both their heads in that direction, but nothing stirred in the forest.

"It's time to go," Cole said.

"Are we going to explore the rest of the Gloaming, like Underhill?"

"There's no need. We got most of the residents out of Underhill, but the dragons were descending on it as we were leaving. Nothing of it remains."

Lexi didn't ask about all the wild horses residing there; she'd prefer not to know. She was sure some had survived and would once again flourish there, and that had to be enough.

"What about the other areas of the Gloaming?" she asked.

"We did the best we could for them too and got out as many as we could. The Lord's men and the dragons would have already gone through those areas and destroyed them too. One day, we will destroy him and reclaim this land, but it won't be today."

"Yes, we will," she murmured.

"Let's go; there's nothing left to see here."

CHAPTER SEVENTY-EIGHT

"You shouldn't have gone without me," her dad muttered from across the table where they'd gathered for dinner.

It wasn't the first time he'd uttered those words since learning she and Cole had returned to the manor and the Gloaming. She was sure it wouldn't be the last time either.

He scowled as, between his fingers, he twisted the stem of his golden goblet. The blood-filled goblet scraped against the table as it turned.

It was just one more thing adding friction to an already tension-filled room. The only one who wasn't staring morosely at their food, was Orin, and that was because he wasn't there.

Niall was at least four glasses of wine deep. Staring at the wall, Varo wasn't eating, and Brokk stabbed at the meat on his plate. After learning about the destruction of the manor, Sahira had gone quiet as she pet Shade, who refused to leave her side.

Maverick drummed his fingers on the table as he contemplated everything they'd revealed to him and Niall about Lexi's ancestry. Kaylia sat with her chin in her hand, tapping her finger against it as she stared over Maverick's shoulder.

Sitting beside Lexi, Cole ate the potatoes on his plate, but she sensed his irritation in the stiff set of his shoulders. She nudged her potatoes aside with a fork before lifting the roll from her plate.

She pulled the bread apart and slowly ate one of the smaller pieces. The displeasure radiating from her dad was a definite appetite killer, but her stomach was rumbling before she sat at the table, and she required food.

"We were perfectly safe," Lexi assured her dad, not for the first time.

His scowl deepened, and he shot Cole a look. They'd always been close, and she didn't want that to change. She worried it might, if her father thought Cole wasn't protecting her or if Cole believed her dad might interfere in their relationship.

"I would never put her in unnecessary danger," Cole said. "We made a decision *together*, and we will do so from now on. She's to be my wife; we're a team."

Some of her father's scowl vanished, and a ripple of astonishment emanated from the others. Lexi smiled as she tossed a piece of bread in her mouth.

"What do we do about the Lord?" Kaylia asked. "Now that he knows about Lexi, he'll prepare for anything we might have tried against him. And I'm sure, since he's also a warlock, he knows about the legend of the Shadow Reaver and recognizes Cole as such."

"Maybe that madman is too far gone to recognize anything," Maverick suggested. "You didn't see him at the ball. He was thirsty for blood, and he didn't care what he had to do; he was going to get it. Except, he most certainly did *not* get it in the way he expected."

Cole smiled. "No, he didn't."

Lexi's chewing stopped as the bread turned to sawdust in her mouth.

"There's not much understanding left in Andreas," Maverick said. "The throne's power has rotted his mind completely."

"Even if he's too far gone to recognize what Cole is, he's still in touch with the warlocks, and I'm sure there were some at the ball," Kaylia said.

"Yes, there were some there," Cole confirmed. "And they'll tell him what the Shadow Reaver is."

"Does anyone really know what it is?" Niall inquired.

"No," Kaylia said. "It was always a legend, and now it's a reality. Like Lexi's powers, we will have to see how it all unfolds."

Lexi threw down her roll as her appetite vanished.

"So, he knows about you two, which means our biggest weapons are compromised. He also knows we have no army, and he's scattered what remained of Cole's," Kaylia continued. "What do we do now?"

"I have men who will fight," Maverick said. "My pack is safe. They knew there was a possibility they would have to prepare for war again."

"Circe and Talon were at the ball too. I'm sure they realize that this time, if they plan to stand against the Lord, it will have to be in open rebellion of him. There will be no more coalition, no more secret planning; it's outright war or nothing," Cole said.

Varo finally looked away from the wall to focus on them. "Do you think they'll go for that?"

"I'm not sure," Cole admitted. "They're against the Lord and everything he's done. However, we're in a worse position against him now than we were before, and we couldn't stop him then. If they do decide to stand against him, they'll have fighters too."

"It's still not enough," Kaylia said.

"We also have the surprise of Del, Orin, and Varo being alive," Sahira reminded them. "He doesn't know about them."

"That's not much of an advantage," Brokk said. "That's more likely to piss him off when he learns we tricked him."

"It's still something," Lexi said.

"I hope I'm there when he discovers the truth," Cole stated.

Lexi hoped he wasn't, and then a thought occurred to her.

"I still have the harrow stone!" she blurted. "I can make duplicates of immortals, so it looks like we have an army."

"That could help," Kaylia said. "Even if they don't move, they'll be a distraction."

"I could open a portal into the palace and kill him," Lexi said.

"First, you don't know where he is at any given moment in the palace and you can only open a portal to places you know," Cole said. "Second, he'll keep himself surrounded by dragons and fighters now. Even if the dragon at the manor seemed repentant about breathing fire at you, that doesn't mean they won't try to kill you."

"And as a warlock, he'll put up spells and safeguards to keep himself safe from such a thing happening," Kaylia said.

Lexi propped her chin on her hand and settled her elbow on the table. "Oh."

"We need fighters," Brokk reminded them.

"And we don't have nearly as many as the Lord," her dad said.

"We can find more," Cole said. "It might take us a while, but there are many who will be willing to stand against him. We just don't know about them yet because they're too afraid to come forward."

"You risk us coming into contact with people who will betray us if we start openly recruiting fighters," Varo said. "Not to mention, I'm sure we all have a bounty on our heads... or at least those of us the Lord knows are alive."

"Kaylia might be the only one who could return to her realm without any repercussions," Niall said.

"The crones will help," Kaylia said. "They may have retired from the rat race of the realms, but they'll help in *this*. It's time that monster is taken down; it's time the death stops, and it's beyond time an arach takes their rightful place on the throne again. From what I know of Lexi, the realms will be a far kinder place with her there. That's something we *all* want."

Lexi shifted uncomfortably when all eyes turned toward her.

They all expected so much from her, yet she still considered herself little more than a simple country girl who loved nothing more than spending time with her horses and family.

She was aware she had no other options and believed she *could* master her powers with more training and time, but the idea of failing was like an albatross around her neck.

However, failure was *not* an option.

They just had to figure out how to raise an army to win.

CHAPTER SEVENTY-NINE

"I THINK recruitment is the way to go," her dad said.

Lexi's eyebrows shot into her hairline. "Really?"

His jaw clenched, and his nostrils flared; then he took a sip of his blood, wiped his mouth, and set the goblet down again. "Yes. We'll start with the members of the coalition, see if they have any interest in going public with their battle, and then spread out from there."

"What are you thinking?" Cole asked.

"I think we do this slowly. We recruit in small increments and in the populations that most avoid. We give those forgotten immortals an arach, and we give them hope. And hope is a powerful weapon that the Lord will never wield."

"Very true," Varo murmured.

"You want to use Lexi to do this?" Cole inquired.

Her dad's teeth scraped together before he grated out. "Yes."

"Are you nuts?" Kaylia asked.

"No. We target those most hurt by the Lord, but also the ones who the Lord wouldn't recruit."

"Like humans," Kaylia said.

"Sure," her dad said.

"The humans wouldn't survive five minutes in the Shadow Realms," Brokk said.

"With some of their weapons, and if they have immortals looking out for them instead of trying to destroy them, they'll last longer than anyone will expect. I'm sure they'd also be happy to fight for a chance to be free of the Lord's oppression."

"That's still not going to help us much," Varo said.

"There are others," her dad reminded them.

"The sirens might help," Cole said.

"Why do you say that?" Lexi asked.

"One of them told me not to die at the ball."

"That is extremely kind for a siren," Niall agreed.

"Then we will also try the sirens," her dad said. "And maybe the zombies."

"Holy shit!" Maverick blurted. "Have you lost your mind?"

"They've been pushed aside throughout all this and relegated to a shitty outer realm."

"With good reason!"

Lexi kept waiting for Cole's protests, but he didn't speak as he rubbed his chin and stared at the far wall.

"The zombies will turn on everyone," Sahira said.

"Maybe not," Del replied. "They've been labeled as outcasts and monsters throughout their entire existence, but they can be rational."

"They can also be brain-eating monsters," Niall reminded him.

"The Lord would never expect it." Then her dad focused on her. "We find the outcasts, the marginalized, and we give them hope. We give them an arach, a *true* leader, and one who *is* good. We offer them an opportunity for a better life. Many would jump at that opportunity."

"What do we do with the zombies if we win?" Maverick asked. "They can't wander openly around others; it would be chaos."

"No, but they also don't have to be shoved into their hideous realm and locked away like they are now. They *can* be rational."

Maverick didn't look convinced by this, and no one else looked happy about it either.

"But we will stay away from the zombies and leave them be," her dad said.

"Good," Brokk said, and everyone at the table nodded.

"However, there are other, forgotten communities out there as well as outcasts from our own communities. The incubus and succubus were also ostracized since the arach fell. Many of them would jump at the chance to have a normal life again."

"This sounds like a horrible idea," Kaylia muttered.

"Yes, but he's right, and we have no other options," Cole said. "It's amazing what a little bit of hope can do for people and immortals. We have to give it to them."

"And the best way to do that is to let them see and speak with Lexi. They have to know she's real, and she's a viable option for defeating the Lord," Del said.

"Then we start recruiting," Brokk murmured.

No one cheered this plan. Instead, they all looked more unhappy than when they first sat at the table.

When they all fell silent, the only sounds filling the room were the occasional scratch of silverware against a plate and a sip from a goblet. Lexi continued to pick at her food as she pondered their options or lack thereof.

As soon as any of them went anywhere in public, they would have to watch for someone seeking to turn them in or trying to kill them.

She took another bite of her bread as Orin breezed into the room, whistling while he walked. Lexi glowered at him as she contemplated heaving her bread at his head. She had a feeling he'd only laugh at her, and that would irritate her more.

They all scowled at him as he strode to the head of the table and plopped into a chair. The dining room of the prison was relatively small, but there were a few other tables in it. They were the only ones in the stonewalled room, but she would have preferred if Orin sat somewhere else.

Lexi was not in the mood for him tonight.

Orin clasped the stem of the goblet Varo had set out earlier in case his brother decided to grace them with his ever-annoying presence. He lifted it in the air, took a sip, and sat back in his chair.

The table shook when he propped his feet on the end of it and crossed his legs. Lexi released her bread and picked up her fork. She should eat, but food had become completely unappealing.

"Why are all my chums so glum?" Orin inquired as he clasped his hands on his belly.

"Trying to figure out our next move, brother," Varo answered. He was the only one in the room not ignoring Orin. "Things seem a little hopeless without an army."

"I see," Orin said.

No one else said anything as they returned to their dinner and drinks. After a few minutes, Orin grew tired of the quiet.

"I bet I can make all your frowns turn upside down," Orin said in such a cheerful way that Lexi's teeth clamped together. "Okay, I can see you all need a little pick-me-up, and I'm just the superb, ever-so-handsome dark fae to give it to you."

He paused, but no one gave him the satisfaction of biting the heavily baited hook he'd dangled before them. Lexi's hand tightened on her fork. Stabbing her future brother-in-law probably wasn't the best way to ingratiate herself into the family, but she didn't think his brothers would mind.

Orin sipped his wine again before speaking. "I have a dragon."

Lexi winced when Brokk's knife scraped across his plate. For a long moment, no one spoke, moved, or *breathed*. Then, almost as one, their heads turned toward Orin.

He smiled smugly as he finished his wine.

∼

Turn the page for a sneak peek of book 5, *Shadows of Destiny*, or download now and keep reading: brendakdavies.com/SDewb

∽

Stay in touch on updates, sales, and new releases by joining to the mailing list: brendakdavies.com/ESBKDNews

Visit the Brenda K. Davies Book Club on Facebook for exclusive giveaways and all things book related. Come join the fun: brendakdavies.com/BKDBooks

LEXI'S HEART thumped like a rabbit's hind leg when it scratched at fleas. It took everything she had not to turn and bolt away from the cave looming before her like a dinosaur looking to swallow her whole.

And considering what was inside that cave, many might consider it a dinosaur. Lexi refused to shiver, but the chill running up her spine cooled her skin.

She glanced back at Orin who still wore that damn, smug smile. He didn't seem aware of how punchable it made him... or he didn't care, which was as likely.

Standing beside Orin, Cole's eyes were the color of liquid mercury. Though his lips were clamped shut, the outline of his lycan fangs was visible behind them.

Her father and Sahira stood behind Cole with their jaws clenched and their hands fisted at their sides. Lexi wondered if they were contemplating punching Orin too.

Behind them, Maverick, Brokk, Kaylia, Varo, and Niall stared at the cave with different expressions of curiosity, unease, and fear. This situation amused Orin, but it had the rest of them on pins and needles.

The sun beating down on them baked the rocks of the barren realm Orin had brought them to. The jagged formations were the color of apricots as they rose and fell over the land. She had no idea if this outer realm had a name, and she didn't care.

And then something stirred deep within the cave. She couldn't see it, but the loud scratch of stone—or something as hard as a rock—scraping against stone came from the darkness.

Instinctively, Lexi knew it wasn't a stone making that noise but a claw that could decapitate her in one swipe. The image of such a thing happening was so clear she almost placed a hand against her neck to make sure her head was still attached.

What the hell am I doing here? Why are we all *here? This is insane.*

But she already knew the answers to those questions. She *had* to be here. She needed to do this because they had to learn how this dragon would react to her. But that didn't mean everyone else had to come and put their lives in danger.

However, they had all refused to remain behind. Not that she could blame them; she'd want to know too... if it was someone else facing a creature who could eat, toast, or smash them with one big, *giant* front paw.

Lexi gulped. She hoped it didn't kill her. She enjoyed her life and was in no rush to become splattered pancake bits all over the cave.

"You don't have to do this," Cole said in a gravelly voice she'd come to recognize as the one that came through when he was trying not to change into a lycan.

"I know," she muttered.

But they both knew it was a lie. She didn't have a choice in this, and everyone here knew it.

Her eyes met her dad's red ones before flitting away when a small snort and a rustling came from inside the cave. It almost sounded like the dragon Orin caught was settling in.

For a second, the shield she'd erected to keep her arach glow hidden from the world crumbled beneath the weight of her terror and the sun burning down on her. To her, that was even worse than facing a dragon.

Her secret was out; the Lord knew an arach still survived and was a threat to his claim on *her* homeland, but she still couldn't lose control. The Lord and those at the ball had seen her, and she was sure pictures of her were circulating throughout the realms, but she could remain hidden if necessary.

She couldn't do that if she were walking around glowing like some kind of overcharged Glo Worm. Lexi scrambled to get her shield back into place, but it was hard to concentrate when the breaths of the creature within were creating a small breeze that tickled her face.

Finally, she managed to regain control, and her glow completely vanished.

"I should go in alone," she said. "It's probably scared and angry."

It was probably terrified and *pissed,* but having this group tromping in wouldn't make things better for the frightened, murderous creature. She tugged at the collar of her fae tunic but released it when Cole's eyes latched onto her. He would never agree to let her walk in there alone, but she didn't need so many going with her.

"I'll go with you; everyone else can stay here," Cole commanded.

"The dragons don't like you," Lexi reminded him.

"I don't care."

Of course, he didn't, and it was probably best if he stayed out of there, but he would never be dissuaded either.

"Keep her safe," her dad said.

"Always."

When Cole turned toward her, she swore the silver of his eyes burned hotter, but at least the shadows weren't swarming around him. They stirred on the ground but didn't creep any closer.

She didn't make the mistake of thinking Cole wouldn't turn them loose on the dragon if it tried to attack. She wouldn't let that happen. It was a murderous beast, but it was also frightened, and she didn't want it hurt.

When they stepped into the cave, Orin followed.

"You should stay out," Lexi said sharply.

"I put my ass on the line for this; I'm going to see what happens," Orin replied.

When Cole rounded on his brother, Lexi's hand shot out and caught his arm. "Don't," she whispered. "Just leave him be. It's not worth it."

She hated Orin's arrogant grin as she glowered at him, but he wasn't worth it. Lexi wasn't going to stand there and fight with him when she had a dragon to meet.

~

LEXI CLASPED her hands tightly before her and squeezed as she put one foot in front of the other while walking through the dark. The cool air of the cave caressed her skin, and somewhere in the distance, water dripped from the rocks into a pool she couldn't see.

Though darkness surrounded them, the flickering glow of a distant torchlight drew her onward like a pot of gold at the end of the rainbow. Except at the end of this rainbow was a dragon who wouldn't give her gold but might smash her to bits with a pot if it got the chance.

Stop it!

Freaking herself was not going to do any good. She had no idea what lay ahead or what would happen, but her turbulent thoughts weren't helping. When they got to the dragon, she would see what happened then.

She didn't ask Orin how he'd managed to pull this off. She didn't want to know the answer that he would be more than happy to give.

Another snort and scrape came from ahead of them as the dragon shifted in the darkness. Did it know they were coming? Had it smelled or heard them?

She suspected, like most animals, it had amazing senses that helped keep it alive, so it had to know they were on their way. Somehow, that made it even worse. It could be up there, preparing for them.

Though, she supposed it might be worse to *surprise* a dragon. She doubted that ever went over well.

When the dragon shifted again, and the torchlight illuminated more of the cave, the shadows on the walls twisted as Cole drew them closer. "Don't," Lexi said to him. "There's no need to call on them."

"I'll do whatever it takes to keep you safe," Cole growled back.

"We're not going to need them."

He grunted in response. Orin wisely remained quiet as a stone crunched beneath her feet. If it hadn't known they were coming, it did now. She guessed that was better, or she hoped so anyway.

Her foot caught the corner of a stone, and Lexi bit back a gasp when her ankle rolled. Staggering to the side, she nearly went down, but Cole grasped her elbow and held her up. She rested her hand against the wall to steady herself.

"Are you okay?" he inquired.

"Yeah," she muttered. "Stupid rock."

When she pushed away from the wall, Cole kept holding her arm. Needing to connect with him, she wrapped the fingers of her free hand around the ones on her arm as they continued.

Love swelled in her as Cole's skin warmed beneath hers, but so did a growing certainty... If they didn't walk out of here with answers, they would never get them.

With every step, the torchlight grew brighter, and the dragon released another snuff. She glanced back to see the faint light of day illuminating the end of the tunnel before focusing forward again.

She didn't think she'd been looking back for that long, but she almost gasped when they turned a corner and saw what awaited her. Her hand flew to her mouth as she caught sight of the beautiful creature wrapped in chains embedded in the ground and cave walls. It looked as if it didn't have much room to move.

This should never be!

The protective, hostile wave that washed over was so fierce that it took her a few seconds to breathe again. No one should ever treat a dragon like this. These magnificent animals should *never* be bound in such a way.

But then, the Lord had also bound them. Maybe not with chains but in other ways. These poor creatures had been held captive for far too long, and it was time to set them free.

She had no fear it would hurl a wave of fire at them as even its mouth was bound with thick manacles that kept it pinched closed. A padlock locked the chains together.

"What did you do?" she gasped.

"I caught a dragon," Orin replied.

"*Why* did you do this to it?"

"To avoid being eaten," he said slowly and like she was an idiot.

Lexi's hands fisted as she spun on him. He smiled as he leaned casually against the wall with his arms crossed over his chest. "You're an asshole," she told him.

"But I'm an asshole who's still in one piece and didn't get torched by *a dragon*."

"Where is the key?" Lexi demanded. "I'm going to set it free."

"Like hell you are."

"How can I know anything about what I can and can't do with dragons if this one is chained like a prisoner?"

"It *is* a prisoner," Orin replied. "And you can work with that monster while it's in chains."

"You're more of a monster than it is."

Orin shrugged. "I'm fine with that."

Turning to Cole, Lexi decided to ignore Orin. "I have to go closer, and I have to do it alone. It needs to be just me."

"That's not going to happen."

"I have to. Stay back here and watch, but don't come any closer."

"Lexi—"

"I'm not arguing about this. It's already chained down; it doesn't need all of us approaching at once. I'm going alone."

A muscle jumped in his cheek, the shadows on the wall shifted, and the dragon snuffed again before jerking against its chains. Lexi's heart raced even as she forced a serene smile to her face. She wasn't fooling Cole, though, as his eyes narrowed on her face.

"Cole, I have to go alone."

"Lexi—"

Rising onto her toes, she clasped his cheeks and kissed his lips before releasing him and stepping back. "I'm going alone."

Before he could protest further, she released him and stepped away. She took a deep breath and wiped her sweaty palms on her pants before starting toward the dragon.

"Don't get too close," Orin warned. "Those chains have some range to them."

〰

As Lexi cautiously approached the dragon, it lifted its head and narrowed its eyes until she found staring into the black, glistening center of its slitted pupils. The sound it released was a cross between an irate cobra and a cornered tiger.

When she was only twenty feet away, the creature lunged forward. Lexi gasped and staggered back, but the manacles bolted into the wall caught. They jerked the dragon back.

A startled hiss escaped the creature as it slammed into the ground with enough force to shake the cave. Seeking to help it, Lexi lunged forward before catching herself and skidding to a stop.

She felt sorry for the poor thing; no creature should be treated like this, but she didn't want to be its breakfast either. Though the chains around its jaws should hold, she wasn't taking any chances.

The dragon lifted its head to glower at her. A puff of smoke escaped its nostrils, each one of them was the size of her head. The dragon was smaller than most of the others she'd seen, making her think it was younger, but its youthful age didn't mean it wasn't as lethal.

Its green scales shimmered with yellows and oranges that resembled a starburst of color when it moved certain ways in the torchlight. The dragon was enraged... *and gorgeous.*

Her fingers twitched with her urge to pet it, comfort it and connect with it, but she balled them into fists to keep from reaching out to the creature. That would probably be a surefire way to end up dead.

"Hi," she whispered, and the dragon released another puff of smoke. "My name is Elexiandra. Most call me Lexi; my dad sometimes calls me Andi."

She didn't get into the fact that the rebels she helped save knew her as Andi; it didn't seem like the dragon was impressed with her words. In fact, she thought talking to it might be annoying it even more.

Its talons scraped the stone as it tried to wiggle closer. The nails on a chalkboard sound made her wince as her bladder clenched, and she resisted the impulse to run.

Those narrowed eyes moved closer; its nostrils were only feet away when another puff of smoke billowed into her face. If there was supposed to be some connection between her and the dragons, this one sure as hell didn't care about it.

But then, she wouldn't be too receptive either if someone tossed her into chains and threw her in a cave so someone could explore with her.

∼

COLE'S CLAWS dug into his palms, drawing blood that pooled into his hands as Lexi stepped closer to the dragon. His breath hissed out through his clenched teeth; his shoulders hunched up as the creature lunged at her with a rattle of chains.

Once again, its bound legs gave out beneath it, and the cave's floor shook as it hit the ground. Lexi gasped, and her hand flew out; as it did, the dragon surged toward her.

Around the dragon, the shadows on the walls crept closer while Cole kept his focus on the animal who would love nothing more than to eat his fiancé. Those shadows would tear this beast apart before it got the chance to hurt her. He would make sure of it.

"I worked hard to catch this dragon; don't you dare destroy it," Orin said to him.

"Then you better hope those chains hold," Cole growled.

"They will."

Lexi's head spun toward him, and her shoulders went back as she frowned at the shadows. "We don't need the shadows," she said.

"As long as it doesn't hurt you, I won't hurt it," he said.

"You shouldn't be calling on the shadows."

Because the more he did, the deeper they dug into his soul, and the more their darkness spread through him. They were both aware of that, but no matter how much they affected him, he would use them to keep her safe...

No matter the cost.

"I'm not a concern right now; *you* are," he told her.

Her slender nose scrunched in annoyance; he had excellent eyesight, but from here, he couldn't see the freckles dotting the bridge of her nose. Freckles that he knew were all scrunched up in the adorable way they had when she was irritated with him.

In the torchlight, the deep red strands in her auburn hair were the color of blood. The ominous color made his claws dig in deeper as he resisted the impulse to shift into a wolf and remove her from this cave and away from the monster. He'd witnessed one of these fuckers eat his father; he wouldn't lose her to this thing.

"Why is it being so defensive around her?" Orin muttered. "It should recognize her as an arach. It shouldn't want to *kill* her."

"We have no idea what the arach connection to the dragons was," Cole reminded him. "For all we know, it all came from Dragonia, or the throne, and there's nothing she can do with them."

"I refuse to believe that."

"Just because you insist on something doesn't make it true."

Orin glowered at him before shifting his attention back to Lexi and the dragon. He'd never admit it, but Cole had expected something more between her and the dragons too. He didn't know what that was, but he hadn't expected it to have the same reaction to her as it would to all of them.

"I'm not going to hurt you," Lexi whispered as she edged closer.

"Don't," Cole warned her.

She froze, and her eyes darted toward the shadows on the walls as they surrounded the dragon. If she kept getting closer, he'd have the shadows pull her away from the beast. He didn't like them touching her, but if they could save her life, so be it.

The dragon lifted its head, so they were eye-level with each other. And those eyes said it wanted her dead.

Cole was so focused on her that he didn't hear the shouts coming from the cave entrance until they rebounded all around him. Footsteps slapped against stone, harsh breaths ricocheted off the walls, and Lexi turned toward him even as he moved around the corner to see the others.

"Incoming!" Del shouted.

Cole didn't know what he meant until a small thud sounded outside the cave, and wings settled into place with a rustle. Then, the light of the outside world vanished as another dragon stuck its head in the cave.

∾

Continue reading *Shadows of Destiny*:
brendakdavies.com/SDewb

∾

Stay in touch on updates, sales, and new releases by joining to
the mailing list: brendakdavies.com/News

Visit the Brenda K. Davies Book Club on Facebook for
exclusive giveaways and all things book related. Come join the
fun: brendakdavies.com/BKDBooks

FIND THE AUTHOR

Brenda K. Davies Mailing List:
brendakdavies.com/News

Facebook: brendakdavies.com/BKDfb

Brenda K. Davies Book Club:
brendakdavies.com/BKDBooks

Instagram: brendakdavies.com/BKDInsta
Twitter: brendakdavies.com/BKDTweet
Website: www.brendakdavies.com

Bound by Fate (Book 8)

Bound by Blood (Book 9)

Bound by Love (Book 10)

The Road to Hell Series

Good Intentions (Book 1)

Carved (Book 2)

The Road (Book 3)

Into Hell (Book 4)

Hell on Earth (Book 5)

Into the Abyss (Book 6)

Kiss of Death (Book 7)

Edge of the Darkness (Book 8)

The Shadow Realms

Shadows of Fire (Book 1)

Shadows of Discovery (Book 2)

Shadows of Betrayal (Book 3)

Shadows of Fury (Book 4)

Shadows of Destiny (Book 5)

Shadows of Light (Book 6)

Wicked Curses (Book 7)

Sinful Curses (Book 8)

Gilded Curses (Book 9)

Whispers of Ruin (Book 10)

Secrets of Ruin (Book 11)

Tempest of Shadows

A Tempest of Shadows (Book 1)

A Tempest of Thieves (Book 2)

A Tempest of Revelations (Book 3)

A Tempest of Intrigue (Book 4)

A Tempest of Chaos (Book 5)

Historical Romance

A Stolen Heart

Books written under the pen name Erica Stevens

The Coven Series

Nightmares (Book 1)

The Maze (Book 2)

Dream Walker (Book 3)

The Captive Series

Captured (Book 1)

Renegade (Book 2)

Refugee (Book 3)

Salvation (Book 4)

Redemption (Book 5)

Vengeance (Book 6)

Unbound (Book 7)

Broken (Book 8 - Prequel)

The Kindred Series

Kindred (Book 1)

Ashes (Book 2)

Kindled (Book 3)

Inferno (Book 4)

Phoenix Rising (Book 5)

The Fire & Ice Series

Frost Burn (Book 1)

Arctic Fire (Book 2)

Scorched Ice (Book 3)

The Ravening Series

The Ravening (Book 1)

Taken Over (Book 2)

Reclamation (Book 3)

The Survivor Chronicles

The Upheaval (Book 1)

The Divide (Book 2)

The Forsaken (Book 3)

The Risen (Book 4)

ABOUT THE AUTHOR

Brenda K. Davies is the USA Today Bestselling author of the Vampire Awakening Series, Alliance Series, Road to Hell Series, Hell on Earth Series, The Shadow Realms Series, A Tempest of Shadows Series, and historical romantic fiction. She also writes under the pen name, Erica Stevens. When not out with friends and family, she can be found at home with her husband, son, and pets.

Printed in Dunstable, United Kingdom